What I
Couldn't
Tell
You

Praise for WHAT I COULDN'T TELL YOU

"Faye Bird should be congratulated on giving such rare but accurate insight into the little-known but distressing condition of Selective/Situational Mutism."

Lindsay Whittington
Co-ordinator and Founding Member
Selective Mutism Information & Research Association
(SMIRA)

What I Couldn't Tell You

Faye Bird

USBORNE

First published in the UK in 2016 by Usborne Publishing Ltd., Usborne House, 83-85 Saffron Hill, London EC1N 8RT, England. www.usborne.com

Cover photography: Grunge background with floral element © Veronique G/ Shutterstock; couple running ©oneinchpunch/Shutterstock; grass © Irmak Akcadogan/ Shutterstock; plant contours © trucic/Shutterstock.

The name Usborne and the devices 🎈 👑 are Trade Marks of Usborne Publishing Ltd.

A CIP catalogue record for this book is available from the British Library.

ISBN 9781474903073 JFMAM JASOND/16 03902/03.

Printed in the UK.

Part One

Laura and Joe
Eight weeks before

Laura and Joe

"I love you."

She said it.

She just said it.

She'd been waiting to say it, and there it was. She'd decided she absolutely wouldn't say it first, but the feeling of loving him, it engulfed her. The words followed the feeling and there was nothing she could do but say it.

Joe smiled and he held her face in both his hands and he looked at her, and he kissed her.

"I feel the same," he said.

We are such stuff

As dreams are made on...

That was what came into her head.

Where was that from?

For a moment she couldn't remember.

She completely forgot.

"Laura," Joe said, and she opened her eyes and looked back at him. "Thank you."

Laura thought it was strange that Joe thanked her for loving him, but then she dismissed the thought, as quickly as it came.

They kissed again.

"What time do you have to be back?" he asked, gently sweeping her hair off her shoulder. They were in the park. They'd been there for hours. It felt good to be there with him. The exams were over; there was what felt like weeks and weeks before the results were out – Laura wasn't going to start worrying about grades and university places yet. She wasn't going to let the almost constant arguments she'd been having with Mum about seeing Joe ruin anything. She was going to enjoy the summer. She was going to spend it with Joe. It didn't matter what Mum said. She was going to live and love and be loved.

"Oh, I don't know…what time is it now?" Laura said.

She didn't want to leave. She didn't even want to think about leaving.

"It's gone six thirty."

"We don't have to go yet, do we?"

"I was kind of hoping you'd come to mine…"

"Really?"

She'd not been to his before. Joe had always said the flat was small, there was no space – his brother was always around, his mum too. He'd always said there was nowhere for them to be.

Joe looked at her.

"My mum said she'd be out. My brother should be too. That's…well, why I thought of it… And there's something else…well, actually, I won't say… It'll be a surprise."

Laura leaned forward and kissed him, slowly, softly. She couldn't help herself. She couldn't wait to get to the flat, to be alone there, together. They'd only ever managed to be together before by sneaking around – the park, the garage a couple of times when Joe had borrowed the key to the outside store round the back, and once when they'd gone to hers and Mum had nearly caught them. Joe had had to jump out of her bedroom window onto the flat roof of the kitchen below to escape.

"Come on," he said, and he stood up and he put his hands out to pull her up off the grass and she let him. She felt light-headed. It was the beer. How much had they drunk? She wasn't sure. They'd been there for hours.

"If my brother's around, then I've got a backup plan," Joe said.

Laura nodded, and smiled. Joe seemed kind of serious all of a sudden. She hadn't met his family and he'd never talked about them much, but then they'd only known each other five weeks. Five blissful weeks. There was no rush to do the family thing.

"I hope they're all out," she said, smiling.

"Me too," Joe said, and he pulled her into him and

kissed her again. "Let's go."

When they got to the flat Joe's brother was there. The TV was on – loud. He was playing some game she'd seen before. Guns, zombies, soldiers. She couldn't remember the name of it.

Laura felt disappointment drop through her like a stone down a well. She tried to stop the ripples of annoyance showing on her face. She tried to look less bothered. But she knew Joe had seen. He shrugged and turned away from her towards his brother.

"You alright, Bill?"

"Yeah," Bill said, looking at Joe and then at Laura. "I'm okay." But for a moment Laura thought he looked like he was on edge or something – startled. She reckoned he must be about fifteen. Joe was twenty. He was younger than Joe. Definitely younger. Joe hadn't talked about him much. There was something about him that made her feel uneasy. Because he was looking at her all the time. He kept turning from the game to look at her, and she didn't know where to put herself in the room. Maybe it totally showed that she was gutted that he was there. She wished she was better at hiding her feelings.

"What are you playing?" she said to try and break the atmosphere in the room.

He didn't answer.

He turned and called out to Joe who had gone through

the archway into the kitchen. "What's the key for, Joe?" he said.

Laura looked. There was a chunky key on the side table next to the sofa.

"I'll show you later," Joe called back.

His brother sighed, and rubbed his hand against his nose. He looked different again, like a child. He glanced at Laura, and then he slung the controller onto the sofa.

"I'm going out," he said, and he stood up, leaving the game hanging, walking over to his shoes.

Laura could hear Joe opening and closing cupboard doors in the kitchen, like he was looking for stuff. She felt awkward standing in the middle of the room. She felt like she was in the way. She knew if she asked Joe's brother he'd agree that she was.

"There's nothing in, Joe," he called through, tying up his laces now.

"I'll get us something while I'm out, Bill. You hungry? Can you hang on until I get back?"

Laura stood still waiting for some kind of reply, but there was nothing, and Joe's brother left the room. She heard the front door slam shut. She waited for Joe to come out of the kitchen. The TV was still talking, screeching. The game was asking over and over for players. Laura looked around her. There was hardly anything in the room. Nothing on the walls. Nothing on the table but the key.

No books, no ornaments. Nothing. Just the furniture, beige, pushed against the walls. It didn't feel like a home. And for a second Laura wondered about Joe; she'd told him she loved him but she wondered now – did she really know him? Maybe she didn't know him at all.

Joe came out of the kitchen with a rucksack. It looked full, weighed down.

"What have you got in there?" she asked.

"Nothing. Just some stuff. Let's go."

"But we could stay here now..." Laura said. "Your brother's gone, you know?" She moved towards him. All she wanted to do was kiss him again.

"Yeah, but Mum's left a note. She'll be back any minute. I didn't realize she'd be back so soon. And anyway there's something downstairs I want to show you..." He grabbed the key off the table, and then Laura's hand. "Come on."

When they got out onto the street Joe dangled the key in front of her face.

"This," he said, "takes us anywhere we want to go..." And he smiled, pulling her over towards a motorbike.

"This?" Laura said. She knew she didn't sound impressed. Not impressed enough, anyway. Joe's brother had gone out. They now had the flat to themselves. Why didn't Joe want to stay with her at the flat? She didn't care about going on a motorbike.

Joe was pumped up, excited.

"Look at it. What d'you think?"

"Yeah, it's nice, I guess… It's yours, then?"

"Shit, Laura, don't you like it? I've been dreaming of taking you out on it. Taking you out to some place that we haven't been before." He wrapped his arms around her waist. "Just you and me."

Laura smiled. He just had to touch her, like this, and she was his again.

"It's nice," she said smiling. "Really nice."

"It's a classic. Vintage. A Kawasaki. And I want to take you out on it. So let's go, yeah?" he said bending down towards the bushes that ran along the front of his flats alongside the pavement, and pulling out two helmets from underneath.

Laura knew her mum would kill her if she even thought she was considering getting on the back of a motorbike, especially with Joe.

"But where are we going to go?" she said.

"Anywhere! Does it matter?" Joe said, climbing on and handing her a helmet.

She stood for a moment and looked at him.

"Do you even know how to ride one of these?" she said.

"Yeah. I used to deliver pizzas, you know? This engine isn't much bigger than one of those scooters. You impressed?" he said, and he smiled.

Laura took the helmet, and sat behind him on the bike, pressing herself close to him so their bodies made one shape, one shadow, one line. It was the only place she wanted to be.

"It doesn't matter where we go!" he said. "Let's just…go!"

Joe pulled away and out of Ford Green onto the Wellbridge Road, weaving in and out of the cars so they tipped towards the ground, left and then right. And each time they tipped Laura clung tighter to Joe. She'd never been on a motorbike before, and she wasn't sure that she liked it. Her heart was pounding. She could feel it thumping in her chest, beating in her ears. "Not so fast!" she shouted into Joe's ear, but she knew he hadn't heard her.

They stopped at some lights.

Joe turned to her. "What do you think?" he called in the lull. "It's brilliant, isn't it?"

"Yeah!" Laura said as the lights turned to green and Joe sped off again. But really, she wasn't all that sure.

They rode for about half an hour. Laura thought she'd been this way before, but not for ages. She didn't exactly recognize where they were.

"Do you know it round here?" Laura said to Joe at the next lights.

"Yeah. There's a place we can stop just a bit further up," he said. "I want to show it to you." And for a moment all Laura could think about was kissing him again.

Joe pulled up on a road bridge over a small river. There was a sign. It was the Tren. Laura could see loads of trees all along the river. It was dense, bushy, and yet the road they were on was so busy. The traffic was building up behind them where Joe had stopped on the bridge. Cars were trying to get round them. Joe pointed across to the other side of the road where there were steps from the bridge to the river. "It's down there," he said. "You cross over first and I'll wheel the bike and follow."

Laura got off and looked for a space in the traffic to cross. She wondered where she was. There were office buildings and warehouses further along the road, a few homes. It felt industrial, and yet when she got over the road and down the steps and onto the path, a meadow sprawled out in front of her alongside the river. Pale tall grasses and beyond that a viaduct – huge, brown, incongruous – a slow line of containers being pulled across it by a train. She was sure she must have seen it before – she wasn't that far from home, was she? – and yet she didn't remember.

She turned back to the steps to look for Joe. He was standing with the motorbike at the top, bending down towards the front wheel, like he was checking something.

She pulled off her helmet to talk to him.

"Joe? You alright?"

"What?" he said. She knew he wasn't listening to her. He didn't look up and he was gazing at the bike. He loved the bike. It made her smile to see how much he loved it.

"How are you going to get it down here?" she said.

"Just watch me!" Joe said, and he started it up again, and got on.

"No, Joe! Joe! No!" Laura screamed as she watched him ride it down the steps towards her. "Shit, Joe…" she said, laughing as he rode straight past her across the path where she stood and into the grassy meadow, doing a loop before coming back to her again on the path. "I cannot believe you just did that!" she screamed again, laughing.

"Why?" he said, smiling, taking off his own helmet now. "Come here and let me kiss you," he said.

And she let him. And then she kissed him back, leaning into him on the bike. It was bliss.

"How do you know this place?" she said.

"Used to live not far from here," Joe said, getting off the bike.

"When was that?"

Laura wanted to know, but Joe didn't answer. He took her helmet and wheeled the bike over to the wall of the road bridge. He leaned the bike against the wall and set the helmets down on the grass.

Laura looked along the river while she waited for him to come back. The path continued alongside the water. It seemed to follow the twists and turns all the way to the viaduct.

"So what did you bring in the bag?" she said as Joe came back over to her.

"God, you're asking a lot of questions all of a sudden," Joe said.

Laura felt struck. It was the way he'd spoken to her. Like he was telling her off or something.

She looked at him. Why was he being like this?

"So what do you think of the viaduct?" Joe said taking her hand and leading her off the path and into the meadow. Laura nodded, and smiled. She didn't know what to say.

They sat down. Joe looked back, checking the bike was okay.

Laura turned to look at the viaduct again. It should have been ugly, but somehow it wasn't. She still felt like she didn't know what to say about it. She looked back at Joe. He was pulling some beers out of the rucksack.

"Come on. Let's have a drink," he said.

Laura wasn't sure where Joe had got the beers from. They'd finished the cans she'd bought earlier that day when they were at the park. Joe's brother had said they had nothing in. It struck her as weird that Joe now had a bag full of beer. But she didn't feel she could ask any more questions.

"Here," Joe said, passing her a can.

Laura took it, and then three or four gulps, fast. Joe did the same and turned back to look at the bike again. "She's gorgeous, isn't she?" he said.

Laura smiled and nodded and took another sip of her beer. She wanted Joe to stop going on about the bike now.

She looked around her. She could see a gap between the trees by the river a little further along the path as it headed towards the viaduct. "What's down there?" she said. "Shall we go and look?"

Joe was finishing up his beer. He squeezed the empty can in his hand and dropped it by his bag, and reached in, pulling out another. Laura wanted to stop him drinking. She wanted to stop him looking at the bike. She wanted him all to herself again. "Come on, let's go down there. To the river…"

She kicked off her shoes as she ran through the grass to the path to find the gap in the bushes that led down to the water. "Come on, Joe!" she called, slipping her bag off her back and leaving it in the long grass as she went. "Leave the bike, come on!"

Joe wanted the beer. All he wanted was the beer. That happened when he'd had more than two. With the two he'd had before in the park, and the one he'd just finished, he'd already had three. This was his fourth now. He didn't want to slow down, but he still wanted to be with Laura, to have sex with her if he could. Now he had her here, with the bike, at this place that he'd wanted to show her, and he had the beer, he felt happy.

He looked over again at the bike.

God, he loved that bike. He'd felt so good riding it with Laura on the back. It was just like he'd imagined it would be. Things in life didn't usually work out that way for him. Usually stuff never happened like he imagined it would. Never.

He'd have to clean the bike before he took it back to work. The wheels were dirty now from the mud on the path, and from the meadow. It was pretty immaculate when he'd finished working on it yesterday at the garage. All shine and spin. He'd made it that way. He'd been working on it for weeks. His boss was impressed with what he'd done. The guy who owned it was picking it up tomorrow. He'd enjoy washing it down later. Cleaning it up. His brother might even do it with him. Be good for Bill to get away from the screen, out the flat. They hadn't done anything together in ages.

Joe looked up. He could hear voices. It struck him he didn't know exactly where Laura had gone, and just as he started to look around for her, he saw where the voices were coming from; three kids were walking towards him. Three kids from Wellbridge; three kids whose faces he knew, and whose faces he'd hoped never to see again.

"Bloody hell, its only bloody Joe McGrath..." That was

Kyle. A tall boy with dark eyes and an attitude to match. He looked stoked.

Joe started to walk towards the road bridge, towards the bike. He didn't want to see them, talk to them. He just wanted to get out of their way.

"Hello, stranger," said Kris. They were right behind him now, and Joe was almost in reach of the bike. "I thought you'd gone and died. Seriously, Joe. What's happening? What you doing here, eh?" Joe stopped and turned to face them. Kris looked older. Joe didn't remember Kris being older than Kyle, but he looked it – today, anyway. Maybe he'd been working out. He looked solid, strong, like he'd thickened out.

"Didn't we give him strict instruction? Were we not clear enough?" And that was Marky. Wherever Kyle and Kris were, there was Marky, lurking just behind like a bad smell, always having the last word. "I thought we were clear enough. What do you think, Kyle? Were we not clear enough the last time?"

They were all around him now, closing in. Joe backed himself up to the bike. He immediately wished he hadn't. He didn't want them anywhere near the bike. Shit, if they did something to the bike. He could handle whatever they might do to him, but not the bike. He knew he was in a shit place. Just under the bridge. No passers-by. He prayed Laura wouldn't come back. Fuck. If Laura came back and saw this, it would be over. He'd lose her. He felt sick. He swallowed, hard. He could taste the beer in the back of his throat.

"Yeah, you were clear," Joe said. "I didn't think I'd see you here. I'll move on. I'll go – you know, I didn't know this was your…"

"Ah – he's scared," said Marky, laughing.

"He should be after what his old man did," said Kris, looking at Kyle like he wanted permission or something. "You haven't forgotten about that, have you, Joe?"

Joe shook his head. He didn't want to think about his dad, and what he'd done. Not ever. If ever he remembered he blocked it out.

They all stood for a minute and no one said anything.

Joe prayed they wouldn't mention the bike.

"That yours?" Marky said, pointing at the bike.

"Kind of…"

"Let's see it then," Marky said.

Joe stepped towards them, and away from the bike. He didn't want to, but he knew he had to. Where was Laura? Where was she?

"It's nice," said Kris. "Really fucking nice. Where d'ya get it?"

"Does it matter?" Joe said. As soon as he spoke he wished he hadn't.

Kris grabbed him, hard, around the neck, pressing his forehead against Joe's. He could smell Kris's breath.

He could feel the warmth of it mingling with his own panicked shorter breaths. He had a pain where Kris was holding him. He didn't want Laura to see him like this. He thought he was actually going to be sick.

Kyle came up behind him and pressed himself against Joe's back. He whispered into his ear.

"Do you need a little reminder of why we don't ever want to fucking see your fucking face again?"

Joe grunted. He'd meant to say *No* but it came out like some kind of cough. It was pathetic. He knew it was.

"Was that a yes or a no, Joe? We didn't hear you. And we really need to hear you. All of us."

"No," he said. "No. It was a no…"

"Because, if a little reminder would help, I'm sure Kris would be more than happy to oblige."

"No," Joe said again. "No reminder. I get it. I understand."

Kris let go of him, and Kyle thrust his hand into Joe's front jeans pockets as he did, pulling out the key to the motorbike, along with a whole heap of wrappers and receipts and general crap, leaving Joe's pockets hanging inside out over the top of his jeans like limp dead fish.

"I just want to have a go on this machine, Joe," Kyle said. "You owe me that. It's sick. Totally sick. Then we'll leave you – yeah?" he said, his hands on the bike now, as he wheeled it over the path to the meadow – to where Joe had been sitting with Laura.

Joe followed them. He was looking at the ground. It was spinning. The whole world was spinning.

"You got a girl here, Joe?" Marky said, from up ahead. He was kicking Laura's bag. "This her bag? These her shoes?"

Joe looked up but he didn't answer.

"Nice one, Joe. Didn't think you had it in you," Marky said, kicking the shoes and tipping the bag upside down so everything fell out onto the grass.

"Don't do that, Marky. Please," Joe said.

"Where is she then, your girl? She gone and left you here all alone? She left you already?" Marky said, and he picked up Laura's wallet, taking out the cash and looking at her phone. "Nice phone," he said. "We'll have that," and he turned it off before putting it in his pocket with the cash.

Joe shook his head, and then he heard the bike start and Kyle and Kris scream – they were on the bike and Marky was chasing them now. He lifted his eyes to see them… Marky chasing Kris and Kyle on the bike around the meadow… Where was Laura…? They were on the bike, they were on it, they had it… Laura was gone… They couldn't take it… They couldn't… Everything had turned to shit… Just like it always did… And where was Laura…? This wasn't how it was meant to be… He felt sick – and everything was still spinning – and shit, they were coming towards him now on the bike – he had to get out the way but his legs – they wouldn't move fast enough – and he saw what was going to happen before it happened – he saw it before he could stop it – Kyle's right fist coming at him – on the bike – coming at his face – in his face – and then it was there – a blow – fast, hard, like a thud to the brain – and a pain in his eye burning like radiation – and he knew he was going to hit the ground – and then he did.

Laura found a gap in the trees, the one she'd seen before, and walked down the narrow bank and into the river. It was shallow. She could paddle in it almost all the way to the middle. The water was cold, but it felt nice. Fresh. She looked behind her for Joe. Where the hell was he? Why hadn't he followed her when she'd called him? She'd had too much beer. She knew that. They'd started drinking hours ago, in the park. She didn't even like beer that much. She walked in the river for a few minutes, towards the viaduct, the road bridge behind her now. She guessed the river must widen further up and go under the viaduct. She felt her feet tingle with the cold. She looked at her watch. It was almost 7.30 p.m. She stood still in the water and wriggled her toes, shifting the mud, shifting some rocks, relieving the pins and needles in her feet. Hopefully this might sober her up – the coldness, the ache of it on her skin. It almost hurt where it reached – right up to her knees.

She could hear the bike – he was on it again… He'd had too much beer to drive now. She was sure he had. And she needed to get home… How was she going to do that? She'd have to let Joe drive her. They'd sober up and then they'd go. She'd be late, really late, but that's what they'd have to do. Mum would go mad. She'd said she'd be back to eat with everyone tonight. She'd have to call. Stop Mum worrying. She never wanted Mum to worry. But she knew she always did. Maybe she'd call Ella. Pretend she'd been with Ella. Get Ella to cover for her. If Mum knew she'd been out on a motorbike drinking with Joe…well, she couldn't know that. Ella would help her think of a way out, an excuse… Everyone needed a best friend like Ella… But still, this wasn't good. It didn't feel that good being here like this. She was drunk. She didn't want to be this drunk or this late. She needed her bag and her shoes. She'd left everything in the grass. What had she been thinking? She needed to get back, get back to her stuff, back to Joe.

She began to wade a little further up towards the bank where there was another clearing between the trees. She reckoned she could get up the bank more easily there and onto the path alongside the river. Everywhere else at this part of the bank was so densely overgrown. But as she waded she saw some boys up ahead, and she stopped. They were loud, jibing each other, messing about. They looked pumped up, like they'd done something they shouldn't.

They were in the clearing she was heading for, between the trees, and she couldn't go there now. She stood still. They were loud. She didn't want them to notice her. Was it better to stand still or keep walking? She wasn't sure. If she turned round and waded back the way she'd come, would they see her? Would they ask her what she was doing? Was she better to just keep going, face up to them? They wouldn't be interested in her anyway, would they?

"Oi – you alright down there?"

They'd seen her.

There were two of them now. When she'd seen them first, she was sure there'd been one more.

"What the fuck?"

"Ah, just leave her will ya, Kyle?"

Laura didn't move.

"No! I wanna talk to her. What the fuck are you doing down there?" the one called Kyle said again.

A third bloke appeared from behind a tree, his trousers open like he'd just been for a piss. His pants just about held up around his waist. "Hey – maybe it's Joe's girl? Oi! You! You Joe's girl?" he said, leaving his trousers still hanging open as he called across to her, his hands on his belt.

They knew Joe. How did they know Joe?

The big guy, the one up front telling the mouthy one to leave it, spoke next, stepping forward towards Laura as he did.

"Listen, if I were you I'd fuck off home, yeah? Like now. Before one of us changes our mind."

"Ah, don't say that, Kris. Look at Marky, he's just had a piss – he's ready – ready for some action. Don't let him miss out. She's smoking – she's hot – look at her – and she's Joe's girl – right? Fuck – she's Joe's girl. She's fucking perfect. This is fucking perfect, right?"

There was quiet. The boys all looked at each other. They were gauging each other, working out what they were going to do next.

Laura didn't move. She couldn't feel her feet now – they were numb – she was numb – all of her. What did they want? Shit – did they want to hurt her, mess about with her – what? She didn't know. She didn't want to know. And they knew Joe? Where was he? This wasn't making any sense. She wanted to go. She knew she had to go. She let her eyes scan the rest of the bank. Was there somewhere else she could get to, to get away, fast, before them? The other side of the river was fenced off. She couldn't get out on the other side. She couldn't see how she might get away.

"Yeah, Kyle," the one called Marky said. "I could seriously do with a bit of Joe's girl…" and he stepped forward towards the water, towards her, as he spoke. "Let me do it, Kris. It don't mean nothing to you if I do, does it?"

"Just fucking go, will you?" the big one, Kris, said to Laura again.

She had to go. He'd given her a chance to go. She didn't know why. But she turned anyway towards the bank. She took his word and she walked away from where they stood, wading, looking back at the big one all the time, to check that he was letting her go, that she wasn't going to be hounded or chased. Her head was banging, but she just kept wading. She'd find a way through the bushes. She would. She'd just find a way. Back to Joe. Her hands started shaking as she tried to grab hold of some of the grasses and reeds by the bank to pull herself up out of the water. She didn't want to cry, but she felt like she might. She bit her lip hard, too hard. Should she scream? Could she? She wasn't sure that she could. She pulled at some loose roots, but they were slippery, wet, in her hands. She couldn't hear any voices now. Where were they? Had they gone? And where was Joe? Where the hell was Joe? She didn't look back. She couldn't. She pulled again on the roots and got up to where she needed to be on the bank. Was Joe looking for her? Had he gone? Had he left her? Would he do that? Leave her? It was so quiet now. She couldn't hear the bike. She wanted to hear the bike, to know he was still there, he was still her Joe, that things were still okay.

Out of the water now, she climbed through some low bushes. Her feet were caked in mud. The stuff was clinging to her toes in great clumps. She didn't want to stop and bang it off. She wanted to keep going. Get back to the bridge. Find Joe. It was completely quiet now. The boys must have gone. She couldn't hear their voices. She looked back, quickly. She couldn't see them. They'd gone. But where was Joe? Had they hurt him? Had they done something to him?

She stepped out of the bushes by the river and onto the path alongside the meadow. She knew she had to go in the opposite direction to the viaduct to get to the road bridge. She was on the path now. She hadn't waded that far. She could see that. She was close. She wanted to run, but she was too scared. Inside she was running. Inside she was running and screaming and running and screaming and her heart and her head were both throbbing.

She saw the bike on its side by the steps of the bridge.

"Joe?"

She walked towards the bike.

"Joe?"

Her voice cracked as it got louder.

She got this feeling like she was about to come across something bad. She looked around for her shoes, her bag. She had this plunging feeling in her chest. She knew it was the beer. It was just the beer making her feel this bad. She told herself it was okay. It was just the beer...

She bent down to look for her shoes – she needed them – she didn't remember where she'd left them – and as she leaned over someone grabbed her hard from behind.

She was jolted backwards – two solid hands had her around the waist – she lost her breath – she was turned around – firmly – and there was no scream except the one she thought she was screaming in her head – and there he was – it was Joe.

"You bastard!" she screamed. "You fucking bastard." She tried to push him but he didn't let her go.

"What? What?" he said, still holding her tight. "It was a joke!"

She tried to push him away again, and he let her go this time.

"You scared me, Joe!" she said and she tipped herself forward so her hands were on her knees and she could catch her breath properly.

"Shit, Laura…I'm sorry…"

She stood up to look at him. He was drunk. Completely drunk. She could see it in his eyes. She hadn't seen him look like this before – and one eye – it was all puffed up, red – but he was all hands and arms, touching her, grabbing at her, her skin, her clothes, where she stood. She wanted to make him stand still, to check him, to look, to see if he was okay. Was his cheek bruised? It looked like it was.

"What happened to your eye?"

"Did I scare you?" he said. "Really?" And he looked like he might laugh.

"Yeah, you did," Laura said, and she punched him hard

on his arm. "I'm serious. Don't laugh. Where were you? I thought you were going to follow me down to the river…"

"You left your bag and your shoes. I thought I better look after your stuff… Shit, Laura," he said again, rubbing his arm where she'd punched him. "That hurt…"

Laura felt bad for a moment that she'd hurt him. She looked across to the meadow where she'd left everything in the grass. All she'd wanted was for him to follow her down to the river, but he'd stayed – to look after her stuff. He was good. He was kind. She knew he was, and she was cross with herself for a moment that somehow, in the middle of all this, she'd doubted him.

She turned to look around for her bag, but Joe was holding her again, holding her arms tight, each of his hands wrapped entirely around each of her upper arms. She could hardly move.

"Come here, I'm sorry…" he said, and even though his hold was too tight, suddenly he looked so sorry, so completely sorry, that Laura let him hold her. "Come on, this way," he said, and he started to pull her with him along the path towards the viaduct, away from the road bridge and the meadow and the bike and all her stuff still lying in the grass.

"Joe, I think we should go…"

"No, not yet," Joe said, kissing her so gently. "I wanted to bring you here. Show you the viaduct. There are bats there. It's kind of freaky – but amazing. Just walk with me, and we can be here, together, alone…"

Laura looked at Joe. She wanted to be with him – together, alone – but not like this.

"What happened, Joe? To your face? Was it those boys?"

"What boys? There weren't any boys," he said and he moved his face close again, into hers to kiss her.

"Joe…" Laura said, pulling back. She didn't understand why Joe had said there weren't any boys. Had he not seen them? From the way they'd talked it was obvious they knew him. And she wanted to tell Joe what had happened to her when she'd seen them – what the boys had said, how they'd made her feel, but suddenly she wasn't sure how to say it.

"Joe…" Laura said again, gently. "I saw them – those boys…"

"Listen, Laura. There are no boys, okay?" Joe's voice was louder now, his hand gripping her wrist. "It's us. It's you and me, right? Just you and me." And as much as Laura made out like she believed him, nodding her head in reply, she didn't. She'd seen the boys. They knew Joe. She didn't understand why he was pretending it was any different.

"Joe, you wouldn't lie to me, would you? You wouldn't do that, would you?" she said.

"Just come with me, Laura – please," he said and he stopped and pulled her in close, more gently this time, and he kissed her, slowly, on the mouth. "Please…" he whispered.

Laura kissed him back.

She couldn't not.

"Five minutes, Joe. For you to sober up," she said. "And then we're going." She knew he couldn't sober up in five minutes, but she just wanted to go. Get away from this place. She needed him to get her home.

Joe took her hand, and looked at her, and he smiled. "Come on then, this way."

"But I haven't got my shoes…?" she said, looking down at her feet. She half hoped Joe might suggest they give up, go back to find her shoes, go back to the bike.

But he ignored her, pulling her with him along the path towards the viaduct. And she followed, because she felt like she had no choice but to follow. And because she wanted them to be together – together alone. Still, as they walked along the path, past the clearing on the bank where she'd seen the boys, she looked for them again to make sure they had gone. She didn't want to see them again. Not now. Not ever.

When they got to the viaduct Joe guided Laura off the path.

"Come on, this way," he said pulling her over the mud and the rubble between the bushes and branches that ran alongside the viaduct walls. Laura could see that other people had been this way before. The undergrowth was trampled. There were beer cans, crisp packets, empty bottles, but they were off the path and it was getting darker. She didn't like it. Joe tugged her along behind him, and as she occasionally slowed, his hand gripped hers firmly. Laura counted the arches as they walked. One, two, three, four – how far along was he going to take her? They were in what felt like a wood. The path, the river, the meadow, it was all out of sight and there were trees and bushes all around. There was a low rumble, and then the sound of a train moving fast as it went over the viaduct above them. She felt the sound reverberating in her chest like it was right on top of them. Too close. It made her want to scream. She looked behind her. What if those boys came back? What if they were here and they came back now? There was no way of getting help, of being seen. Laura wondered why Joe was so intent on taking her here. What was it that he so wanted her to see? Had he said something about bats? She thought he had.

"Just here," Joe said at last, leading her under the sixth archway as another train sped over their heads. They were way off the path now. Without her shoes Laura was sure she would cut her feet. He led her further in again. There were smashed bottles, an old shoe and the remains of a fire – a charred musty pile on the ground. It smelt of stagnant water and piss. As soon as they arrived Laura wanted to leave.

"Joe, listen, I – I haven't got my wallet, my bag—"

"Come on…I want to kiss you…here…just here…"

"Joe, you're drunk – please, let's not do this here. I need to get my stuff—"

"But I want to show you this place. There are bats here. Me and Bill used to come here all the time."

"Okay, Joe. I've seen it now."

"We used to have to get away, you know? When there was shit happening at home."

Joe was holding her hand so tightly now. Laura was struggling to understand what he was saying, what he was doing.

"What do you mean?" she said trying to pull her hand away, but Joe didn't let her.

"My dad… Bill's seen stuff… Stuff a kid shouldn't see. Bad stuff. Because of my dad. His dad was nice, you know? Not like mine. But he disappeared when mine came back on the scene. I needed to get Bill away sometimes. Protect him, you know?"

Laura didn't know. And she didn't want to know. Because she just wanted to go – to get away – to leave this place and go before Joe passed out on her – or the boys came back for her – or for Joe.

"Will you let go of my hand, Joe, please? I need to get my bag, my phone. I need to get my shoes. Will you take me home now? I don't like it here. I don't like the way you are…I just…"

Joe let go of her hand but pushed his whole body up against her, circling his arm tight around her waist. For a moment she wondered if he was going to push her to the ground.

"Shit, Laura. I thought we were okay."

His voice had never seemed so loud before.

"I thought you liked me, Laura. You said you loved me. I'm sure you said you did. Or were you lying? Do you lie about shit like that? Do you?"

Laura took a step back, and Joe let go of her, willingly.

"What do you mean, Joe? This was a good day – it was… I thought it was…" Laura said, and for a moment she thought she might cry, because she was confused. Had this been a good day? She thought it had. She'd told Joe she loved him. He'd said he felt the same, but then being here, now – it wasn't how she'd imagined it. It wasn't how she wanted it to be.

"Yeah, I thought it was a good day too… And then it changed. You changed. I'm not as good as you thought I was, am I? I'm not good enough…"

Laura stepped forward and took his hand in hers and squeezed it.

"I don't know what you mean, Joe."

"Oh shit – I don't want to do this," Joe said, rubbing his head.

"Look, can we just go? Please."

"No. Not yet. Just give me a minute," he said. "Just a minute." And he wandered over to the wall and he leaned against it and was sick. Over and over. Laura could hear him retching, but she couldn't see him. It was getting really dark now, and it was so much darker under here.

"You alright, Joe?" she called out. "I can't see you..."

Joe didn't answer.

"I'm going to find my shoes, Joe," she said. "Are you coming?"

Laura walked back over the rubble, back the way she and Joe had come. She wished she had her phone. She couldn't believe she'd been stupid enough to follow him, to let him lead her – with no shoes, no phone, all her stuff by the bike – when he was drunk. She'd been drunk too, but at least she felt more sober now. That was a relief. Another train rumbled above her, and as the noise of it died away she could hear a phone ringing. Only two more arches to walk past now. She was counting. Two more arches and she would almost be back at the path by the river. She didn't want to meet anyone here. She didn't want to see anyone. She wanted to get back to the path, to the bridge, to the road... The ringing was getting louder now, and then she saw it – Joe's phone on the mud in front of her. He must have dropped it. She bent down and picked it up, fast, to try and answer it. She looked at the screen – and then she stopped...

Ella calling…

Ella? Ella calling Joe? Ella's number in Joe's phone? She didn't know that they spoke, that they were in each other's phones…

She swiped her finger across the screen to try and answer it, but the ringing stopped. She'd missed the call.

Laura turned to look for Joe, the phone still tight in her hand.

"Joe?" she called again, louder this time.

There was nothing.

She turned round. She looked ahead of her. For a moment she wasn't sure where she was. She thought she only had one more arch to walk alongside before she was back on the path, but as she started walking again she wasn't sure what direction she was heading in. Had she come off the path to pick up the phone? She wasn't sure but her feet were stinging as she tried to step over all the stones and rubbish and branches. She wanted to run but it was too rough under her feet. And it was too dark to see where she was, what was on the floor. But she had a phone now. It was going to be okay, she told herself. She was going to be okay. Except she'd left Joe. She knew she shouldn't have left him. But he'd gone so quiet. And it was so dark. She couldn't go back now. She couldn't. She was sure he'd be okay. She called out for him again as she stumbled on – back alongside the viaduct – along the path – she was on the path now – and she kept walking – hoping she hadn't gone wrong –

"Joe? Joe? You alright?"

She called out again.

And suddenly she heard her words echo back around her, and a force – she felt a force – a blow – a crack – on her head – in her head – all over her – and there was pain –

At first she didn't know if it was just the noise of another train going over the viaduct – the rumble, the jolt, and then the force of it –

– in her head – it was like the train was going right through her –

screeching black pain –

pain – pain – pain –

and then black –

nothing –

and she felt herself slip away.

Part Two

Tessie
Eight weeks later

Tuesday

1.

"Who's going to the hospital today?" Mum said. "Dad's back to work. I need one of you to come with me."

I looked at Jake. We were sitting across the table from one another eating breakfast. He had to go today. He just had to. I'd been yesterday and I wasn't sure I could handle it again today.

Laura had been lying there for weeks. First with tubes in her nose and her stomach and her arms, and the pumping, the pumping that was breathing for her, keeping her alive. Then she was out of the coma, breathing on her own but still unconscious – still not Laura. She looked like she was sleeping, but the difference was just that she never woke up. And it was the same now, almost eight weeks on. Still, she was sleeping.

"Jake – will you come?" Mum said.

Jake looked at me quickly as Mum turned back to the toaster.

"Will you – please?" I mouthed across the table to him,

so Mum couldn't hear.

He blinked back at me. In the blink there was a yes, but he shook his head. He didn't want to go at all.

"Yeah, Mum. Sure," he said, standing up and walking to the sink with his cereal bowl. He dropped it in with a clatter and I knew in that moment he hated me for not stepping up. I followed him over and picked his bowl and spoon out of the sink and put them in the dishwasher before Mum had a chance to have a go at him. That was my thank you.

"We'll go after school," Mum said. "I don't want you missing anything. I'll meet you there, at the hospital. By the main entrance."

We'd only just gone back to school. We'd been back a week. Mum said she wanted us there for the first day of the new year – sixth form college for Jake, Year Eleven for me. She wanted us to start the term just like everyone else. That was why she wanted Dad to go back to work too. She wanted things to be more normal. And he was fine with that. As soon as Mum suggested he should think about it, he agreed, and said he'd go in on the Monday. He went straight to his laptop to email the office and let them know. He'd almost looked excited. Mum had watched him walk out of the kitchen and she'd put her hand to her mouth as he went. When she saw me looking at her she turned and gazed out of the kitchen window. She didn't want me to see her tears. I just went up and hugged her from behind. She let me, but she didn't hug me back. That was the week before last. It had been like that with me and Mum for a while now.

The thing is, Dad wasn't good at being at home. And part of what was so "not normal" about the last seven or eight weeks was Dad not working; him being around all the time just felt wrong. I know that sounds weird, but I think I wanted him to go back to work too. I figured that if he did, then it was only Laura not being there that was different. If Dad was at work then you could actually kid yourself that nothing had changed. Mum would be upstairs folding the washing or something – because these days she was always at home. She'd stopped working last year. It was stress. That's what they'd said. Jake would be in his room with the music on and I would be watching TV or reading or something. We'd all be doing what we normally do. And Laura could have been out with her friends. I could pretend that she was out. And then I could pretend that none of the horrible stuff that happened had actually happened. But whilst Dad was home, there was a constant reminder that something was wrong, and not least because he didn't know how to *be* with us.

Every day he'd get up and try and suggest things we might do together. Stupid things. Things none of us wanted to do – like going for a walk, or a coffee, or visiting someone we hadn't seen in ages – things that just felt wrong when Laura wasn't there. And of course all that did was make it worse. Because the thing about Laura lying unconscious in the hospital was that there was literally nothing anyone could do. Nothing. But at the same time not doing anything, and leaving Dad pacing around the house, that wasn't right either. Dad being at home was just a constant reminder of the really bad place we were all in.

"*Like normal,*" Mum had said. "*I want us all to try and just get on like normal.*"

I was up for that, I really was, but part of me wanted to remind her that things weren't really that normal before. It was like everyone had forgotten that. But I hadn't. I hadn't forgotten at all.

2.

I texted Max when I got upstairs to my room after breakfast.

Walk in together? Tx

I'd known Max since primary. He'd been my friend when I talked and my friend when I didn't, and that made him my best friend in all the world. My only friend. And he lived just over the road.

He texted straight back.

Yeah. Knock for you in 10.

Max knew that when he knocked for me and the front door was open I wouldn't speak. The front door has to be PROPER SHUT for me to speak in my house. That's just the way it is for me. The way it's almost always been, since I was five years old. And no, I don't know what started it and no one else knows either. I was shy. I was always a bit shy. I didn't really talk much. I don't think anyone even noticed that at first. But then I just stopped talking when I wasn't at home, and when I was at home I only talked to the people I knew really well – like my family and really close family friends. And by the time everyone noticed there was nothing I could do. If anyone talked to me, asked me to speak, I couldn't. In fact that made it worse – much worse. I mean if you're scared of spiders and I give you a spider, it's not going to make you better, is it? And it's the same with me and talking. If you try and talk to me, or ask me a question, you're going to make it worse because all you're doing is pushing me to try and do something I really can't do.

I'm selectively mute. Selective Mutism. That's what they call it. SM for short. Some people think I don't have SM. They just think I'm really rude or really stubborn. They think I am choosing not to speak. And I guess that is how it looks – to them. But I really don't have a choice. No one knows how I feel when I'm outside my house. And the nightmare is, I can't really tell them. I can't explain. I guess I've always felt the world is a scary place. Even before what happened to Laura. And people have tried to make me feel better about that, like my mum, my dad, and my speech therapist, Anya. They've all told me that if I speak – if I find a way through my fear about talking – then everything will feel better. They truly believe that. But I don't see how the words make anything better. There is nothing good you can say to make a bad thing less bad. If anything, what happened to Laura just proves that I'm right – that I've always been right; the world is a terrifying place. There are no words that can make it better.

When I opened the door to Max he was getting out his headphones.

"Hey, Tessie," he said.

I smiled, holding the door. He'd had his hair cut. All short at the sides and kind of floppy on top. It looked like he'd used gel on it or something. He looked nice.

"We should go," he said. "I want to get a sausage bap before we start. Had band practice last night. We finished really late. Didn't eat after. Woke up hungry, had breakfast, still hungry."

I smiled and nodded and pulled the front door shut behind me, and Max passed me an earbud.

This was our routine. Every morning. We walked, and we listened to music together. One earbud each so we could hear the same thing. We'd been doing it since the middle of Year Seven, after Max told me he found it awkward walking to school together in silence. I am fine with the silence. Silence is safety. It's my cocoon. But I know I'm different, and Max doesn't like it that way. I do get that.

"Today it's all about The Who," he said. "Lead singer Roger Daltrey, guitarist Pete Townshend, bassist John Entwistle, drummer Keith Moon – who died of a drug overdose and was replaced by Kenney Jones. One of the best rock bands of the twentieth century, in my opinion. I won't say any more for now. You tell me what you think later, yeah?"

I listened. It sounded tinny. Old. But all Max liked was old music. It was his dad's music. Max's dad had died of cancer five years ago, and the thing that had got Max through that first year without him was playing his dad's vinyl. Max genuinely believed he was born in the wrong generation. I never argued with him about that. I'd always nod like I thought he was born in the wrong generation too, but inside I was really thinking how the music just brought his dad back for him – in a good way. It didn't matter if it was Pink Floyd, The Stones, Santana – if it was from the seventies with serious amounts of guitar – it was all he needed. And now I was becoming an expert too.

I looked over at Max as we walked. He seemed happy. I'd forgotten what happy looked like. In that moment, happy, for me, was Max. Seeing Max. I wondered if that was what love was? Being with a person, doing nothing in particular, and just feeling happy. When I'd asked Laura she'd said it was more than that. She said you had to fall to know, and that when I fell – like she'd fallen for Joe –

I'd know. And she had this smile on her face that lit her up. That was the week before her attack. I guessed that meant I didn't love Max. I didn't feel any fall. But still, I wasn't sure, because somehow what I felt for Max felt something like love. There wasn't another word I could think of to describe it. And anyway, right now, all I could see in Laura's version of love was pain.

Joe was the police's main suspect in the investigation into Laura's attack. He was missing. He'd not been seen since. All that lay between Laura and Joe now was a whole heap of the horror of what had happened – and somewhere – we didn't know where yet – him lying low, alone, with his guilt. That wasn't love. It wasn't what Laura meant when she talked about falling in love with Joe.

I took a deep breath in.

None of us wanted to think about what had happened to Laura, or what Joe had done. It hurt too much. But I couldn't stop; every thought I was thinking seemed to end up with her.

"You okay?" I felt a hand on my arm.

I nodded.

"You know if you ever want to talk to me about Laura when we get back to yours, one day, or at mine, after school or something – then…well, you know you can… Can't be easy coming back to school after this."

Max didn't look at me as he said it, but I put my hand

on his arm, just like he'd done to me, and I smiled and nodded back.

The words that I would have said if I could have said them were: *Yeah, I know, Max. Thanks. I know.*

3.

When we got to school Max headed straight for the canteen and I followed. Holly and Kat were up ahead. Seeing them was something I dreaded, and the feeling of wanting, no, needing to avoid them, never went away. Each September when we returned to school I'd wonder whether this would be the year that they'd finally give up having a go at me. It was constant through Years Seven, Eight, Nine and Ten and now here we were in Year Eleven. I prayed that today was the day – the day that they'd get bored of me – that they'd find someone else to bully.

"Squeak like a mouse, Tessie. Can you squeak like a mouse?"

That's why Max had started walking with me to school and back three weeks into Year Seven. He'd caught up with me one day at the bus stop when they'd had me pinned to the bench.

"Has the cat got your tongue, Tessie?"

"Has she even got a tongue?"

"Show us your tongue, Tessie! Show us your tongue!"

And then they'd started pinching me hard to see if they could get me to make a sound, chanting "*Squeak! Squeak! Squeak!*" and some of the other kids at the bus stop thought it looked like fun and started to join in.

It was Max who stopped it.

He'd been walking by and seen them having a go. He pushed his way through everyone and said, very gently, very quietly, "*Come on, Tessie. Let's go.*" And everyone just automatically moved out of the way. I can't believe how brave Max was. I'm not that brave. I could never have done anything like that. And seeing Kat and Holly in the canteen now brought back just how weak I felt.

I swallowed.

My mouth was dry, and I could feel my heart begin to race. I walked quickly towards the breakfast bar and picked up a juice, swiping my lunch card and sitting down at the end of one of the benches, where I hoped no one could see me. I couldn't drink the juice. I wouldn't. I couldn't eat or drink in front of people. That was the SM. When I ate people looked at me. I knew they did, and I couldn't eat because I didn't want people looking at me. But I needed to have a drink in front of me, something to occupy me, some reason for being in the canteen while Max had gone ahead to get in the queue for his sausage bap. I put the juice down on the table and looked for Max over at the hot food counter.

He was chatting to Mia in the queue. Mia had joined our tutor group at the end of last year. She'd moved from another school because her parents had split up. She liked Max. I could tell. And she was pretty. Really pretty. I wasn't sure what was stopping him asking her out. He seemed to act like he liked her too. They were both slightly softer around each other, if that makes sense. That's what I'd noticed. I think that's what made me think there was something there. Like they were showing each other their kindest side.

Kat and Holly joined the queue behind Max and Mia. They didn't look over. Maybe they hadn't seen me. Maybe they weren't interested in me any more. Had the moment I'd been wishing for finally come? I mean, I had a sister in hospital – a sister on the brink of life. No one wants to talk to you when you've got a sister about to die, do they? They don't know what to say. No one does. That was the best protection I had against them all now. Except as soon as I had that thought I felt bad – bad for even thinking it. Laura was lying quietly in the hospital and here I was, relieved that somehow her being there made things better for me at school. I wished I'd never thought it.

I looked over again at Max. I was pretty sure the bell would go before he made it over to sit with me, so I got out my book. It was the closest I could get to hiding. But as I started to read I couldn't focus on the words. I felt like someone was watching me.

I looked up.

Max and Mia were still chatting in the queue. Everyone else was talking, coming in and out. There was a hum. A general hum. Kat and Holly had sat down on the other side of the canteen. I wondered what everyone was talking about. Everyone always had something to talk about. Was it all stuff that mattered?

I looked down again at my book.

Still, the feeling was there.

Someone, watching me.

I felt myself go hot. I picked up the juice, closed up my book. My heart started racing. I had to get out of the canteen. I put everything in my bag. Someone was looking at me. Everyone was looking at me. Everyone. They were all looking. I knew I shouldn't have bought the juice. I stood up to go, but I wasn't sure I could move. I felt my face getting hotter and hotter. Everyone was looking. I was sure. I had to go. I had to. I took a deep breath and stepped away from the bench. My legs were shaking. And as I walked through the wide canteen door and out into the corridor, I saw him. A boy with a shaved head and eyes so blue they sparkled. He was new. I'd never seen him before. And he was looking at me. He had been looking at me. And the minute I saw him I knew that he wasn't just anyone. I knew that before I even knew his name.

4.

When I heard the doorbell after school, I didn't answer. Mum was at the hospital with Jake. I was on my own and it was hard. It was the anticipation of someone coming to the door or the phone ringing, even though I knew I didn't have to answer it, or do anything I didn't want to do, it still made me feel uncomfortable.

The doorbell rang again.

I swallowed. I felt like I might cough. And then I did. My nervous cough. My blip. I was under threat – of speaking.

I stood completely still just inside the sitting-room door. I didn't move in case whoever was at the door could see me somehow through the glass. I felt my heart beating in my ears.

The letter box lifted, and a voice called through.

"Tessie, it's me – Ella. Are you there?"

Ella. Laura's best friend.

"Let me in, will you? Please! I won't be long…"

No one was saying they blamed Ella for what happened to Laura, but deep down you knew everyone in my family had thought about that at least once. Ella had met Joe first. As soon as she'd met him she hadn't stopped telling Laura how amazing he was, how gorgeous, how he worked at the garage down the alley along from the cafe where she worked. She'd describe in detail how he came in every day for tea and a toastie. When she was at ours with Laura, after school, it was all she talked about. And then two weeks later Ella had introduced them. She was stocktaking at the cafe one night after closing. Laura said she'd turned up to keep Ella company, that she was messing around with her iPod in the cafe's dock when Joe banged on the window. She said that as soon as she saw him, she knew she liked him. She never told me exactly what happened that night, except that Joe ended up walking her home. They talked. And I guess that was when she began to fall. Maybe if Ella hadn't ever introduced them none of this would have happened. I'd never heard Mum actually say those words, but I knew it was what she thought.

"It's important, Tessie. It's really important."

I walked towards the front door. I could feel the stretch in the skin around my neck, the tightening in my throat. I couldn't reply, I couldn't say anything until Ella was inside and the door was PROPER SHUT. Ella knew that. She knew. I didn't understand why she was pushing me to talk back to her like this, through the door.

"Tessie, is your mum here or is she at the hospital?"

I opened the door quickly and let Ella in.

And then I closed it again.

PROPER SHUT.

Ella hadn't been round for weeks. We'd hardly seen her at all since Laura had been in the hospital. It seemed almost odd seeing her now.

As I turned to walk into the sitting room I remembered the day the police had come to say there'd been an incident, that they thought something had happened to Laura. I remembered that evening so well. Ella had phoned. She'd phoned almost as soon as the police had arrived. We'd all jumped when the phone rang. We were so on edge. The police had barely had a chance to tell us what was going on, but they'd indicated to Mum that she should pick up, and we'd all heard her side of the conversation.

"Oh, Ella, it's you!" Mum had said when she answered the phone. "Have you heard from Laura? Have you heard anything from her this evening at all?" I remember the desperation in Mum's voice, the hope that somehow the police had got it wrong, the hope that Ella was calling to say Laura was with her, they were on their way to ours, she was bringing Laura home. "I have to go… We have to go…" Mum had said quickly, just as soon as it was clear that Laura wasn't with Ella. "The police are here. They think something has happened to Laura. We'll call you…" And she hung up.

I remember thinking Mum hadn't left enough pauses in the conversation for Ella to really answer. That's the thing about not being a talker; when you don't talk that much you listen more. You see the gaps in the conversation. You can read them like the words in a book. I'm really good at doing that because I'm listening all the time. And when you listen, you hear everything. You hear things in the silences, in the sighs, in the blank spaces of the conversation too.

"Is your mum here?" Ella said again, bringing me back to the present.

"No, she's at the hospital, with Jake," I said, quietly.

I could talk to Ella at home. Ella and Laura had been friends for so long and Ella had spent so much time at our house, she was almost like family. It was people who weren't family, or as close as family, that I couldn't talk to, even at home.

"It's just I promised my mum I'd pop this round," Ella said. "And well, I sort of forgot."

I nodded and took the bag Ella was thrusting into my hands.

"It's just some of Laura's stuff. A top, a book, some make-up – all stuff she lent me. Your mum asked me for it, wanted anything I had of Laura's back." She paused for a moment. "I looked to see if there was anything else, but there isn't. This is it."

I nodded, taking the bag into my hands. I wondered why Mum would be doing that, looking through Laura's things, looking to get stuff back. She must have been going through Laura's room. The rest of us weren't even allowed in there. Mum had made it out of bounds. Was that because Mum was somehow trying to put the room back together? Make it perfect. Make sure nothing was missing, because Laura was.

Ella and I stood in silence in the hall for a moment. I wasn't sure why she wasn't saying goodbye and leaving. I waited. Did she have something to say? And then her phone rang, and as she started looking in her bag for it, she spoke.

"Have they found Joe's phone, do you know?" she said, lifting her eyes up to mine, looking at me intently, whilst scrabbling around in her bag. "Have they said anything about it? The police?"

"No," I said. "It's been switched off since the night Laura was hurt. They can't trace it."

"I wish they'd hurry up and find it," Ella said, pulling her phone out of her bag, looking at the screen. "Because then we'd find him and we'd discover the truth of it – I mean what actually happened that night."

Ella had missed the call.

She looked up at me again. "I mean that's what's so terrible about all this, Tessie, isn't it? No one knows what happened – except Laura, and she can't tell us." She paused. "And I don't know where Joe is, or what he's doing right now or what happened. I wish I did, but I don't."

"Yes," I said. "I know." But I didn't understand what Ella was saying or why she was saying it. No one had suggested she knew anything about Joe or his phone or what happened that night. Had they?

Ella looked down at her phone again.

"Listen, I've got to go. I'm meant to be at the cafe, like now... I'm closing up for Leila. Tell your mum I came round. Give her that stuff, won't you?"

I nodded, because Ella had opened the front door to leave and she was still talking to me as she went. I couldn't speak now.

"I'll see you soon, yeah?" Ella said. "Come and see me in the cafe, Tessie. Any time, yeah? I mean it, I'd be glad to see you. I've no one to talk to these days..."

I nodded.

I knew what she meant.

It just wasn't the same for any of us without Laura here.

5.

I switched on the TV after Ella left. I didn't know what else to do. There was just something about the way she'd come round, and the way she'd been, that seemed odd. But it had been so long since I'd seen her. And I couldn't pretend that seeing her without Laura wasn't weird. Laura and Ella had done almost everything together, before – well, before Joe anyway.

And watching TV made me feel less alone. I liked the sounds of the random voices. If I stayed downstairs and had the TV on loud enough there were people with me all the time, even when I went into the kitchen to get something to drink or eat. I liked that. And then Mum's voice joined the throng almost as soon as her key was in the door.

"I don't know what we're going to eat tonight, Jake. Honestly, just let me get in and put down my bag and I'll work out what there is…"

Mum was snapping, stressed. I stayed in the sitting

room and heard her go into the kitchen. The kettle flicked on. I didn't move from the sofa. I wanted to know how Laura was, and I didn't want to know, all at the same time.

Jake appeared at the sitting-room door.

"Alright?" he said.

I nodded. "Was it okay?"

"Oh, you know, the same…" he said.

Jake found it hard to really say how anything was. That didn't mean he didn't feel anything. I could see on his face what he felt, but he wasn't going to say things were "terrible", because if he did I guessed he might have to think about what that meant or what might happen. I mean if you admit something is terrible, where do you go from there? I guess maybe you fall apart. And none of us could fall apart, because that was what Mum did. She'd fallen apart before a few times, and I never knew why, but I knew it was happening again now. And Laura was usually the one who made it better for Mum. She somehow always knew how to help Mum, in the same way that Dad did. When Dad was at work Laura seemed to step into his role and, when I think about it now, I don't know what it was that Laura did that seemed to make everything just a little better, but me and Jake knew that we had to work it out somehow, and try to fill her shoes.

Jake turned and went upstairs. I heard his bedroom door shut and the music come on and I guessed I wouldn't see him until the morning – unless at some point there was food. I needed to go and see if there was food.

I stood up and went into the kitchen.

"Don't ask me if there is anything to eat," Mum said as soon as I walked in, her back to me, "because I haven't had a chance to look."

That was the first she'd spoken to me since I'd seen her this morning. I felt wounded, though I knew that if Laura had been here she'd remind me that this irritation was just a normal part of Mum's low.

"I was just going to see if I could make something," I said.

She didn't reply.

I opened up the fridge door – a red pepper, some old ham, a jar of mayonnaise. I closed it again.

"Beans on toast," I said. "That would work, wouldn't it?"

"Maybe," Mum said, her voice quieter now. "I'm not sure I feel like eating."

I nodded.

The kettle clicked off, and Mum just stood still, looking into space, out through the kitchen window.

I got a mug and a tea bag and the milk and I made the tea and handed it to her.

"Thanks, Tessie," she said, breaking her stare, and turning towards me. "Thanks, darling." And she took the tea and stroked my face with her hand and it was like she'd come back to me. But I knew she was thinking of Laura, not me, and that she was about to break down and cry. Still I was glad that she'd seen me. In that moment at least, I knew she had seen me.

The front door opened and slammed shut.

"Hey, everyone!"

It was Dad.

"I got pizza... Who's for pizza?"

That was the brilliant thing about Dad. That's why we needed Dad. He knew how to make things better in an instant. He knew what to do to make things right when they felt completely wrong.

Jake's footsteps thundered down the stairs and Dad came into the kitchen.

"Grab some plates, Tessie. Come on, let's eat while it's hot," he said, and Mum smiled. We all pulled out chairs to sit down together at the table, and even though we were all thinking about Laura – I knew we were – none of us mentioned her. And somehow, that was okay.

Wednesday

6.

"So I've put together a new playlist, and I guarantee that after today you'll see the genius that is The Who."

Max. He was at the front door, raring to go – to walk me to school and listen to music.

"I know you didn't love what I played you yesterday. But today, I'm starting with "Substitute". This one's a classic. It may be all I need to convince you. Ready?"

I looked at him. The world was always okay for Max. It never seemed to dip or turn. Even when he lost his dad he seemed to accept the sadness in a way I knew I never could have done. *"He was ill, Tessie. It was harder seeing him ill and suffering than accepting, now, that he's gone."* Why was life like that for some people? Why didn't it make sense like that for everyone?

Max passed me an earbud, and I stepped out of the house and closed the front door behind me. The air was slightly cooler this morning. The first hint of autumn. I breathed out to see if my breath might form a cloud. No, not yet. I closed my eyes and wished. I wished for Laura to wake up before autumn came, before I got out my winter coat, before my breath could form a cloud.

I listened to The Who as we walked. I didn't think there was any way I was going to call this genius, even if I heard it again and again for the rest of my life. But I decided I wouldn't tell Max that just yet. He was singing the words as he walked, tapping me to grab my attention when he wanted to let me know a really good bit was coming up.

When we got to the gates he put out his hand so I could pass him back the earbud.

"I won't ask you if you liked it. I mean I'll ask you later." He paused. "Listen, my mum said your mum was picking you up after school, so you don't need me to walk with you. I guess you're at the hospital tonight?" he said. "I might go with Mia to the cafe after school, it's just...you know... well, I said I would...and..."

I wanted to interrupt him. I wanted to make him stop talking. I wanted to say: *It's okay, Max. Of course it's okay.*

Except even though I was thinking those words, somehow, somewhere I was a little unsure that it did feel okay. I felt a kick in my chest, like a thump. What was that? I think it was panic. A little thump of panic, and I knew then that I really wasn't that sure at all. Were they going to start seeing each other? Max and Mia? Was this a date?

Max was looking at me, searching my face for an answer,

so I nodded quickly. I just nodded. And even though I felt the urge to touch him, to squeeze his arm, I didn't. Because people were streaming around us, coming into school, and it would have looked too weird. So I stopped myself. I just turned and went. And inside I felt like something was slowly dying. But this was a feeling I knew; the gaping sadness that's left when you miss the moment to say the thing that you really want to say. I knew that feeling as well as the shape of my fingers, the lines on my hand. It engulfed me. It was choking me now. But it would pass. So I walked on and I didn't look back and I trusted that Max understood me enough not to read too much into it, and wonder why I had just had to walk away.

I headed inside along the corridors towards the lockers. My bag was heavy and I wanted to offload some of the books I didn't need until the afternoon. I'd grab them back at lunchtime, and that would also give me something to do. Lunchtimes were always difficult. So much time with literally nothing to do but avoid everyone.

I dumped the books I didn't need in my locker and slung my bag back across my shoulder. And as I walked along the corridor I saw Kat and Holly coming towards me.

I wasn't sure whether to stop.

If I kept walking, maybe they'd just carry on too.

That's what I hoped as I approached the doors – that we would just pass each other – go through the doors –

with everyone else – we'd all just pass on through.

I kept walking.

I felt myself go hot, hotter, my heart speed up.

I didn't want to feel like this. I wanted the feeling to go, to be over.

I pushed the door open wide, a pain in my throat, tensing as I did.

"SQUEEAK!"

Kat was there, in my face, screaming, pressing me up against the open door.

"EEK! EEK! EEK!"

Holly now. Her face so close to mine that her hair was in my mouth, up my nose, making me want to spit and cough.

I pressed myself up against the open door to keep myself back, so they'd back off, but there was no room to move, to breathe. I wanted to get away.

"Hey, Mouse!" they both squealed together. "Hey, hey, hey!" they squealed again before moving on, laughing, moving away.

Everyone else was passing through the doors now, laughing, commenting, talking to me – but just for a laugh, because they knew I couldn't speak back, that there was nothing that I could say. And I stood still, to let them pass. I didn't move. I waited. And when everyone had gone, and the bell had sounded, and the corridor had emptied out completely, I stepped forward. I let the door close gently behind me in the quiet, and I turned back and pressed my hands and my forehead against its cool glass panels, imagining I was somewhere else. I closed my eyes to imagine it. Another place. In the cool, and the quiet.

Count to ten. Take a moment and count to ten.

That's what Anya would have said.

So I did.

I counted to ten.

And then I opened my eyes.

And there he was –

The new boy –

The one with the sparkling eyes –

He was standing on the other side of the door.

And his hands were pressed to mine, touching mine, through the glass.

And his words – he mouthed the words – asking me – if I was okay.

I lifted my forehead away, slowly, from the glass, but I left my hands against it, against his, because I couldn't move them. I didn't want to take them away.

And we stood, and we looked at one other.

He stood.

And I stood.

Looking.

And then he smiled.

A shy smile.

A smile that looked like it came from a faraway place.

A place that was hard to find.

And all I wanted to do was ask him.

I wanted to open the door and ask him his name.

7.

Mum picked me up in the car after school. When I got in she passed me a packet of biscuits.

"I'm guessing you'll be hungry and there's nothing worth eating in those vending machines at the hospital."

Mum hated travelling in the car with me. She didn't understand why I wouldn't speak in the car. I had tried to explain to her when I was having my sessions with Anya that it just didn't feel safe. That people could see me, if the windows were down, they could hear me. *"But you're with me,"* Mum would say. *"I don't understand why you can't talk when it's just me and we're not outside. We're in the car!"*

I didn't want to say that it wasn't about her, that it was about me, because I knew she'd take it the wrong way.

I opened up the biscuits and passed one over to her.

"No, thanks," she said. "I got them for you."

I didn't want to eat. My stomach was tight with nerves.

I hated the hospital. I hated going there, I hated seeing

Laura, I hated the nurses who were always trying to talk to me, to jolly me along. I hated that Mum always cried and Dad wasn't there to make it better. But I knew all that was selfish. It wasn't about me, it was about Laura, and I had to go, for her. I had to go and try and be there, to make things better, even if I couldn't do anything to help because I couldn't say a word.

I held onto the biscuits on my lap.

"So you're not going to eat one?" Mum said, as we pulled into the hospital car park.

I shook my head as she parked up.

Whatever I did, it was wrong.

"God, you're hard work, Tessie," she said, turning towards me. And then she leaned down and picked up her bag from by my feet. "We'd better go straight in," she said, and she looked at me in a way that made me think I'd be sick with the strain of trying to make things right with her and always somehow failing.

There was a nurse by Laura's bed when we walked into the ward. I didn't recognize this one. The first few weeks, when Laura was in ITU, we had Magda. Magnificent Magda, and Brilliant Brenda. That's what Dad had called them. They'd made us all feel that, despite the hell, Laura was going to be okay. And, unlike the ward, it had been so quiet in ITU. Muted, hushed – all the noise came from the machines – the whirring, the swishing, the sighing – and it matched the sounds of sadness in my head. There was a symphony of life in that ITU, but with no variation – no crescendo, no pauses, nothing. Those first few weeks I found myself listening for breathing, waiting for something to happen – some change – but nothing did. No life. No breath. No voice. No change.

"No change."

That's what the doctors said.

"She's doing well, but no change."

We were all waiting for change, but we were scared of it too. Because a change could be for the better, but it could also be for the worse.

And then it happened. There was a change. Two and a half weeks after the attack. Mum and I were at the hospital and Laura coughed.

She actually coughed, and she started pulling at all the tubes and her legs and arms were flailing and she looked like a diver rising too fast from the deep. Reaching, reaching, reaching for the surface, reaching for the air out of the watery blue. Suddenly nurses were everywhere. There was noise. Life. I had to step back. I was crying. And Mum was saying, *"Is she dying? What's happening? Is she dying?"* and no one answered. No one said a thing. And I remember thinking that someone needed to say something.

They really needed to say something. But it wasn't – it couldn't be – me.

Laura was moved to the ward about two weeks after that, as soon as she could breathe entirely on her own. That was in August. She had coughed her way out of ITU, but she remained unconscious still even now. "In a severely decreased level of consciousness." That's how the doctor described it. She still looked like she was in a coma to me. But she could breathe on her own and she was now on a general ward. And on the ward it felt like there was a different nurse on a different shift every time we came to see her, but I'm sure that wasn't true. It was just that the nurses there didn't talk to us in the same way as the ones in ITU. They didn't know Laura like Magda and Brenda knew her, and they didn't know me, about my SM. They would often try and talk to me. It was hard.

"Pull over that chair, darling," one of them said to me now. She was standing by Laura's bed straightening the sheets as Mum and I came across the ward. "I'm nearly done."

I did what the nurse said and pulled the chair over. I thought it would get easier in time, coming here, doing this, but it seemed to be getting harder.

"And Mum, you alright sitting over there?" the nurse said. She was so jolly, so completely at ease. "You could go and get some tea. I'm nearly done. Then you can sit down here."

"Oh yes, I'm fine," Mum said. "Good idea. I'll get us some tea, Tessie. You stay with Laura, I won't be long." And she left.

"Her blood pressure is stable today," the nurse said, looking at me.

I looked back at her and swallowed. I felt a lump in my throat like a rock. It was the anticipation that she was going to ask me something, ask me a question. I could feel the heat building in my face.

The nurse stroked the sheets down at the end of the bed as she passed by me.

"Tell her you're here," she said. "She can probably hear you, you know. I'm sure you've been told that before, but talk to her," she said, and at last she left, pulling the curtain around the bed as she did. "Give it a go."

She was right. I'd been told to talk to Laura a million times before by a million different nurses since Laura was on the ward. The fact that I couldn't was what made coming here so hard. I knew it helped to talk to her. They'd told us that in ITU. "*Talk to her,*" Brenda had said. "*It doesn't matter what about. Tell her about your day. Hold her hand. Tell her a story. It will help just knowing you are here.*"

I looked at Laura. All I was doing was letting her down. I'd never be able to speak to her here. Never. What was the point in coming if she couldn't see me, if she couldn't hear me, if she didn't know I was there?

I could feel my throat thickening, my ears pumping, like there was hot sticky lava gliding through my throat, my neck. I knew I should pull my chair in closer towards her, say something. But all I could do was think the words. I couldn't say them. And I didn't want to touch her. I was afraid to touch her. She was still so pale, so fragile, so not the Laura I knew.

"*Don't touch me!*"

That was one of the last things Laura had said to Mum before the accident. They'd argued. That's all they'd been doing since Laura had started seeing Joe. It was constant.

"*He's not good for you, Laura,*" Mum had said.

"*How can you possibly know that, Mum! How? You've met him once. Once!*"

Mum hadn't answered, and Laura had carried on, giving it back. She was so angry. I was sitting at the bottom of the stairs. I had my hands cupped over my ears but I could hear every word.

"*You can't stop me seeing him. You can't do that!*"

"*I know, but I'm your mother, and I can tell you how I feel, and what I think. I can tell you that I don't want you to see him. He's not good for you – I can see that – the way you are – the way you've been – since you met him…*"

"*You mean he's not good enough for me? That's what you mean, isn't it? Not good enough. You're just not saying it because you know how wrong it is to judge him because he* works at a garage, because he isn't going to university. I can't believe—"

"I don't want him to hurt you, Laura."

"I'm eighteen, Mum. This is my life. And I'm seeing him. I'm seeing Joe. And there is nothing you can do about it. Nothing!" and Laura walked into the hall and I remember she grabbed her bag off the banister and her face was flushed and she looked beautiful, so completely alive and beautiful. And Mum tried to grab her, to pull her back.

"Don't touch me!" she screamed as she moved away.

And then she saw me, sitting on the stairs.

"I'm sorry, Tessie," she said. "I can't stand it. I can't do this any more. I have to go – get out for a bit…"

And she left.

But when she said that, she hadn't meant that she wasn't coming back. She hadn't meant she wasn't coming back at all.

8.

"Hello, Mrs Green. Do you have a minute?"

It was the Family Liaison Officer, May Grover. She'd arrived within ten minutes of me and Mum getting home from the hospital. We hadn't seen her for over a week. When it first happened she was here every day, sticking her nose into everything. That's how it felt anyway. She was meant to be here to support us, to guide the family through the investigation – the kind face of the police. No uniform, soft voice, good at making tea. But I hated her being here. Because when she was here she took over my family. She took them all away from me. I couldn't speak anywhere those first few weeks, not even at home, because my home had a stranger in it – May Grover – as well as all the other people who seemed to have to come and go. I spent most of that first week in my room. There was literally nowhere else for me to be.

"Is there news?" Mum said.

I stepped away from the front door and backed myself

up towards the stairs. Just seeing May made me do that. Instinctively I wanted to move away.

"Can we come in, Mrs Green? Just for a minute? It won't take long. I've got DI Campbell with me. He's just finishing a call in the car. Is that okay?"

If Detective Inspector Campbell was coming in that meant there was news. He was leading the investigation. He was in charge of everyone and everything to do with it. I stopped where I was on the stairs. Mum looked back towards me.

"Tessie, why don't you go up?"

I turned, and did as she said.

"Mrs Green." I could hear his voice. DI Campbell. He was coming in from outside. "Sorry to disturb—"

"No, no – it's fine," I heard the need in Mum's voice – the need for news, for word of something. It was why I was sitting at the top of the stairs now, hidden just out of view. I didn't want to be in the room, but I also didn't want to miss out on hearing what they had come to say. I craved news as much as Mum did.

"We just wanted to update you. Can we come in?"

"Yes, of course – come through," Mum said, and they all moved towards the kitchen. "Have you found something? Her phone?"

Mum was desperate for them to find Laura's phone. We all were. We were sure it would give the police stuff they needed to know about Joe and about what had happened that night. Laura lived on her phone. There had to be something there.

I crept quietly down the stairs so I could listen.

"We haven't found any new evidence, Mrs Green, I'm sorry. The search for Laura's phone, and Joe's too, will be ongoing, of course, but I wanted to let you know that the search unit feel that they are coming to the end of their job now."

"What?"

I could hear the shock in Mum's voice as she spoke.

"The search around the river and the viaduct has been extensive," Campbell went on. "As you know, we had a unit there day and night for the first couple of weeks, and the searches have continued, albeit with a scaled-back team, since then."

"So you're giving up?" Mum said. "Is that what you're telling me?"

There was emotion in Mum's voice now. She was going to cry.

"No, Mrs Green, not at all. But our search for evidence, in that particular location, is coming to an end at this point in the investigation. It doesn't mean we won't stop looking for evidence elsewhere, of course."

"So what have we got? What happens now?"

"Well, we have a motorbike crashed and abandoned on

the Wellbridge Road, which was reported stolen from the garage where Joe McGrath worked as an apprentice the morning after Laura's attack. Given Laura's relationship with Joe we are working on the basis that the motorbike is a significant piece of evidence. Joe going missing within the same timeline continues to make him the person we are most eager to speak to about the case. In this respect, nothing changes, Mrs Green."

"Yes, but what about the evidence collected at the scene? You said you were going to go back to that for further tests. Will you still do that, given that Joe is still missing?"

"Yes, Mrs Green. We have done, and this is partly why May and I are here today. Look, despite the rain that evening, forensics have managed to get some DNA evidence from the motorbike, which is a great result. And the evidence confirms that the crashed motorbike on the Wellbridge Road had also been in the meadow by the viaduct. There are traces of soil and spores from the grasses by the River Tren."

"So is that good news?" Mum said.

"Yes, it is, Mrs Green. It helps. Obviously what we are really looking for here is evidence of who was riding that motorbike at the viaduct on the evening of Laura's attack, and then later that same evening on the Wellbridge Road. The evidence from the helmet found at the scene isn't giving us anything conclusive right now."

"But you said there was a witness on the Wellbridge Road? Someone who described a young man fitting Joe's description – height, build – crash the bike and run towards the West Way…"

"Yes, but that doesn't prove that it was Joe, Mrs Green, or indeed that it was anyone specifically known to us."

Mum was silent, as if she was waiting for more information, anything more. I could feel her desperation through the walls from where I sat on the stairs.

"Mrs Green, the most compelling evidence we have so far is the beer cans we found in the meadow. They were swabbed by forensics, as you know, immediately after the attack. They gave us some DNA that didn't tally with any existing records on the database, but we did go back to them for fingerprints just this week, as part of our general forensic review of the evidence in this case. We did the same with the bike, and we've been lucky. We've recovered a clear print from one of the beer cans that does tally with one of the elimination prints taken at Joe's locker at the garage. Obviously this strengthens our need to find Joe McGrath."

"So the prints are Joe's?" Mum said.

"No. The prints we've taken are sitting on our database as unidentified right now, because they don't tally with any existing prints in the system. As soon as we question Joe and are in a position to make an arrest we'll be able to cross-check the evidence we've collected to establish whether we have the person to whom those prints and that DNA evidence belongs."

"But what about the CCTV?" Mum said. "You must have something from that, surely? The world is full of bloody CCTV!"

I wanted to go to Mum.

I could feel her anger, her frustration.

But I couldn't. I was meant to be upstairs, in my room. I looked down at my hands and saw they were curled into tight little fists in my lap, like tiny hedgehogs.

"Mrs Green, as I think you know, there is no CCTV in the area where Laura was attacked and whilst the CCTV along the Wellbridge Road is useful, in as much as it shows us the movements of the bike that evening with timings, and the number of riders at particular points, it isn't conclusive evidence. We cannot identify the riders from the footage, given both riders were wearing helmets. Even if we could, it still doesn't tell us who attacked Laura. Look, I'm sorry I can't come to you with more than this right now…"

It went quiet. Were they talking more quietly or had the room gone silent? I couldn't quite tell. I inched my way a little further down the stairs, my fists still in my lap.

"What would really help," Campbell said, "would be to get some witnesses to come forward. I'm pressing for the reconstruction to happen this week. We're ready to go, we have everything in place, including the media, but I'm just waiting for the okay from the powers that be at the station. Murder cases take priority, and we're looking at attempted murder here, or possibly grievous bodily harm, but given where we have got to in the investigation we have good reason to get a go-ahead for the reconstruction. We need some new leads. Obviously, if we get anything in the meantime we'll be following them up, but right now our search team, and forensics, who gathered the prints and any DNA evidence, feel they've got all they can from the area surrounding the viaduct. It's frustrating we haven't found a weapon or either of their phones, I admit."

"So where can they be? I mean, the phones must be somewhere. They can't have just disappeared off the face of the earth. I understand it's common land, it's not easy to search, it rained – I get all that – I understand, but Joe – he's got to be somewhere. Someone must have seen him, seen something, found his phone. There's all the technology, I mean…"

Mum sighed. It sounded like she'd lost all her fight. I was surprised how strong she'd been up until now. She didn't usually ask so many questions, push for so many answers. It was usually Dad who did that.

May Grover spoke up.

"Mrs Green, has anyone in your family had any contact with Joe McGrath at all in the last week or so?" she said.

"No, of course not! Why would you think...?" Mum said.

"I'm sorry, Mrs Green. We just have to ask."

"If we'd heard anything – anything at all – don't you think we'd have been straight on the phone to you? Just like you asked?" Mum said.

"That's good to know, Mrs Green. Thank you," Campbell said.

I slipped down to the bottom step to get closer still. I could hear Mum make a half laugh, half hiccup noise with her throat, and I knew she was about to cry.

"I'm sorry, Mrs Green. I really didn't mean to upset you," May said, and I heard her chair scrape against the kitchen floor as she must have got up to go to Mum.

"So you have nothing more at all to tell me about Joe?" Mum said.

"We are continuing our search, Mrs Green," Campbell said. "Our investigation doesn't stop here. He is still our main suspect."

"We are working on it," May said. "I know it's hard to believe that when you don't see the day-to-day effort that involves, but let me assure you we are doing all we can to find Joe McGrath."

It was quiet.

I stretched my hands out from their fists, spreading my fingers wide, and lifted my head, straining to hear. I guessed Campbell and May were about to go. I'd need to start moving back up the stairs.

"Just one more question, Mrs Green," Campbell said. "Are you certain that there isn't anyone else in Laura's circle of friends who knew Joe McGrath or spent time with him? There isn't anyone else you can think of?"

"No," Mum said. "I told you. They met in the cafe – where Ella Taylor works. Joe was a regular there once he started working around the corner in the garage. They got chatting. Ella introduced Laura to Joe. There wasn't a circle of friends. Joe wasn't part of Laura's life – I mean at school, with those friends. I'm not even sure if any of her other friends ever met him. Just Ella, and of course Ella left school after her GCSEs. She's been working at the cafe, saving to go travelling or to college, maybe train to be a nurse. She's not part of Laura's scene at school any more. Laura hadn't been seeing Joe for long – five, maybe six weeks. Only Ella knew him, had met him. But I told you that. I've gone through all this before, so many times."

"And how friendly were Ella Taylor and Joe? Did you ever get a sense of that?" May asked.

"Once Laura got together with Joe it was very much all about Laura and Joe. They really didn't hang out with anyone, not as far as I know. They didn't even really see Ella.

Why? Why are you asking about all this again, now?"

"No reason, Mrs Green. We're always revisiting things, in case you remember something. Sometimes things that don't seem important at the time come back to you later on. It's always worth bearing that in mind," Campbell said. "But thank you for your patience."

I heard the chairs moving again against the floor and guessed the police were leaving.

"Ella's a good girl, you know," Mum said. "Laura couldn't have had a better friend."

I stood up and started to turn to go back up the stairs. I didn't want to be seen, listening, hovering at the bottom of the stairs, but I wanted to hear what they were saying about Ella.

"Well, I'm sure that's right," May said, "and as I said, we're just revisiting things. Always revisiting."

I could hear the chairs being pushed back under the kitchen table, now. They were trying to finish up – Campbell and May Grover – but Mum didn't want them to go. She wanted to keep them there, with more questions. I could feel it.

I walked slowly, quietly back up the stairs and made sure I was in my room, the door closed behind me, before they came into the hall.

I rested my head against the door. I wanted to see Max. To go over to his house and fill my head with the noise of

The Who, or whatever it was he was listening to right now, and hang out with him.

Then I'd go back to Mum, and soothe her. Because I guessed that was what Laura would have done. But right now, I couldn't be at home. Not once Campbell and May had left. Because I knew Mum would fall apart. She'd go over and over what Campbell and May Grover had said, and she'd want answers to all the questions she'd asked, and when I couldn't answer them she'd get angry and upset. And even though I knew she wouldn't be angry or upset with me, I couldn't be there for that right now. I couldn't take it. I wanted them to find Joe, and I wanted them to find the phones and I wanted all the answers too. But if I said that, if I showed her I felt the same, it would make things worse not better. She only wanted the answers, and I didn't have them. And right now it seemed like no one did.

9.

When I knocked on Max's door his mum answered.

"Hi, Tessie. You looking for Max?"

She always did that. Asked me a question she knew I couldn't answer, but I knew she didn't do it on purpose.

"Why don't you go on up. He's in his room."

And then she'd always answer her question – straight after she'd asked it. She was alright really.

I climbed up the stairs to the loft. Max's room was at the top of the house. The closer I got to him the louder the music became.

I knocked on the door, and then pushed it open. Max immediately looked up.

"Hey!" he said. "You alright?"

I closed his bedroom door tight behind me. PROPER SHUT.

"Yes," I said.

It always felt strange – the first few words I'd say at Max's house – because I wasn't at home. But Max's room was okay. I'd worked really hard with my speech therapist, Anya, on making some "safe spaces". That's what she called them. Places where I could talk outside of my house. Anya said if I could start to build one or two "safe spaces", then by the time I left school I'd be well on my way to talking everywhere again.

I'd talked a few times at the cafe, but then one day Ella hadn't been there to take my order and it had all felt too hard. The girl covering for Ella was really abrupt; she kept asking me what I wanted, and when I didn't answer she told me I was rude – and the more she asked me the worse it got – and then the pain came in my throat and the not being able to talk – and in the end I ran out the cafe and everyone was looking at me and I heard people laugh. I'm sure the whole cafe laughed. Anya wanted to come with me after that, to try and help me build on all the good talking I'd done at the cafe before then, but Mum said she didn't see the point of Anya helping me any more if it was just going to upset me. I don't think she really understood what was going on, and when I'd tried to explain she didn't really listen. That was kind of the beginning of things going really wrong between Mum and me. But thankfully it was different at Max's. If I was in his room, with him, just him, and the door was PROPER SHUT, then I was okay to speak, and nothing had got in the way of that. Although I always thought my voice sounded different somehow when I spoke in Max's room, but Max said it didn't. He promised me that. And I believed him.

I went and sat down next to him on the floor.

"What are you doing?"

"Well, I'm meant to be doing this maths," he said, pointing to an open book spread in front of him on the carpet. "Have you done it yet?"

I shook my head. I hadn't. I needed to though.

"I haven't got very far," he said.

"Really? You do surprise me," I said, smiling.

"Don't be so sarcastic, Tessie! You haven't even started it yet. At least I'm sitting here with the book open. That's more than you've done, isn't it?" And he grabbed me and pinched me around the waist as he said it and I wriggled to try and get free of his hand. It tickled. But I liked it.

"Don't try and change the subject," I said, pushing him gently away. "We were talking about you, remember?"

"Well, yes, okay. I was pretending to do it, and I was listening to music and I was…well, kind of, dreaming actually."

Max looked over at me.

I nodded.

It felt awkward for a moment.

I wasn't sure why, but then I didn't know what to say. I guessed Max was waiting for me to ask him what he was dreaming about, but I didn't want to ask. I didn't want to know, in case it was about Mia. They'd been to the cafe together today after school.

I leaned across him to pick up the record sleeve so I could try and change the subject.

Max listened to his music at home on vinyl, even though everyone told him he was mad to do that. He wanted to keep using his dad's decks. He said he loved the vinyl and he wasn't ever going to change the way he listened to his dad's music at home. He was kind of stubborn like that.

"Ian Dury," he said, before I could ask him what he was playing.

"Noise," I said, and he laughed and pushed himself back and started banging his feet on the floor in time to the music.

I lay down on my back next to him, so our heads were side by side, and he reached over and grabbed a handful of pencils that were sitting on his books, and passed a couple over to me.

"Drums. Now let's go," he said.

And we drummed the air with our pencils; we drummed and we drummed and Max stamped his feet and Max sang, "'Hit Me With Your Rhythm Stick'..." and we started laughing until I was laughing so much I couldn't stop. That was what I loved about Max. That we could do this stuff together, and it felt so…normal. Not like being with anyone else.

"What the hell was that?" I said, still laughing, when the song came to an end.

"'Hit Me With Your Rhythm Stick', of course!" Max said into the silence after the song.

"Put it on again," I said, still smiling. "I want to do it again!"

And then I turned my head to look at Max, and as I did he shifted onto his side so his face was really close to mine.

"Tessie?" he said.

"What?"

There was silence. Was he waiting for me to say something? I wasn't sure. His face was serious now. He wasn't smiling any more. He was looking right at me. It felt awkward again.

"You want me to go, don't you?" I said, trying to fill the quiet. "You need to do that homework? You've got football later?" I said. "I should go…"

I went to sit up.

"Tessie, stop," he said and he put his hand on my arm and guided me to lie back down next to him. "Tessie, you have no idea how much I would love for the others to see you like this."

I turned my head away quickly, and looked up at the ceiling, away from him.

"The others?" I said.

I knew what he meant.

He meant everyone at school – all his friends who didn't understand why I didn't talk; all his friends who didn't understand why he was friends with me.

I wished he hadn't said it.

Why had he said it?

We were having fun.

He'd ruined everything.

I pulled myself up to sitting and passed the pencils back.

"Tessie? Don't go weird on me," Max said, sitting up now too.

"I'm not," I said.

"I'm sorry…if I shouldn't have said that."

I didn't say anything.

"It's just, it's hard for me too sometimes, you know?" he said.

I looked over at him and I nodded.

"I know," I said. "I do know that." But when I said it I couldn't look at him because, however hard it was for him, it was way harder for me, and I was always going to win if we were going to make it a competition. And I didn't want to make it a competition. Not with Max. He was the one who understood me better than anyone. Or at least that's what I thought – until this moment – until right now.

Max stood up and went over to the player, and chose another record.

I wondered whether I should just go, get back to Mum, but really I wanted to stay – just for a bit. I wasn't ready to leave yet.

When the music came on again, I spoke.

"Campbell just came over," I said.

"What's going on? Any news?"

I shook my head.

I loved that Max knew that Campbell coming over was a big deal, that it meant there might be news.

He came and sat back down next to me.

"I just wish they'd find Joe, you know?"

"I know," he said.

"Laura was mad about him, and he hurt her – we all know he did – even the police. They need to find him."

"And still no witnesses?"

I shook my head. "Campbell said he wants to do a reconstruction, but it depends on his boss or something. It may happen this week."

"A reconstruction would be weird," Max said.

"I know," I said looking at him. "I don't want to be around when it happens…" I paused. "But if it means they get something more, then I guess it would be worth it."

I looked at Max, for reassurance, I think. I was trying to be positive, but the thought of them reconstructing what happened to Laura that night made me feel sick.

"So they haven't found any more evidence?" he said.

"They say they've got some, but it's not enough or it's not good enough. I don't know…"

"But they're still searching around the viaduct, aren't they? They'll find something."

"Not any more. That's why Campbell came over. They're stopping the search. It's common land, a public space. They can't keep it closed off for ever. The paramedics trampled on it anyway, when they came to find Laura. May Grover told us that before. I don't even know how much evidence they had in the first place. And still no one can find Joe… Maybe they'll never find him? Maybe we'll never know what happened to her."

I looked at Max.

He didn't say anything.

"She loved him, Max. I think she really loved him." And as I said it I remembered sitting on Laura's bed one evening, the week before the attack, watching her get ready to go out. She was sitting at her desk with a small mirror propped against some books, leaning on her elbows with her back to me. Her face was close to the mirror and she had an eyeliner in one hand, while her other hand propped up her cheek as she carefully drew a solid black line above her eyelid. I always enjoyed watching her put her make-up on. Her hands steady, her face transforming as she worked the liner into the corners of her eyes and the mascara across her lashes. I didn't wear eyeliner, but I knew that when and if I did I'd never be able to do it as well as her. And I remember asking her if she was going out, and where she was going, and she turned to look at me with a smile so wide I thought it would leap off her face, and she said, "*I'm seeing Joe.*" And I saw it then. That she loved him. I knew that she did.

"I can't believe she got him so wrong," I said, looking at Max head-on.

"Maybe she didn't get him so wrong. Maybe it isn't him, Tessie? If they don't have the evidence they can't say that it's him, can they?"

"But if it wasn't him, then who was it? I mean, it has to be him, doesn't it? The fact that he's disappeared, he's gone. And none of us knew him, apart from maybe Ella, and even then she didn't know him that well. No one did…"

Max leaned forward and picked up my hand.

I looked down at our hands entwined together.

"I don't really know what to say," he said. "I mean it's not easy to know what to say."

I nodded, and I thought about Ella and I thought about what I'd just said, and for a moment I wondered how well she knew Joe. Really knew him.

Max squeezed my hand. I looked up at him.

It felt awkward between us – sitting together on the floor, holding hands – this had never happened before. I didn't know if this was a friend thing or something different. For a moment I wasn't sure if I wanted it to be something different. I felt uncomfortable.

I waited for Max to say something, but he didn't.

"Listen, I – I'm not sure – I mean – I'm not sure what's going on…" And before I could finish trying to say what I wanted to say, and loosen my hand from his, Max's face was close and his lips were on mine, and my words disintegrated into his lips, and the feeling of his kiss was so…unexpected and so new and for a moment I felt like I couldn't breathe…and without thinking, I pulled away.

Max looked flustered, embarrassed.

"Max – I'm sorry – I don't know – I just don't know about this, how I feel, I – there's just so much going on and…"

I stood up.

I thought for a moment about Mia. I thought Max liked her. Not me. Had I got that wrong?

"I should go…" I said.

"Tessie, please. Don't go. Not like this. I like you, you know? I really like you…"

"Yes, because we're friends. We're friends, aren't we?" I said.

"Well, haven't you wondered if we might be…oh, I don't know, more than that?" he said.

"Well, yes, sometimes, but no…I don't know. I don't know how I'm meant to feel. I don't know if how I feel about you – if it's what it's meant to be – if that's what this is – if that makes sense? Because we're friends."

"Tessie, it doesn't make sense. What you're saying, you're complicating it. Didn't it feel nice, just now when we kissed?"

I looked at him.

I didn't know how it felt. I'd pulled away, hadn't I? It hadn't felt like Laura described it, like how it was meant to feel – like how she'd said it would feel – a fall.

I didn't say anything.

My head started scrambling for words – for words I could say – because I was here, in Max's room – and I could actually say them – I could speak them – except the words, they didn't come – and there was silence – and I knew it hurt.

It hurt Max, and it hurt me.

I could feel the hurt, there in the room.

I wanted to make it better.

"Listen," Max said, standing up, running his hands through his hair, looking down, away from me. "I should probably get on with this maths…"

"Okay," I said. "Me too. I should go back, make a start. I'll…I'll see you in the morning, yeah?"

And as I went towards the bedroom door to open it I

felt so sad inside. Like I'd stepped on something precious, something fragile. Like I'd broken the thing I cared about most in the world. And I hadn't meant to do that with my silence, but I knew I had. And I knew that Max – well, I could see – he felt the same way too.

Thursday

10.

It was awkward the next morning. Max knocked for me as usual, but when I got to the front door he was already along the front path, at the gate, ready to head out into the street.

I walked towards him and he hardly looked at me. He seemed impatient as he passed me the earbud; there was no explanation or introduction to the music today, and he started walking fast. I could hardly keep up.

I struggled to put the earbud into my ear as we walked and when I did I heard adverts and chat. It was the radio. I hated it. All the talk, the competitions, the adverts, more chat. I wanted the music – Max's music. I didn't want to hear these voices.

I looked at him as we walked, to try and see if he might look at me. I was sure that if he looked at me he would say something. I wanted him to say something, anything. I wanted him to say the words I couldn't say. My head was full of the words I wanted to say, all the things I wanted to say to make what happened yesterday better, but I couldn't say them. Not now. And Max wouldn't look at me. He ignored me. His eyes were focused on the street ahead as we walked. It was almost as if I wasn't there.

When we got to the school gates he left me without a goodbye and so I guess I shouldn't have been that surprised when he didn't show up at our usual place in the corridor outside the school office at the end of the day. But still, I waited and I waited because I didn't know what else to do. And I watched the second hand tick around the clock on the corridor wall in front of me and I told myself that once fifteen minutes had passed I would come up with a plan. I told myself that I wouldn't think about walking home on my own, or getting past the bus stop, until the fifteen minutes had gone. I told myself that once the fifteen minutes had gone, I'd think about walking a different route. But every time I thought about the fifteen minutes coming up, I felt a sickness roll over in my gut. It made me swallow until my throat hurt.

I couldn't walk home on my own.

I couldn't do it without Max.

I swallowed again, and shifted on my feet.

I probably deserved this.

I should have been nicer to Max. Kinder. I shouldn't have pulled away. Maybe if I'd let him kiss me properly, it would have been okay. Maybe I'd have liked it. But I'd had so many other things running through my head.

My legs started to shake.

If I started walking someone was bound to try and talk to me. I couldn't risk that. I couldn't risk seeing Kat or Holly. Or anyone.

I took a deep breath, to try and steady myself. Just like Anya had taught me. I took the breath, and as I did I could sense someone, close by.

Watching me.

I could feel their eyes on me.

I thought about the boy in the corridor and how he'd pressed his hands up to mine through the glass, how he'd asked me if I was okay, how he'd smiled at me.

I liked the way seeing him had made me feel.

Was it him again – watching me?

I didn't want to look back, but eventually I couldn't do anything but look.

And he was there – walking towards me now – close.

I held my breath for a moment, without thinking.

He took a step towards me.

"You," he said. "I was looking, I mean…I mean… I wanted to find you."

My neck seized up – stiff, hard – like someone had opened up my mouth and poured a bucketful of dry pebbles down my throat. And it hurt.

He took another step towards me.

"What's your name?"

I wanted to shake my head. I wanted to say: *Don't talk to me. I can't talk. Don't try and make me talk. You have to leave me. You have to go away. You have to leave me alone.*

But I couldn't – and I couldn't take my eyes away from his.

I was burning, hot.

I could feel the heat rising from my chest, to my throat.

"Will you tell me your name?" he said again, coming closer to me.

He was tall. For a moment I imagined him opening his arms, enveloping me, holding me. Was it that I wanted him to do that or just that he looked like he could, like he would? I wasn't sure.

I blinked.

My cheeks hurt from the heat in my face – but his eyes – I could have swum in his eyes – in my head I was swimming in the cool clear blue of them – and it was okay – everything was okay.

Mr Gardiner's voice boomed down the corridor.

"If you aren't heading into drama or football or the library then you should have gone home by now. Go on. Out you go."

The boy looked back over his shoulder towards the sound of Mr Gardiner's voice.

"Are you going?" he said.

I nodded.

"Come on then," he said, and I followed, moving alongside him as he started to walk out. "Were you waiting for someone?"

I swallowed and the words didn't even form in my head. There was just a whirring in my ears like the machines in the hospital and a feeling like I might faint.

"You don't have to tell me," he said. "Just wondered…" And his eyes dropped to the ground as he stepped away from me to go. Then he looked back up. "I guess I'll see you tomorrow?" He almost smiled. "I'll be looking…" he said.

And he went.

I watched him go.

And I didn't take my eyes off him.

Not even once.

And when he'd gone, completely gone, and I was standing alone, in the middle of the street, I thought about my nearest safest place, and I walked there. I walked there as fast as I could, catching my breath as I did.

11.

Ella looked up as soon as I pushed open the door. The cafe was the nearest safe place to school, and I could get there without passing the bus stop. Well, at least it had been safe once, and that was enough for now. I was relieved to see that it was empty as I walked in. Ella was wiping down the counter. I knew she wouldn't be closing up for at least an hour.

"Hey, Tessie!" she said. She sounded like she was really pleased to see me. It surprised me. Ella was Laura's friend. Not mine. But then she'd said she was missing Laura. I got that. We all were.

I managed a smile.

"Do you want something to drink?" Ella asked.

I went and sat down in the booth at the back of the cafe. When I'd spoken here before that's where I had sat. The booth was still the only place I wanted to sit now, but I knew I wouldn't be able to talk here again. Not now.

Ella grabbed two Cokes from the fridge and followed me to the booth.

"I'm on my own – Leila's at the cash and carry. If someone comes I'll have to serve," she said, sitting down opposite me. "I'm guessing a Coke will do?"

I nodded, and took the can from her and sat it in front of me. I wouldn't drink it, but I wanted to have it there.

We sat in silence for a minute or two. I wasn't uncomfortable. I never was in a silence. But I could tell Ella didn't quite know what to do.

I should have told her that I'd only come to the cafe because it was closer than home. That I'd only come here because I didn't have to walk past the bus stop to get here. But there was no way I could say all that.

Ella sighed. The kind of sigh that was begging me to ask if she was okay.

She opened up her Coke and it hissed at us both.

"Does your mum know you're here?" she said, after taking a sip.

No one knew I was here. Mum would be at the hospital with Jake. She thought I was walking back from school with Max, like I always did.

"Maybe drop her a text?" Ella said. "You know how she worries. Then she'll know you're okay."

I pulled my bag up off the floor, took out my phone, and messaged Jake. He checked his phone more than Mum. He'd see a text straight away. I didn't like messaging. I only did it when I had to – for practical stuff. Like where to meet and what time, simple stuff. Yes and no answers. I'd never message to say what I thought or what I was feeling or what I was doing. Not like everyone else. I was hardly on my phone. To message all that stuff every day – it was the same as talking. At least it felt that way to me.

> I'm with Ella at the cafe. Meet me here from the hospital? Tx

Mum and Jake would be on their way back from visiting Laura pretty soon. They could pick me up on the way.

I put my phone on the table and looked up at her.

"Good," Ella said to herself, smiling.

There wasn't really any reason for her to say it, but sometimes people did this when they were with me: said the stuff that maybe I was meant to say. It was a way of filling in the cracks of the conversation, filling the silence.

Ella sipped her Coke again.

I could tell she was still feeling awkward.

She looked up, and around the cafe again, like she was almost nervous, and then she leaned in towards me to speak.

"I just feel so bad about Laura," she said. "I can't believe she's still not conscious, still in this coma… I keep thinking about what happened to her, and I keep thinking about Joe, and I keep thinking about whether there was anything…well, you know, I could have done, that was… well, different."

I shook my head.

What did she mean?

"I just can't stop thinking about Joe, you know? Have they found his mobile yet? Do you know?"

I swallowed.

Spit sat hard, in the base of my throat.

She'd asked me that before. Why was she asking again?

"I keep reading the papers, searching online, but there isn't anything in the papers any more. I mean, I wonder, if they found his phone, would that even make it into the news now? I have no idea. It's like it's not being reported any more. Not like it was."

My neck was stiff and it hurt now. Ella was asking me too many questions. Questions I couldn't answer.

"I shouldn't ask you all this stuff. I know that, Tessie. I'm sorry. It's just…I haven't been sleeping. My mind's been racing. All the 'what if's, you know?"

I swallowed again. It hurt. I wasn't sure what Ella meant. I didn't know.

"I feel like it's all my fault. I mean, when Laura and Joe met it was mad. They literally looked at each other and it was like you could feel something had changed in the room. It was that strong – the way they felt."

Ella looked at me, and bit her lip, looking down again

before she carried on talking.

"That night in the cafe, when I was stocktaking. It was meant to be me and Joe – just me and Joe," she said, looking up at me, and then looking back down again quickly, like she wanted to hide her face as she talked. "Joe said he'd keep me company. I was going to be there most of the night. I'd got some beers, and I was really looking forward to…to spending time with him, just him and me. Laura wasn't meant to come at all. But then…well, she turned up – before Joe… Joe was late and I…well… I wanted to see Joe, but I wanted to see Laura too… So I figured we'd just make it fun, hang out together, you know? I'd told Laura about Joe. And I really wanted her to meet him… But when he knocked on the window for me to let him in, and I opened up, and Joe and Laura – they saw each other – that was it."

I thought about the boy with the sparkling eyes. The way he looked at me. How it made me feel.

Ella looked up at me, her face hard.

"It started right there, Tessie. And after that it was like I didn't exist any more. And any chance of it being me and Joe again – well, it was over. It was gone."

I looked back at Ella. Was she saying that she and Joe had been together? Before? Before Laura and Joe? I wasn't clear, I wasn't sure.

Ella was cradling the Coke can in both her hands now,

twisting it back and forth between her fingers rhythmically. She pressed her lips together. I couldn't tell if she was going to cry.

"I've tried ringing Joe's phone. I know I shouldn't have, but well… It's just I really want to talk to him. I want to know how he is. I mean, how do we know he's okay? We don't. He's missing. Maybe he's hurt somewhere? Maybe whoever hurt Laura hurt him too? He could be somewhere right now, needing help, you know? I don't think anyone has thought about that. His phone is dead…but maybe that's because he's in trouble, because he needs help, not because he's run away. I just can't believe he would do anything…to Laura. He wouldn't…"

Ella was talking so fast now I was struggling to keep up with her. And the more she spoke, the more her face darkened. As the words spilled out of her it was like all the light in the room was being sucked into a cloud.

"I've got to go to the police station tomorrow," she said. "They want to question me. Officially, like under caution. Mum's coming with me. Did you know?"

I swallowed.

I didn't know.

The swallow sounded ugly in my ears – a loud gulp, like a wet click. I knew Ella had heard it.

"They don't know about Joe and me. No one does. And I can't tell them. It looks too bad."

I blushed. I went hot. Completely hot. It was panic.

"If I could just speak to Joe, you know? I could tell him he needs to come back and sort this out. Because he could do that. He could sort this out for me, for him, for all of us. I know he could. And until he does, I'm not saying a thing."

I wanted to ask Ella why she was talking to me like this, telling me this, but I couldn't. I tried to swallow away my frustration but it was stuck in my throat like a rock. I shook my head to try and dislodge the pain in my throat, to make it shift.

Ella grabbed my hands, hard. She held me still.

"Joe is innocent, Tessie. I don't know why the police think he's guilty. We're not involved in this – neither of us. I swear. I can see what you're thinking, but we're not. Not in the way you think we are."

Ella was shaking her head now, like she was flicking the words she'd just said away, away from her, away from me, like she knew she'd said too much. "We" – she was talking about her and Joe as if they were together, a couple. I wanted to grab her words, use them, flick them back at her, and ask her the questions I had in my head.

I pulled my hands away.

They were hot.

I looked down at the can of Coke in front of me. There was condensation all over it. I ran my fingertips through the droplets of water to cool them down. I wished I could crack the can open and pour the cold liquid down my throat, to soothe it.

The cafe door banged opened – loud.

We both looked up.

An old man came in and headed noisily to the counter to be served.

"It was too much," Ella whispered, leaning in towards me across the table, pulling my gaze into hers. "The way they felt about each other – Laura and Joe. It was too strong. It wasn't a good thing. I mean something that starts that strong – it's bound to end like this…in some fucking mess. We should have known. All of us. It's like every movie you ever see. We both read fucking *Romeo and Juliet*. We should have known…"

My phone buzzed next to me on the table. It made me jump.

"That's probably your mum," Ella said, and she stood, picking up her empty can, leaving mine unopened in front of me, and walked over to the counter to serve the old man. "You should reply."

I looked at the message.

It was from Jake.

Just leaving. Be there in about 5 mins.

And I looked up again at Ella at the counter. She was

chatting, talking, setting the coffee machine to start grinding, and I was glad of the noise, because it drowned out my thoughts and it drowned out the words that Ella had just said. And for a moment that was a relief.

12.

I saw Mum and Jake pull up outside the cafe before Ella did because I was sitting watching, waiting.

I stood up quickly, picked up my phone, put it in my bag, and walked to the door.

It was good to move.

I hadn't realized it, but the whole time I'd been there I'd felt trapped. It was the way Ella had talked to me. It was the way she didn't even give me a chance, a choice, not to listen.

She followed me to the cafe door, and Mum wound the car window down on the passenger side to talk to her across Jake, who was sitting next to her in the front. It was dark outside now. The threat of rain had drained the light from the sky.

"You alright, Ella?" Mum called.

"Yeah – fine," Ella called back.

Ella was so at ease with Mum. It was almost as if she hadn't said all the things she'd just said to me. It surprised me.

I walked over to get in the back of the car and Ella followed, leaning her face through Jake's window.

"You must come over soon. With your mum. Have some tea with us or something," Mum said. "It's been ages."

She always said stuff like that, invited people over, but when it came to it she never really liked people coming round. We hadn't had anyone over for ages.

"Sounds lovely," Ella said. "I'll talk to Mum."

Mum smiled, and Ella went to move, to go.

"Oh, and thanks for dropping over the stuff," Mum said. "Laura's stuff. Tessie passed it on."

Ella nodded. She looked awkward suddenly. Different. Was it because Mum had mentioned Laura?

There was a moment's quiet.

"Laura's doing okay," Mum said. "We've just been to see her, at the hospital. She's the same really…but she's doing okay…"

Ella's eyes flickered over to look at me in the back of the car, and she nodded.

It was guilt.

That's what that look was.

"You should go and see her some time," Mum said. "I think – I think Laura would like it."

Ella nodded again.

I looked down at my hands in my lap, willing the conversation to end.

"They say she can hear, feel, touch—"

"Look I better go. Almost time to cash up, lock up...I'm on my own just now," Ella interrupted, looking back over her shoulder at the cafe. "I shouldn't really be out here. Leila would kill me if she saw me. She's due back from the cash and carry any minute."

"Sure," Mum said, and Ella stepped away from the car and walked back to the cafe door, fast. And then she turned back round, and waved. But she looked at Mum. She didn't look at me at all.

Mum pulled away.

It was a few moments before she spoke.

"I don't understand why Ella hasn't been to see Laura. Brenda always said that friends were as important as family. Laura needs Ella, just as much as she needs us. She needs to hear her voice, know she is there."

Jake began to wind up his window. He didn't say anything.

"They were inseparable. Best friends," Mum said. "She needs to go and visit."

"Well, maybe now she will," Jake said.

It was the most diplomatic answer he could have come up with. I didn't know he had it in him. He almost sounded like Laura, soothing, placating.

"Well, I hope so," Mum said. "I really do."

I looked out of the window and thought about Ella and what she'd said about Joe.

I wished I'd never gone to the cafe.

I wished she'd never told me.

Jake turned round to look at me in the back of the car. "Alright, Tessie? Everything alright?"

I knew he was trying to protect me from what Mum had said about talking to Laura, about Laura needing to hear Ella's voice, because Laura would never get to hear mine and he knew that would upset me. But right now all I was thinking about was Ella going in to be questioned by the police tomorrow, and how she seemed to care more about what had happened to Joe than Laura, and how she'd left me with a secret. Why had she done that? Was it because she knew it would be impossible for me to tell?

13.

When we got home I followed Jake up the stairs and into his room.

He slung his bag on the floor and slumped down on his bed, turning to face me.

I shut his bedroom door behind me, and leaned against it.

"Thanks," I said.

"For what?"

"You know? In the car."

"It's nothing, Tessie."

"Do you think it's weird that Ella hasn't been to the hospital?"

"I don't know," Jake said. "I mean if I didn't have to go I seriously wouldn't. Not because I don't love Laura or anything, it's just…"

"I know."

"It's just shit seeing her like she is. And you know it's going to be shit before you get there, and still that doesn't make it any better. In fact it almost makes it worse. It's always way worse when you're there than you even imagine it's going to be, even if she is looking better and responding to treatment and out of ITU now. It doesn't matter. She's still lying there unconscious. She's still not responding to us. She's still not Laura."

I went over and sat next to him on the bed and we sat in silence for a moment. I knew exactly what he meant, but still, it wasn't right that Ella had never been.

"I miss her," I said.

Jake nodded and started picking the skin around his fingers.

"Do you think this is it? Do you think this is just how it's always going to be now?" I said.

"No change," he said, doing an impression of one of the nurses at the hospital.

I smiled.

"She's doing well, but no change," I said copying him back.

Jake smiled too, although it didn't really feel like the sort of thing we should have been smiling at.

"Things with Mum are just so hard too," I started to say, but Jake interrupted.

"Listen, we just have to do our best with Mum. She wasn't that great before all this happened. You know that, right?"

I nodded. I had known that, but I never really knew why. No one ever explained. No one ever talked about it. It was just one of those things that Dad and Laura and Jake just accepted, so I did too. It was like everyone knew why she was like that, but me. And I never asked, because really I wasn't sure that I wanted to know. Was it because of me and my SM? I guessed it was, in which case it was easier not to know. The thought that I'd made Mum so stressed and so sad – that was a thought I really didn't want to have. And right now it was a thought I could easily bury; something I could choose to ignore.

"We just have to do our best with Mum," Jake said. "And I know it's hard. It's hard without Laura being here. She was always so good at helping Mum, stepping in and just doing stuff, making everything better, when Mum wasn't coping. She somehow made it okay. I think I've only realized that since she's not been here. But *we* have look after Mum now. For Laura. We have to be good to Mum, because it will help Laura too. You see that, don't you, Tessie?"

"Yes," I said. "I get that. I was thinking the same thing."

I liked Jake when he talked like this. I liked him more than I'd ever liked him before. When Laura was around I'd always felt like the annoying younger sister. Laura and Jake got on really well, and there I was, the youngest, making life harder for them, for everyone, just by being there –

and that was before my SM. When Jake talked to me like this I didn't feel like that bad annoying person any more.

He put his arm around me, and I looked up at him.

"Do you think Laura will ever wake up?" I said.

Jake tipped his forehead so it rested against mine before he spoke.

"I don't know, Tessie. I just don't know."

Friday

14.

Max knocked for me in the morning to walk in, but he was quiet and it was the radio again. No Who. No Zeppelin. No nothing. It just made me feel sad. I missed him talking to me. I missed his stupid music. I wanted to tell him that at some point. I imagined what he'd say when I told him I'd missed The Who. Probably something like – *I told you it was genius, Tessie. It was only a matter of time before you heard the genius too.*

We got the whole way to school without Max saying a word. I wondered whether he might be trying to teach me a lesson, show me what it felt like to be with someone who didn't speak. Pay me back for my silence. But I didn't think he'd be that petty.

When we got to the school gates I lifted my hand up to the earbud, to take it out, to give it back to Max, and I could feel someone watching me.

I looked around for him – the new boy.

I hoped it was him.

"I'll see you later," Max said and, without looking at me, he walked away fast, taking the earbud quickly as he went.

And still, I could feel someone watching me.

I felt heat, full in my cheeks, as I thought about him – the boy with the sparkling eyes – just the thought of him could make me feel like this.

I stood by the gates for a moment, waiting.

"Hey," a voice came from behind me.

I turned.

It was him.

And he was close.

"I'll walk you to class," he said. "What tutor group you in?"

I smiled and started walking with him, alongside him, without even thinking. He was tall. So much taller than me. I felt small next to him, but I liked it, just walking with him. And I didn't usually do stuff like this with people I didn't know. Most of the time if someone spoke to me I was rooted to the spot, my feet heavy with the strain. But not with him. Not today. I looked down at my feet. They were walking. I was walking, we were walking – together – and I was smiling – and this was new.

"I'm guessing you remember me?"

My shoulders seized a little, my neck twinged. I prayed that the look in my eyes was enough of a yes, because my neck felt stiff now, and while I wanted to nod, I couldn't walk and nod. I couldn't do it.

I coughed. I didn't mean to. It just came out. A rough little cough, as I walked, and I looked up to see if he'd noticed. He was looking back at me, and he smiled.

"Yeah, I think you do," he said.

I swallowed and even though it hurt, it really didn't hurt that much.

"I forgot to tell you yesterday, that I'm Billy," he said.

I blinked. ONE BLINK. One blink for YES.

One blink for YES. Two blinks for NO.

That's what I would have said to him, if I could have explained.

Billy.

I knew his name.

I was glad to know his name.

The bell rang.

He looked up.

"And you're Tessie, yeah?" he said.

I stopped walking.

How did he know? How did he know my name? I could feel panic, rising.

"Here, come here," he said, pulling me over to the side of the corridor, his hand on my arm, firm, looking up and around us at everyone else in the corridor as he did, crouching down towards me as he spoke, making me feel like I was someone to him, like he was someone to me.

"Listen, I...I asked some people about you. They told me you're shy – like really shy. You don't really speak. Is that right?"

He was whispering now.

I looked away.

I didn't want him to know about me. I didn't want him to know that I was messed up, different. Why did he have to go and ask around? I knew what people would have said. Anyone he'd asked would have said that I was a freak. That I was a freak of a freak of a freak.

"Is it more than that? The way you are – I mean... I just...I just kind of want to know," he said.

I looked up at him, and into his eyes again.

I knew I would never get the chance to explain.

Not properly.

My breath was getting shorter now.

The quiet between us felt suffocating. It always did. My spaces in the conversation, where the words were meant to be, strangled everyone. This was how I killed friendships. This was how it always was with me.

"Well...I guess...I guess I should go," he said after a minute, lifting his hand up to run it over his head as he looked around again at everyone else in the corridor. And for a moment he looked lost.

"I'll find you later, yeah? Another day?" he said, and he walked, his head down, slowly towards his tutor room.

I watched him as he went and I wished, I wished and I wished that I could reply, that I could speak. Of all the people in the world, I wished that I wasn't me.

"Hey, Mouse, you need your PE kit," Kat appeared in the corridor, bashing my shoulder as she passed me by.

Had they seen me with him, with Billy?

I swallowed hard.

"Yeah, Mouse," Holly said, bringing her face too close to mine as she said it. "PE kit!"

They walked on.

I left the corridor and headed towards my locker. I didn't want to go and get my kit until I knew they had gone. But in my head the word *Billy* was swimming up and down, up and down, steady, fast, flipping, turning and repeating again in the pool of my brain. And I liked it. It was keeping me safe.

"Hi, Tessie."

It was Mia. She was getting her kit. Her locker was right next to mine.

I clicked open the padlock on my locker door, and reached in to pull out my bag. My trainers were on the shelf. I'd slung them back in after PE the last time, and they were filthy from the field. Still laced up; a tangled mess of dried mud and hard cotton where they lay.

"Come on, I'll walk with you to tutor group," she said. "You got your stuff?"

Mia was standing right next to me now. I wasn't sure why she was being so kind.

I slammed the locker door shut, and looked at her. She was cute. Her wavy brown hair short, but not so short that she looked boyish, her face so completely open. Even when she looked back at me now, even when she knew I couldn't answer any of her questions, she managed to feign an expectation that I might reply, but still make it feel okay that she knew I'd never answer.

"So I'm guessing I'll see you at Max's gig tonight," she said. "I've never seen him play before. I'm really looking forward to it." And she smiled and went to leave, so I would follow, but when I didn't she stopped and turned back towards me.

There was a pause.

"You do know about the gig?" she said. "Don't you?" And then she paused again. "Sorry – I assumed… He said it was a last-minute thing. He only told me about it yesterday. Some other band cancelled. They got the spot, in the back room at The Red Lion. I'm sure he was going to tell you about it…"

The bell went. The one that meant we should be in our tutor room for registration with our kits, ready to go straight to the sports hall and change for first period PE.

I stood still, completely still.

"Oh god, I'm so sorry, Tessie, if I've said the wrong thing.

I – I guess I have," she said, and she turned and left and this time she didn't wait for me to follow.

I bent down and picked up my kit bag. For the first time in weeks I felt like I might cry. A hailstorm of pins pricked my eyes – and I blinked hard and slow to make them go away.

I hated that I didn't know about the gig.

I hated that Max hadn't told me.

I hated that I couldn't talk to Billy.

I closed my eyes and I opened them again.

I had to make it better with Max.

I had to.

That was something I could do. And I had to do it.

It was just, I didn't really know how.

15.

Can we walk back together today?
Tx

That's what I texted. I'd gone into the toilets at lunchtime, shut myself in a cubicle, and sat down on the closed toilet seat and got out my phone and texted Max. Usually I'd be with Max – on the field or in the canteen – but these last two days without him at lunchtime had been impossible. There was literally nowhere I could be.

As soon as I texted him I waited. I so wanted a quick reply. I stared at my phone, willing a message to appear.

And there was a bang on the door.

"Oi, Mouse! That you in there?"

It was Kat. I'd recognize her voice anywhere.

I slowly lifted my bag up and onto my back and raised my legs up onto the toilet seat so I was crouched up in a ball off the floor.

"I know you're in there, Mouse," Kat said again.

I tucked my head down so it rested on my knees.

"We can see your shadow, you know," said another voice. Holly.

Wherever there was Kat, there was Holly too.

I lifted my head up slightly. I could see her shoes in the gap under the door. Scuffed up, raw.

"That new boy, Billy, he's been asking about you, you know?" Kat said.

I took in a breath.

"You got a boyfriend, Mouse, and you didn't tell us," Holly said. "We feel pretty pissed about that."

It was Kat and Holly that Billy had talked to.

Why them?

Holly's foot lifted up and started gently kicking the door, over and over.

"You kissed him yet, Mouse?" Kat said.

"I bet she can't kiss," Holly said. "Her tongue doesn't work, does it? You can't kiss if your tongue doesn't work."

They laughed, and Holly's foot kept kicking, kicking, kicking.

"When you kiss him, Mouse, you have to tell us, okay? We have to be the first ones to know," Kat said.

I felt a cough rising in my throat. I didn't want to cough. I didn't want to make a noise.

"He'll want to kiss you properly, you know. You'll have to use your tongue," Kat said again. "We want to know how it is for you, Mouse, when you actually use your tongue."

"Maybe he'll cure you, Mouse. Cure you with a kiss."

"Like Sleeping Beauty," Kat said.

"Sleeping Mutely," Holly said, laughing, kicking, laughing.

I swallowed.

"He asked us if we knew you, Mouse," Holly said. "We said you were very quiet. We told him you didn't say much. Shy, you know? We told him your name, but we didn't tell him, Mouse. Not everything. We didn't tell him you don't speak at school – not at all – not ever."

"He's very intense, Mouse. Only interested in you. Doesn't talk to anyone else."

"So you're the special one... The one that he wants," Kat said. "But you can't talk to him, can you? Sad, eh? Tragic."

"You'll have to tell him yourself, eh, Mouse? That you can't talk...like *ever*," Holly said now.

"Yeah, we left that for you to tell him," Kat said.

I coughed and retched at the same time. There was no saliva in my mouth, just a dry pain in my throat and a burning shame inside my head.

"Don't be sick about it, Mouse," Holly said.

"We just thought it would be more fun if you told him," Kat said. "Much more fun. For us anyway."

"And I think we did you a favour really," Holly said. "Because it'll be good for you to try, you know, to speak? Good practice."

"And maybe love will conquer all, eh?" said Kat.

"Ah, yeah!" Holly said. "Because he's really into you, Mouse. I mean, maybe he's your prince…"

"Yeah," Kat said. "Maybe he's gonna be the one to save you, Mouse."

I gently bit the sides of my tongue to try and get some saliva in my mouth, and it worked, but my heart was racing.

"Have a nice day, Mouse," Kat said.

"Yeah, have a nice day!" Holly said, and then they left, laughing, kicking all the cubicle doors alongside mine as they went.

My legs were shaking when I stretched them out to stand back on the floor. I wanted to stay inside the cubicle for the rest of the day. I didn't want to leave. I stood up and leaned against the door to steady myself.

My phone buzzed in my hand.

I looked down quickly, hoping it was Max. If it was Max and I texted him straight back he might come and meet me in the corridor outside the toilets. Walk with me. Help me.

Don't forget we're going to the hospital today.
Meet you outside school. Mum x

I had forgotten.

And I never forgot anything to do with Laura.

My head was all over the place.

I'd needed the message to be from Max.

All I wanted was for it to be Max.

16.

Max never replied to my text. I waited, but when it was almost time for the bell for afternoon registration, and still a text hadn't come, I came out of my cubicle. My legs were aching from the pins and needles I'd got from crouching on the toilet seat. I went over to the sinks. Most of them were blocked, full of soap and wet tissues, but I splashed some water from the tap into my hands and straight onto my face. It was cold. Too cold. It made me shiver. I looked at myself in the mirror. My eyes were red, and my cheeks were blotchy. I didn't want anyone to know I'd been crying. I scooped my hair up, tying it with the hairband from around my wrist, but as soon as I got it up I pulled it down again. It didn't look right tied up. And I was sure everyone would look at me, because it had been down before lunch, and I knew they'd notice. I ran the tap again, and checked the mirror once more. I stared at my eyes, and I wondered what it was that Billy saw when he looked at me, when he looked into my eyes.

He's really into you, Mouse.

That's what Holly had said.

I looked again at my phone.

Still nothing from Max.

We told him your name, but we didn't tell him all about you, Mouse.

Everything felt wrong.

Everything.

We didn't tell him you don't speak.

Because it was.

I felt tears well up and I swallowed them down.

I had to leave the toilets now. The bell was about to go. I pulled my bag up off the floor and I slipped out into the corridor just as it rang. I joined a throng moving along, and as I did I felt someone join me, quietly, peacefully, and before I had a chance to look, to see who it was, I felt a hand gently take mine. It was strong, warm, and it held onto me.

"I'll walk you to tutor group," the voice said and I didn't need to look because the way it felt, hearing his voice, the way his hand held mine, I knew it had to be Billy.

"I can wait, you know, Tessie. I can totally wait for you to talk to me," he said, looking ahead as we walked.

I looked up at him.

And I squeezed his hand, tight.

Because he'd made it okay for me not to have the words.

He'd made me feel that way.

And no one had ever made me feel quite so safe this way before.

17.

Mum didn't say anything when I got in the car after school. Not even hello.

We sat in traffic, and I waited to see if she might say something. I wanted the comfort of her voice, her chatter. But I guess I actually hadn't had that for a long time now.

I looked out of the window.

In my head I was still in the corridor with Billy. I had been gliding with the memory of his hand in mine, replaying it over and over, ever since. It took everything away – Kat, Holly – everything. And then Mum spoke.

"Ella's been in for questioning today by the police."

I turned to look at her.

I guessed Heather, Ella's mum, must have called her, told her.

"They questioned her under caution, Tessie. I just don't understand. That means the police must suspect her of something. It doesn't make any sense to me at all."

I shook my head.

I didn't know what else to do.

"Heather said the police think that Ella has been in contact with Joe since the attack. They've taken her phone for evidence because they say they have reasonable grounds to suspect it's been going on for weeks. And they're saying they also have evidence that could put her at the viaduct with Joe."

I took in a deep breath. I felt my heart rush. A twinge of panic.

Ella had said she'd tried to get hold of Joe. She'd said she couldn't reach him. She'd tried. That's what she'd said. But had she seen him? Had she been in touch with him all along?

"Christ," Mum said. "It's at times like this I wish you'd just talk to me, Tessie. Just say something back. Anything…"

I raised my head up and I looked out of the window.

There was nothing I could do to make things better.

Nothing.

Even if I'd had the words, there wouldn't have been anything to say.

I stared right out into the distance, beyond the traffic, down the street, until my eyes stung and watered.

Because then I knew I could cry.

And I did.

Mum didn't say anything more until we got to the ward. We walked in silence from the car into the hospital and when we reached the ward, and walked over to Laura's bed, we stopped – both of us. Because she wasn't there. Laura wasn't there. Her bed was empty.

Mum turned and looked at me and I saw the panic in her eyes – fear fear fear like a siren going off in her brain.

They'd have told us, Mum. They'd have told us if she'd…

That's what I wanted to say before Mum exploded – before the words came flying out of her mouth as fast as she could think them – like wild dogs on the attack. I grabbed her hands, tight, and tried to make her look at me, to stop her from losing it, to try and make her focus, on me.

"Where is she?" she said. "Where is she?" And she turned and looked all around for a nurse, for someone to talk to. "Where is my daughter?" she shouted. "Someone! Please!" And she didn't walk away from the bed. She stood, turning, looking, with everyone else on the ward, turning and looking too – but they were looking at her – and at me – because of her shouting which became screaming which became wailing within seconds – which felt like minutes – which felt like years. I could feel my face reddening, my cheeks burning, my throat constricting.

I wanted to say: *It'll be okay, Mum. Let's just wait. Find someone who can tell us what is going on. It'll be okay.*

But instead I just held onto her hands and I held them tight and I looked at her hard and I shook my head. I'm not sure why I did that. I think I was trying to say: *Don't do this, Mum. Don't lose it here, in front of everyone.*

But I couldn't and the heat of my body fuelled my own fear and my frustration – because where were my words? They were in my head. Like always. They were locked inside my head. And I couldn't help Mum. I couldn't help her. I started my breathing, the breathing Anya had taught me. I needed to stop my panic. I could feel it trying to envelop me whole in the room.

And then I turned, pulling Mum, to take her back towards the nurses' desk at the entrance to the ward, and she followed.

"I left my phone at home," she said. "I knew I should have gone back for it, but we were coming in to see Laura. We were going to be at the hospital. I thought it would be okay... Oh god, where is she? What's happened to her?" and as she talked, she cried, but she let me guide her. She let me hold her hand, and as soon as we saw one of the sisters we'd spoken to before at the desk she let go of me.

The nurse explained that they'd been trying to call, that Laura had picked up a hospital bug, and they had had to move her from the ward. They'd wanted to speak to Mum before she arrived, to explain.

Mum's face was a mess. I could tell she wasn't listening. I could tell she just needed to see Laura. She needed proof that she was okay, that she was still alive. She banged her

144 | What I Couldn't Tell You

fist down on the desk and she leaned in towards the sister and spoke in a voice like a strangled scream. "Just take me to my daughter!" she said. "Now! I need to see her. Now!"

"We had to move her from the ward because she needs to be isolated, Mrs Green," the sister said. "We are giving her antibiotics. The infection is on her skin. That's the best-case scenario with these sorts of bugs. You don't want them in your system. She's in her own room, now. Let me take you. It's literally just here." And she walked us to a door we'd already walked past earlier, just behind the nurses' station, and there, in the bed, was Laura.

"Wash your hands please. Here's an apron. You can go straight in. Just make sure you dispose of the apron in the bin inside the room just there, before you leave. And wash your hands properly again when you come out. There's a hand sanitizer on the wall."

Mum squirted her hands, and then I did mine, and we tied each other's aprons in silence, and went in.

The room was dark, darker than the ward. There was a window but the blinds were down. It was small. There was only space for one chair next to the bed. But it was a relief to be away from the staring tired eyes of the ward.

Mum walked straight over to Laura and stroked her cheek.

"Hello, darling," she said. "Hello. We couldn't find you, darling. How are you today?"

I stood at the door, watching, as the sister left. I felt a sob rising inside my chest, and as much as I tried I couldn't swallow it down. It was relief. To be here, with Laura, to see her, alive. She looked peaceful, calm. She might have had a hospital bug but she didn't look any different. I was glad.

Mum looked up at me.

"Come on, Tessie," she said, her voice short. "Are you coming in or not?"

I stepped further into the room.

The hardness in Mum's voice was back now that she was talking to me. She'd been so soft with Laura just now. I'd loved seeing her like that, like the old Mum. But this was how it always went. An irritability after the crisis, and it was usually directed at me, like somehow I was to blame. I guessed she was angry with me for the things I didn't say. But the feelings we both felt didn't go away just because the words were never said. They lingered between us horribly and came out looking like anger on the other side of things.

"For god's sake, Tessie. Come and sit on the bed. I'll go and see if we can get another chair in a minute." She patted a space on the bed next to Laura but she didn't look at me. I walked to the bed and sat down.

I didn't like it here, in this new room.

Mum leaned forward and kissed Laura on the forehead, and she said, "Here, have my chair, Tessie. I'll go and see if there's another one." And as she stood to go to the door I wanted to grab her arm and scream: *Don't leave me here. Please. Don't leave me.*

But Mum left.

I swallowed hard.

I knew she'd only be gone a minute, maybe two, but suddenly the quiet in the room felt like it would suffocate me. I looked at Laura lying motionless in the bed and then around, back towards the door.

It was PROPER SHUT.

It was just Laura now. Laura and me.

I looked back at her.

I so wanted for her to know that I wasn't like Ella. That I was there, in the room. That I'd always visited. I'd always been to see her.

I looked at the door again. It was definitely shut.

There was no reason why I couldn't talk here now.

This was the first opportunity I'd had to do that, to let Laura know I was here. There had always been a nurse with her in ITU, to check the ventilator, to make sure she was still breathing and it was the same when they were weaning her off it. And then she was moved to the ward and it was a public place; it was full of people. But here, now, in this room, there was nothing to stop me talking. There was no one here but me. Me and Laura. Technically, I could speak. If I could find a way to make this a safe space

– if I worked towards it, then maybe, maybe I could talk to her. But the thought of it frightened me. So much.

I swallowed again and felt the familiar tightness in my throat.

Surely Laura would understand why I couldn't speak to her here? Surely she would know why I couldn't do it? There would be no anger or disappointment. There would be no blame. If she woke up right now, and I didn't speak to her – she'd understand. She wouldn't need me to explain. Would she?

I looked behind me again to check the door.

It was still PROPER SHUT.

And we were alone.

Just talk to her. It doesn't matter what about. Tell her about your day. Hold her hand. Tell her a story. It will help. It all helps – for her to know that you are here.

That's what Brenda had said.

I felt a panic inside my chest. It was rising like a river in a storm.

I should talk to her.

I should.

I thought about Anya, and the sessions we used to have. I thought about how I'd spoken into a voice recorder at home, and brought it in to school for Anya to listen to in one of our sessions. And it was hard, but I remembered how Anya had responded – just a smile – but still a broad, happy one – when she'd heard my voice in the room. She'd tried to hide her reaction, her pleasure in hearing me speak. She knew she couldn't really show how she'd felt when she'd heard me, because it might have set me back, added to the pressure I felt when someone talked to me, or had an expectation of me talking back. But her delight had shown, and I wondered if Laura's would too, if I spoke to her now.

I coughed.

I didn't mean to.

It was my body expressing my fear – despite my lack of words.

I looked down at Laura's hand next to mine on the bed. We were both so pale. There was no difference in the way our hands looked. I stretched out my fingers to Laura's so the tips touched. Her nails were long. They were still growing. They were longer even than mine.

I looked up at her face.

Even if I could speak to her, I didn't know what I would say.

It doesn't really matter what you say, Tessie.

That's what Anya would have said.

Try counting. A shopping list. A poem you have in your head.

That's how it had started with Anya, how I'd started to talk into the recorder at home and bring it into the room

at school so she could hear. We were studying *The Tempest*.
I hadn't got to read a part in class. I couldn't. It didn't mean
I didn't have anything to say about it. It didn't mean I didn't
follow all the words, love the words, hold them in my head
as they were read. It didn't mean I didn't understand.

We are such stuff
As dreams are made on;

That's what came into my head.

and our little life
Is rounded with a sleep.

I pushed my hand a little further along the bed sheet,
and I rested my fingers on top of Laura's.
She was so still.
I wrapped my fingers around hers.
And I held her hand.
For the first time since her attack, I held her hand.
The door opened.
I jumped.
Mum was back.
I let go of Laura quickly, like I'd been caught out.
"All okay?" Mum said.
I nodded, moving off the bed.

"No chairs anywhere. Ridiculous."

I moved over so Mum could get past me to the chair that was already next to the bed, and I made a T shape with my hands and walked towards the door so Mum knew I was heading for the toilet. And when I stepped out of the room, and the door closed behind me, I turned, and I looked through the glass in the door, back into the room.

If I could talk and Laura could wake up, then surely anything in the world would be possible. Anything at all.

Saturday

18.

"You awake in there?" Dad called, poking his head round my bedroom door.

I lifted my head up to see him standing in his pyjamas holding a mug of tea.

"I am now," I said, and he smiled.

He came and sat on my bed. I liked the weekends. I liked having him around more.

"Mum's not so good today."

I nodded. I knew what he meant, and at the same time I didn't. No one ever seemed to really explain. I hated that – the knowing, and the not really knowing.

"I've said we'll all have breakfast, together."

"Is Jake up?" I asked.

"No, I'm about to wake him."

"Okay," I said. I guessed breakfast altogether was Dad's way of trying to cheer Mum up.

Dad lifted his hand up and stroked my cheek.

"I've got to go away, for work." He stood up. "We'll talk

about it over breakfast. Come down once you've had your tea."

I felt disappointment slip over me like a cloak – over my head, around my shoulders, my waist – it enveloped me. I knew how it was going to be over breakfast now. It was going to be hell.

"See you in a minute," he said, looking back at me from the bedroom door as he went. It was the checking look. He knew it was going to be hell too.

I sat up and grabbed my thick socks and a hoody from the floor next to my bed, and bunged them on.

Since Dad had got this promotion last year he'd started travelling with work. He'd never had to before. The trips were usually meant to be short ones, abroad, four or five days, but they always became longer. That's what Mum hated about them. That she never knew exactly how long he'd be away.

"*I'm troubleshooting,*" Dad would say. "*I'm really sorry. It'll take as long as it takes, Kate. It's just the way it is.*" That was what Dad would say to Mum, to try and explain. It usually just made things worse. I never really understood what Dad did in his job, but it was something to do with IT and configuring networks, and streaming and systems. He often used words like that.

I stood up to go to the bathroom before I went down to the kitchen.

I could hear Mum calling for me up the stairs.

"Tessie?"

I opened my door and shouted back. "Yes?"

"Ella's on the phone…"

I stood still. I didn't answer.

I could tell from the tone in Mum's voice as she said it, that she thought it was strange too.

"Did you hear me, Tessie?" Mum said when I didn't answer.

Ella had never called me before. In fact no one ever called me. No one. I never used the phone. Never. Ella knew that, didn't she? I wouldn't use the phone at home or the mobile. My mobile was for texts only. She knew that.

"For me?" I said. "Are you sure?"

"Yes, Tessie. She asked for you. What shall I say?"

"I…I…"

I couldn't quite get the words out. I wasn't ever going to be able to call her back and anyway, I wasn't sure I wanted to know what she had to say.

"Tessie!" Mum said, the frustration in her voice leaking through. "Tessie, I'm going to tell her to try you again in a bit, that we're about to eat…which we are." I heard her footsteps back across the hall as she headed to the phone in the kitchen.

And I told myself I wouldn't take the call.

I wouldn't. I'd be out. I'd make sure I was out.

And I went to the bathroom, and brushed my teeth, and I headed downstairs.

Me and Mum sat at the table whilst Dad served up.

"Ella's going to call back soon. I said to give us half an hour. She's at home."

I nodded. I didn't care where she was. I wasn't going to take the call.

"Where's Jake?" Dad mumbled as he started spooning the scrambled eggs onto each plate. It looked disgusting. Like mangled rubber ducks. I thought it might bounce off the plate as soon as Dad spooned it on.

"I'm not eating," Jake said, walking into the kitchen in his running gear.

"What do you mean? We're having breakfast together. I told you that," Dad said.

"I don't want to eat before I run," Jake said.

"Run later," Dad said. "This is important."

"Look, I know what this is. It's a family meeting to talk about the fact that you are going away with work when everything here is totally messed up. What is there to discuss?"

Mum turned her head very slowly to look at Dad. I knew that look. It was like a challenge and a plea, all rolled into one. *Don't go.* That's what she was saying with it. *Please don't go.*

"It's a week," Dad said. "In fact it isn't even a week. It's five days. I'll be back before next weekend."

"Yeah, well a week feels like a bloody long time right now," Jake said.

No one spoke.

Dad sat down at the table.

"Jake, come on. Sit down. We do need to talk about this."

"I'm not sitting down to talk about it!"

There was quiet again.

"What if the trip gets extended?" Mum said. "Like last time. Like it did when you went to Cologne."

"That won't happen, I promise. This is a quick job. It's a week, tops. I might even get back early, if it all goes well."

"A lot can happen in a week," I said, and when I said it they all stopped looking at one another and they looked at me. Even Mum. I went on. "I mean, what if Laura wakes up?"

It was what we were all waiting for, but we never actually talked about it. Never.

"Tessie…" Dad said, reaching his hand out towards me.

"No, I'm serious, Dad. What if she wakes up and you're not here?"

"He doesn't think she's going to wake up. That's the whole point, Tessie! That's why he's going, working, getting on with his life, why he's only at the hospital once a week – not like the rest of us. He doesn't think she's going to wake up now, but he just won't say it."

"Don't!" Mum said standing up. "Don't say that, Jake!" And as she spoke her face crumpled. She looked like someone had punched her hard, in the gut.

I looked at Jake and I looked at Dad, and I willed one of them to do something, to make it better, to make Mum better. If Laura was here she would have done that, but I didn't because I didn't know what to do.

Dad stood up and walked over to Mum and put his hands on her shoulders, easing her back into the chair, and she slowly sat back down.

I looked at the cold egg on my plate and imagined flipping it, tipping it, ripping it – I imagined throwing it all over the table.

"I'm going for my run," Jake said. "And don't you dare ask me when I'll be back." He turned and headed to the front door, but before he got there, the doorbell went.

Mum looked at Dad. "Are you expecting someone?" she said, standing up again.

Every time the doorbell rang unexpectedly these days, the house filled with panic. Like floodwater, it seeped through the doors, the windows, the cracks and crevices in the ground.

"Let me go and see," Dad said walking towards the hall, but Jake had already opened the front door on his way out, and was coming back through to us in the kitchen now.

"It's May Grover," he said.

Dad put his hand on Jake's arm. "You go for your run, Jake. We'll talk when you get back."

Jake turned and nodded at May as he passed her in the doorway, and Dad beckoned her in.

19.

"Good morning – do you have a minute?"

"Yes, sure. Come on in. Do you want coffee or tea or something?" Dad said. I could tell he was panicking, walking from the table to the sink to the kettle.

"No, no. I won't stay long," May said coming into the kitchen. "Hi there, Tessie," she said nodding.

"Why don't you go up and get dressed?" Mum said. "You don't need to stay here for this, Tessie."

I got up and headed into the hall. I'd started to go before Mum had even spoken. I knew she didn't want me there. She never did.

"Is this about Ella Taylor?" Mum said as soon as I had left the room. "I heard you brought her in for questioning."

I stopped and turned, standing just behind the kitchen door.

I wanted to hear. I wanted to know what Ella had told them.

"No. This isn't about Ella Taylor. But you're right, we did

bring her in for questioning yesterday and she's been released for the moment. I can't say any more just now. No, I came today about a separate matter – we've had a new witness come forward with information."

"Okay," Mum said.

"A woman who was in the park behind the viaduct just after the time of Laura's attack. She was walking her dog."

"And she's only just come forward now?" Dad said.

"Yes, I know. It seems strange, but it often happens. People don't remember things, then they see something, and it's like a reminder, it jogs the memory. Or they don't feel sure about what they think they saw, so they sit on it for a bit. To be fair, that's why I was pushing for the reconstruction, which is looking less likely now as time goes on, but this new witness—"

"What did she see?" Mum said.

"Three lads walking from the direction of the viaduct, just after the time we estimate Laura was attacked. One of them acted like he was going to kick the witness's dog. It jumped up at the lads, wouldn't leave them alone. Our witness says she apologized, tried to get hold of the dog, but they were abusive, said her dog was out of control. They seemed hyped up, she said. Like they were in trouble, looking for trouble. Those were her words. She's provided a pretty good description of one of them in particular, so it's given us something to look for on the CCTV footage for that evening. We've picked these lads up on various cameras at various locations within a couple of miles of the viaduct, both before and after the estimated time of the attack, and the witness managed to identify one of them in particular. His name is Mark Tyler – he's got a previous record for theft, selling on stolen phones and possession."

"I don't understand," Dad said. "Are you saying you think these boys attacked Laura?"

"Does the name Kyle Brooks mean anything to you?" May said.

"No, not to me," Dad said, looking over to Mum.

"No," Mum said. "Me neither."

"Ever heard Laura mention a Kyle?"

"No," Dad said again. "Why?"

I pressed my nose to the crack between the door and the frame to try and see through. The three of them were sitting around the table. Dad's arms were crossed. Mum was leaning on the table, towards May. I could see she was hanging off her every word.

"We can't formally identify Kyle from the CCTV, the images are just too blurred, but he's known to hang around with Mark Tyler, or Marky – that's what his mates call him – and Kris White. The three of them pretty much hang out together all the time. We're as certain as we can be that it was those three that our witness and her dog encountered at the park that evening. In fact, Kyle's of particular interest because we've found a connection between him and Joe McGrath. Obviously we're keen to follow that lead."

Mum looked at Dad. He reached over and took her hand.

"So this Kyle, what's his connection to Joe?" Dad said.

"They went to school together, in Wellbridge. They definitely know each other from inside and outside school. Look, we've got officers out there right now searching for Kyle, to bring him in. Until we've spoken to him I can't say much more. But we think he might bring us one step closer to Joe McGrath. At least, that's what we're hoping. I came today to bring you up to speed on this and the reconstruction and—"

"We can ask Jake," Dad said. "When he's back from his run. You never know, Laura may have said something to him about a Kyle. Maybe she met him with Joe – if there's a connection…I'm just thinking out loud…I don't know."

"Yes, that would be great," May said, standing up from the table. "And if he knows anything, then call me."

I had to move. I had to get out the way. I couldn't be seen, listening.

There was quiet.

"Well, look, it's the weekend. I understand that," May said. "I don't want to intrude. I'll get out of your hair."

"Of course," Dad said, and I heard the chairs round the table scrape across the kitchen floor as May stood up to leave.

I quietly tiptoed across the hall and made a dash up the stairs, and I stood at the top, listening as they came into the hall. May was still talking.

"We're obviously doing all we can to find Joe, Mrs Green. This is where the focus of our investigation lies. It seems he really didn't have many friends, but Kyle Brooks is definitely a lead, so we need to be patient."

"I just still find it hard to believe he hasn't been found," Mum said.

"I think we have to assume that he really doesn't want to be found, Mrs Green – and you wouldn't believe the lengths people will go to if they need to just get away from a situation."

I could tell May was trying to wrap up the conversation. I turned to go back into my room, but then the phone started ringing downstairs.

Ella. That was going to be Ella. Ringing me back.

I had to get out. I had to go. I went into my room, pulled on some jogging bottoms over my pyjamas, dragged a brush through my hair, grabbed my trainers and waited at the top of the stairs. And as soon as I saw Dad close the front door to Campbell and follow Mum into the kitchen, as she went to answer the phone, I came down the stairs and slipped out of the front door.

And I went to Max's.

Because Max's was the only place I could think to be.

20.

When I knocked, Max's mum opened the door, and I almost flew in.

"Everything alright, Tessie?" she said as I passed her and ran up the stairs to the loft room two at a time.

I didn't know what I was going to say to Max. I knew I had to say something. I couldn't pretend that everything was normal, that it had been normal this past couple of days. I didn't know how I would explain why I'd pulled away from him when he kissed me, but I also wondered how he'd explain not inviting me to his gig last night. Remembering that it had been yesterday and that Max hadn't invited me, it actually hurt.

I was almost out of breath when I got to the top of the stairs. I knocked, gently pushed open the bedroom door and stepped into the room. Max looked up and I closed the door behind me, so it was PROPER SHUT.

"Hey!" I said, and my voice came out so light and bright it kind of shocked me. I was so glad to be there, to see him.

I so wanted to make things okay.

"Hey," he said back, but then he looked down again at the magazine he was reading.

I waited for him to stop, to say something more.

There was nothing.

I went and sat down next to him on the floor.

He looked up at me.

He looked nice.

"What are you doing?" I said.

"You can see what I'm doing, Tessie," he said, closing the magazine and shifting away from me, so he could lean against his bed.

Suddenly it felt like someone had turned down all the bright lights that had been shining before.

"I waited for you yesterday, you know? To walk you back after school, and you never showed up," Max said, standing up and putting the magazine on his desk.

For a moment I had forgotten that I'd texted him. But he'd never replied, and then Mum had sent me the message about going to the hospital.

"God, I'm sorry," I said. "I never heard back from you. I..."

"You forgot," Max said.

"Mum picked me up – I, I went to see Laura..."

I'd so wanted him to call or text me back. I'd so wanted him to walk me home. But he hadn't replied.

"Yeah, when you didn't show I remembered it was a hospital day."

I nodded. I didn't know what to say. I was sorry. I really was.

There was an awkward silence.

"How did the gig go?"

Max looked up.

"How did you know about the gig?"

"Mia. She kind of let it slip. She thought I was going."

Max nodded, looking down at his hands in his lap now.

"Look, it was a last-minute thing..."

"Yeah, I know. Mia said."

"I didn't know what to do, Tessie. After the other day, you know?"

"Do you like her – Mia?" I hadn't meant to say it, but it just came out. Suddenly I wanted to know.

"No!" Max said, looking up. His voice came out louder than even he thought it would, from the look on his face. "How can you say that, Tessie?"

"Because she likes you. It's obvious. And you went with her the other day, to the cafe; you invited her to the gig."

"I told you I was going with her to the cafe, though, didn't I?"

"You don't have to ask my permission to go anywhere with her, Max!" The words came out hard, too hard. I'd wanted them to be softer, kinder. I hadn't meant for it to sound like it did. But they had gone to the cafe and he had invited her to the gig, and he hadn't invited me.

"I am finding it really hard to understand what's going on with you at the moment, Tessie," Max said. "One minute you sound like you're jealous of Mia, the next you're—"

I stood up.

"What? I'm what? You know everything that's going on with me. Everything! You know better than anyone what is going on with me!"

"Yeah, well then why do I feel like I'm so completely in the dark right now," he said, standing up too. "I literally do not know what is going on inside your head. You text me to meet you, and then you're not there—"

"You didn't turn up the day before that, Max. Have you forgotten that? You didn't show—"

"I didn't know what to do, Tessie. I kissed you. I kissed you – and you pretty much pushed me away."

"I didn't, Max. I just…"

I stopped speaking.

I looked at his lips. I didn't know if I wanted him to kiss me again. I didn't know if I liked him enough. I wanted to like him. I did like him, but – he was my friend. And then I thought about Billy, just for a second. His face came into my head. And my stomach swirled like someone had pushed me hard and fast on the brightest most beautiful fairground ride and all the colours were merging, over me, around me, through me, and I was lost for a moment in the joy of it.

"What, Tessie?"

Max's voice broke the thought.

I didn't know what to say.

"I – I—"

No words were forming. Not in my head, not in my mouth. All I'd done was make it worse. So much worse. I should never have come.

"I – I just wanted – to—"

"What, Tessie? What?"

Max was angry. He was still angry. Or was it frustration? But there was nothing I could say now that could make it better.

"I should go," I said.

"No, Tessie! Don't go. You always do this. Leave, just when we're about to really talk. Don't go."

"I have to go," I said. "This isn't how I meant it to be. I need to think." And I turned and I opened the bedroom door.

"Tessie!" Max said, and I looked back at him before I went, with the words *I'm sorry* crouching softly, timidly, like they were in hiding, on my lips.

Monday

21.

The weekend had continued very much as it started. It was just made worse by the fact that we all knew Dad was leaving early on Monday morning.

We never finished the family discussion we'd started on Saturday morning, before May Grover had cut us short. Jake went for another run later in the day, and came back puffed out and drenched in sweat, like he'd had a fight with himself and lost. I sat waiting for him at the top of the stairs, but when he got back he just walked straight past me and into the shower. He didn't come out for ages and then kept himself in his room most of the day, asking me to just leave him alone whenever I tried to talk to him.

Mum had gone back to bed and stayed there for the rest of the weekend. I remembered her doing that once before. Maybe twice. I think it was after I was diagnosed with SM, but I don't really remember. I think I just knew things were bad then, and they were bad again now. Dad cooked meals that no one ate and washed clothes that no one put away.

He left them in piles outside our bedroom doors.

He went to visit Laura on Sunday morning. He asked us if we'd like to come, but I didn't want to go with him, and I guessed Mum and Jake felt the same because he went on his own. I watched a lot of television. Endless shows that blurred into one long drone. All I kept thinking about was how I'd messed things up with Max. The feeling of fighting with him, hurting him, was there with me all weekend like a pressed bruise.

Dad's taxi arrived at 7 a.m. to take him to the airport. When we heard it draw up outside the house and the cabbie beeped to let us know he was there, I think we were all relieved. I know that's a bad thing to say, but none of us had recovered from the conversation on Saturday morning. The only way we were going to get back to some sense of normality would be if Dad left us to it. Somehow then, I knew me and Jake would fill the gap that Dad left for Mum when he went away. We'd step up. We'd do the chores. We'd be gentle with Mum. We'd make it okay. Just like Laura would have done, before Joe anyway. I told myself I'd do my best. I'd definitely do my best.

"So, I'll see you all on Friday," Dad said, standing in front of the open front door. There was an edge in his voice that I recognized. It was emotion. He sounded like he was going to cry. I'd only heard him like that once before, when Laura hadn't come home on the night of the attack. Mum had spoken to the police and they'd asked her to confirm what Laura had been wearing that day. Mum had looked at Dad and asked him if he could remember. Dad had said, *Jeans, I think. A striped top – yes, blue and white – a bag, her canvas bag, the yellow one…* And there it was – the edge that warned you he was hanging, about to fall.

Mum stood in the hall in her dressing gown. "The taxi's waiting," she said. "You should go."

"Let it wait," he said. "They often do, you know." There was the edge again. Different this time. Irritation, frustration. But still, he was holding on. "Where's Jake?" he said.

"He's upstairs, in his room," Mum said, and then she blinked, slowly, at Dad and she stepped away. "I'll go and get him."

And I knew that was her goodbye.

And it would be Jake's too.

Because goodbye wasn't a word any of us could say any more. We'd never got to say goodbye to Laura before the attack, not properly. She'd left home on an argument. And if we got to say goodbye to her now it would be because we were letting her go. Goodbye was a word that evaded us all, because maybe if we didn't say it, there would still be room for another hello.

"Come here, Tessie," Dad said as Mum went up the stairs, and he ran his hand over the top of my head and down to my neck and pulled me in strongly for a hug.

I knew I had to be the one to give him that. With the front door open and the cabbie glancing over from the taxi I had no words, but I could give him that. And I did.

"Be good, little Tessie," he said. "Be good." And he held my face in his hands for one last moment, and then walked down the path and got into the cab and was gone.

I closed the front door, and turned round. Mum and Jake were coming down the stairs.

"Come here," Jake said to me, and he put his arms around me, and then Mum put her arms around both of us, and we stood in the hall, holding one another, waiting for the moment to pass.

"We will be okay, you know, Tessie," Jake said, pulling back.

Mum looked at me and nodded, but she didn't say a thing. She just took Jake's hand and squeezed it, hard.

"Let me walk you to school today, Tessie," Jake said, letting go of Mum's hand now. "Max won't mind, will he? It'll give him a day off, eh?" And he jabbed me in the arm as he said it.

I smiled. It was a good idea. It meant I didn't have to face Max just yet. Jake was doing me more of a favour than he knew.

"Great," Mum said to Jake quickly, turning to go back upstairs. "I'm going to get dressed so I can head to the hospital and see Laura this morning. Jake, you'll still come with me later on today though, won't you?"

"Sure," Jake said, and I could see on his face that he was trying. He was trying really hard.

And then the phone rang.

"I'll get it," Jake said, heading to the kitchen.

I stood in the hall where Jake had left me and I prayed it wasn't Ella.

"Tessie! It's Ella for you!"

I had to take the call. I had to take it.

I walked into the kitchen and took the phone from Jake as he headed past me to go upstairs and get dressed.

I put the phone to my ear. Ella's voice was there.

"Tessie, it's me. Listen, did you hear what happened?"

I shook my head. I didn't speak.

"Tessie? It's me, Ella. You there?"

I tapped the phone, as an answer.

"Oh, okay…right…" Ella said, like she was just catching on that I wasn't going to speak. "You're gonna listen, right? Tessie? Please listen."

And then without waiting for any kind of response she started to talk.

"Tessie, I went in to be questioned on Friday, like I told you, by the police, and it's like they know about me and Joe. I didn't tell them anything. But it's like they know. They've got this receipt from the cafe. They found it at the viaduct. I don't know how it got there. Just some stupid bit of paper that I'd scribbled a message on – for him – for Joe – ages ago – before he was seeing Laura – after we'd... spent time together, you know? And somehow this bit of paper turns up there, at the viaduct, and I don't know how... The police are asking me if I was there, at the viaduct. If not that night, then another time, with Joe. They're calling it evidence... You still there, Tessie?"

I tapped.

I didn't want to, but I did.

"It doesn't look good for him, Tessie. They're trying to make out it's a place he took girls, like Laura, like me, like he got together with girls and tried to hurt them. They're asking me if he ever took me there and tried to hurt me. Are you listening, Tessie?"

I tapped the phone again. I was listening but I didn't want to know. I didn't want to know any of it. I tapped the phone and hoped it would block her out, shut her up. I kept tapping. But it didn't.

"I told them Joe wasn't like that, he wouldn't do that. So then they started asking me how well I knew Joe, and how I felt about him. They asked me if I was jealous of Laura and him, if I wanted Laura out of the way, because I was jealous. They said maybe I couldn't control my feelings for him – that we'd planned to do this – me and Joe – together…"

I heard Ella take a deep breath. There was a silence, at last, between us. I closed my eyes, and Ella began to talk again, but this time in a quieter voice.

"The police took my phone, Tessie. They took it. And now they're going to see that I called Joe the night Laura was attacked. In fact I called him loads that night, and before, and after that night too. And it's going to look so bad. But that's not how it was – it's not what they're saying it is – that's not how it's been. It's not. I just want to know he's okay, Tessie. That's all. I just want him to come back, you know? Make it all better. He can do that. I know he can."

I stood still. Completely still.

"Tessie – you still there?"

I was there, and I was listening, but I was finding it hard to take it all in. All the words that she was saying, so fast, so matter-of-fact. And she didn't seem to be thinking about Laura at all.

"If Joe came back he could tell everyone how much he loves her, you know? Laura – " she said – "because he does. He loves her. Not me. It's her he loves."

I didn't move. I didn't tap. I couldn't. I felt numb.

Ella was quiet for a minute.

"Will you come to the cafe after school, Tessie? I don't like talking on the phone at home, like this."

I didn't move.

"Tessie? Would you? Please?"

And I hung up.

Quickly.

Without thinking.

Without waiting for her to say goodbye.

22.

I texted Max to let him know Jake was taking me in, and I kept checking my phone right up until we left the house, but I never got a reply. I guessed Max thought I was still avoiding him. I'd have to find a way to explain that it had been Jake's suggestion, not mine.

Me and Jake walked down the end of our street and turned into the main road.

"I'll come with you to the bus stop, and then head off," Jake said. "That okay?" Jake's sixth form college was another ten-minute walk from my school. The bus stop was the obvious place for him to leave me.

I nodded, but felt my heart beat faster, louder in my chest. I was going to have to walk alone. I'd made it to the cafe after school the other day, but still. I looked up ahead towards the bus stop. I started scanning the street, looking for Holly and Kat. I needed to know if they were there, if they were waiting for me, because that's what they'd do. Get off the bus and see if I was around. If I was, they'd hang on for a game of Kat and Mouse before heading to school. That's what Holly called it. Kat and Mouse.

I needed to work out how I'd get Jake to stay with me, if they were there. I kept looking ahead, my eyes on the bus stop, but I couldn't see them. I looked behind me. There were no buses in view amongst the traffic. Maybe I'd missed them. I kept walking alongside Jake, towards the bus stop, my heart calming a little in my chest. Except I could see somebody waiting up ahead by the wall, just before the bus stop. A boy. In uniform. I recognized the outline immediately. The shaved head, the broad shoulders and the strong back.

As we got closer I knew it was him.

Billy.

My heart started pumping stronger, faster.

Billy.

It was Billy.

I looked at Jake.

"What?" he said.

He could see in my face I wanted to say something. I had turned like I was going to say something. I think I'd almost opened my mouth to speak. I was excited – to see him – to see Billy.

I looked down quickly, away from Jake.

I didn't want him to see my excitement.

"So, I'll see you later, yeah?" Jake said. "After me and

Mum have been to see Laura. If Max isn't around then walk to the cafe after school, yeah? Like the other day?"

I nodded. I just wanted him to go now, to leave me, so I could get to Billy.

And as he peeled off down the side road, I saw Billy stand up away from the wall and hitch his bag onto his back, and he was smiling the smile I'd been trying to keep inside since I'd seen him. And I smiled right back.

"Hey," he said. "I've been waiting for you."

I nodded.

"I saw you go off this way the other day, so I kind of… followed you. Just for a bit."

I looked up at him.

Why did you follow me?

That was the question I had in my head.

"I wanted to know where you lived, you know?" he said, answering my thought almost as soon as I'd had the chance to think it.

I wondered when he'd followed me. It must have been when I was with Max.

We carried on walking.

"I was thinking…" he said, "that we could text or message…something like that?" and he slipped his hand into mine as he said it and smiled, and his hold was warm and strong and it felt right. "You've got a phone, right?"

I looked at him. And I blinked.

One blink. ONE BLINK for YES.

But I couldn't message. Not really. And I couldn't tell him that.

"Then we can chat, can't we?" he said. "In a different way, yeah?"

I tried to smile back, to show him that I'd like that, but inside the panic began, because I couldn't text him – not in the way he'd said, like a chat.

He stopped walking and turned to me, taking both my hands.

"I'm happy to wait for you to talk to me, Tessie. Really, I am..." he said, looking down at me now. "I meant that when I said it before. Because I like you – I just... I like you...and well, you'll talk to me – I'm sure you will ...one day." And as he said it he gripped my hands tighter. "It's just I'd like to know some of what's inside your head, you know? Now, while I'm waiting. This kind of thing... liking someone...liking you, like this...it doesn't happen to me everyday, you know...?"

I nodded. And I blushed. I couldn't help it. This kind of thing didn't happen to me everyday either and I wanted to tell him that, so much. And I wanted to tell him how he made me feel, because he made me feel like maybe it was possible to talk, to talk to him. But what he said about waiting – for me – it panicked me. The panic was raging inside of me now. Because I didn't know whether he could wait that long for me, and the thought that he didn't know just how long he might have to wait, made me lose all the softness I felt inside. My hard edges were back. I knew they were. I could feel my body stiffening with tension, and not just in my neck and my throat – it was all over – and it wasn't going away – it was there in the gaping silent space between us – there, then, now – always – where my words were meant to be.

Billy started walking again, but his hand in my hand felt too tight now. He was gripping on to me... Or was I gripping on to him? I couldn't tell. I looked around. We were close to school now. I didn't want Holly or Kat or any of the other kids in my tutor group to see me. I wanted to let go of Billy's hand, but I wasn't sure how to make it happen, without saying anything. I opened my mouth to try and bring in some air – to gasp – and my neck tightened and my ears started filling with the words I couldn't say:

Let go of my hand.

Let go of my hand.

Let go of my hand.

The words were loud. I was screaming them inside my head now:

Let go.

Let go.

Let go.

I turned my head to look up at Billy as we neared the gate.

I could feel a cough building in my throat, my throat raw with the pain, a cough that I couldn't get out. Could I pull my hand away? I didn't want to and I did want to, all at the same time.

And then I saw Max. He was standing by the school gates, talking to Mia, and they were laughing.

I looked down quickly at the pavement.

I didn't want to see them together, like that.

And I didn't want them to see me, like this.

There was no saliva in my mouth – another cough was building.

I stopped walking, to take a breath.

"That your friend over there?" Billy said, motioning over to Max, and dropping my hand out of his as he did.

I felt a momentary relief and quickly put my hand into my pocket, out of the way of Billy's and I looked over towards Max again, and as I did Max looked over at me, but he didn't smile. He pretended like he hadn't seen me, and I pretended like I hadn't seen him. But I felt a pressure on my chest like a dead weight and it wasn't letting me breathe.

"He goes everywhere with you, doesn't he?" Billy said, and there was something in his voice that sounded like jealousy, but I wasn't really sure if it could have been.

And I looked back again for Max. But he had gone.

23.

"You kissed him yet?"

That's what Holly said as I went to walk out of school at the end of the day.

She and Kat were waiting for me by the gates as I headed out to go to the cafe. I had no choice. I had to go there. I'd done it once before. I told myself I could do it again.

"You kissed that boy Billy who's totally mad about you?" Holly said.

I needed to move. I needed to find a way to move.

I wondered if Billy might be around. I looked, I hoped, but I couldn't see him anywhere.

"He's totally mad about you," Kat said. "You mad about him too?"

I looked at Kat.

"You going mad thinking about him in that tiny silent little brain of yours?" Holly said, tapping me on the head, hard, her hand in a fist. I felt the thud of it, then the pain.

I started to walk, my face tilted towards the floor, my gaze on the tip of my shoes as I took a step, and then another, each shoe disappearing and reappearing again and again. I had to get away.

"Ah, she's all shy," I heard Holly say again. She was walking next to me now. Kat was too, on my other side. "Shy and in love…" I heard her say as I kept putting one foot in front of the other, my heart slamming, my pulse banging.

"I don't think he knows how shy you are, Tessie," Kat said, laughing. "I don't think he has a clue."

"Yeah, you're like completely mute, and he's so stupid he doesn't seem to have noticed," Holly said.

He has noticed, Holly. He has.

That's what I would have said, if I'd had the words.

"Did you hypnotize him, Mouse?" Holly said. "Is that what you did? Did you get him to fall in love with you just by looking at him? Just with that stupid look in your eyes?"

"Mad and stupid," Kat said. "They're both mad and stupid."

"They were made for each other," Holly said, and she turned to Kat. "Come on. Let's go. It's too early in the day for this freak show. We'll catch up later, yeah? Let's go."

"See ya, Mouse! Another day," Kat said, waving, and they left me counting my footsteps, the numbers keeping order in my head, as I walked all the way to the end of the street. And once I was sure I was out of their sight I headed to the cafe to wait for Jake, thinking over and over and over about Billy as I did.

The cafe windows were all steamed up when I arrived. I pushed the door open and felt a cloud of warmth greet me as I stepped in. It was packed. Ella was making coffee, frothing milk, and the dishwasher was wide open, clean, all the white mugs like a mouth full of teeth. I stopped. There were too many people. I didn't like it. I looked through to the booth at the back, but there was someone already sitting there. If it was free, I'd told myself, then I'd grab it and text Jake and wait for him like we'd agreed, but it wasn't...

"Tessie, come in!" Ella's voice boomed over the whir of the coffee machine. "Go down the back. Jake's here..." She looked pleased to see me. She looked happy. She was glad that I had come. But I'd come to meet Jake. Not her. I hadn't come to see her at all.

I stepped forward and looked again down the back of the shop towards the booth. The person I'd seen turned towards me – it was Jake. I wasn't sure why I hadn't recognized him before. He waved me over, and I went to him.

"Hey, Tessie," he said. "You alright?"

I slid myself along the banquette opposite him and put my bag down next to me. He had his homework out on the table. Had he been here a while? Had he not been to see Laura with Mum?

"Ella's getting me a hot chocolate. You want one?"

I shook my head.

"You okay?" he said, moving all his stuff over to the side of the table.

I shrugged. I wasn't sure I could really explain even if I'd been able to.

"Wanna tell me what's going on?" he said.

I shook my head.

"Here we go," Ella said coming to the table with hot chocolates. "That lot have all got coffee now, and I'm on my break so I'm going to come and sit with you. God, what a mad hour that's just been."

I looked at Ella, and she smiled back at me. She'd made me a hot chocolate. I was tempted to take a sip. It looked sweet and creamy. But I knew I couldn't drink it in front of everyone. I looked around. No one was looking this way. I bent down towards the cup and felt the steam rise over my face and I breathed in the smell of it. No – I couldn't do it. I couldn't take a sip.

"So how's things?" Ella said, looking at Jake and then turning to look at me.

There was something so completely upbeat about the way she asked that it felt like she was putting on an act. This wasn't the Ella who'd been on the phone to me yesterday, desperate to see Joe, desperate to talk.

"Well…you know, the same," Jake said. I could see there was no way he could find an answer that matched her overwhelmingly positive mood. "I've just come from the hospital," he said, and then he looked at me. "Mum picked me up just after lunch. I finished early today."

I nodded. Ella nodded too, smiling, but she seemed distracted, fiddling with the rings on her fingers, looking around the cafe, then down again at her hands.

"How is Laura?" she said, more quietly now.

I looked up at Ella. She'd asked. She'd actually asked.

"The same. You should go and see her. I mean…it would be good if you could go see her, you know?"

"I know," Ella said. "I just…"

"It's totally shit…" Jake said, looking down.

"I know, Jake. I know I've been totally shit…"

"That's not what I was saying, Ella," Jake said, quickly leaning over towards her. "I was going to say it's totally shit seeing her like she is, but – that's how it is and we have to go. The family have to go. You don't have to. But she doesn't look so bad now she's out of ITU. She's off a lot of the machines she was on before. Her hair's kind of growing back where they had to shave it. Her face, her eyes – she's less black and blue. She's just unconscious. It's like she's sleeping. And they say she's responding to the drugs they've given her for this bug she got, and well, we're just waiting for her to come around. The hospital say that friends are just as important as family, you know. It's about the people she loves – it's about letting her know we're there. It's not easy – but…"

I looked up at Ella again and her eyes met mine. Her whole face had changed, darkened.

"Tessie's looking at me like she thinks I'm a piece of shit for not going."

I hid my face behind my hot chocolate and looked down. I pretended to take a sip.

"Nah, she's not. That's just how Tessie looks," Jake said, lightening the conversation.

I smiled but I hated sitting there with Jake, saying nothing, knowing the things that I knew.

"Ha bloody ha, Jake. You gonna get him, Tessie? You gonna give him a punch for that? I would." I could hear the relief in her voice as she said it. Jake had given her an out. He'd changed the route of the conversation. She was released.

"Well, you'll have to get me once I get back from the toilet, Tessie," Jake said, and he got up from the table and ducked like I was going to swing him a punch, and Ella laughed, too loud, as he headed towards the front of the cafe to the loo.

As soon as Jake had gone, she spoke.

"I'm so glad you're here, Tessie," she said and she came

and sat next to me on my side of the banquette. I shifted further up into the booth so that my arm was pressed up against the wall. There was no way I could get away now. I was trapped, forced to hear the torrent of her words.

"Listen, I've been thinking," she said. "About Joe."

I didn't want to know what she'd been thinking about Joe.

I reached across the table and picked up a paper napkin. I folded it, twisted it in and out of my fingers, this way and that… I needed something to play with, to hold onto, as Ella carried on.

"He's kind, he's sweet – so sweet, you know… And Laura loved him. And he totally loved her. It was that simple. The police just don't get that. And because they don't have any other names, no one else they can talk to, they think Joe's to blame, and it's just stupid."

I twisted the napkin again in my hands, round, the other way.

I just had to sit and listen and wait for Jake to come back. That's all I had to do.

"If we could get through to Joe, talk to him, then we'd know who did this to Laura," Ella said. "That's the reason I've been trying to stay in touch with him, Tessie. You have to believe me. That's the reason."

I twisted the napkin again.

"I just can't believe there were no witnesses, no one else

who was there that evening, no one who saw anything," she said, and she looked at me. And when she said it the name Kyle Brooks came into my head and I didn't mean to, but I looked up, straight up, and back at her.

"What is it, Tessie? There is someone, isn't there? I can see it in your eyes – there is."

Didn't she know about Kyle Brooks? Had the police not asked her? Surely they'd asked her about Kyle, just like they'd asked us? I wondered if Dad had talked to Jake yet, like he'd said he would. My throat jarred with all the questions that were backing up inside it.

I flicked a look over towards the front of the cafe. I wanted Jake to come back. Now. Where was he?

"You've got to tell me if there's a name, Tessie. You've got to," Ella said.

I looked away again – and down at the napkin in my hands – I twisted it – tighter.

"Here," Ella said, grabbing the napkin from my hands and pulling a pen out of her hair so it fell down around her shoulders, out of its messy twist at the nape of her neck. "Here," she said again, passing me the pen and flattening out the napkin. "Write it down."

I looked over again towards the front of the shop. Jake was answering his phone. He motioned to me that he'd be back in two minutes and stepped outside the cafe to take the call.

"Please, Tessie. If there's a name, you have to tell me. Write it here."

Ella took my hand and put the pen into my fingers and pressed her own fingers down on mine, around the pen.

I didn't want to write.

I didn't want to put anything down.

I didn't do this – write messages. I never did. The school had given me a notepad in Year Seven, asked me to write down the things I needed to say. They thought it would "cure" me. Or at least cure the problem that they had communicating with me. But it didn't. Because to me it felt the same. To write what I was thinking, to write what I wanted to say, it was the same as speaking, messaging. In fact it was worse. Because it was there – it was permanent.

I looked up again for Jake.

"Tessie – please!" Ella said. "Just this one thing. Just do this one thing. Write it down. And I won't ask you again. I promise."

I shook my head but I could tell it hardly moved.

"Tessie! Please! I beg you, before Jake comes back. You have to – " And she pushed the pen in my hand and pulled it along the napkin so it made a mark. The ink on the napkin, bleeding blue, and she whispered – "Just do it, Tessie, just do it," and her hand was over mine and the pen was in both our hands – mine and hers and I did it –

I wrote – and her hand moved with mine and I only did it so she would stop – so she would stop talking to me – touching me – talking at me…

And the words my hand wrote were clear:

KYLE BROOKS

In big fat capitals on the napkin.

And as soon as I saw them, I wished that I hadn't written down a thing.

Ella pulled the napkin away from me.

"Shit," she said, looking up at me. "Kyle Brooks? Are you serious?"

I swallowed hard, still looking at the napkin.

She knew the name. She knew him. She knew his name.

Ella pulled the napkin away from me, folding it up and putting it in her pocket just as Jake started heading back to the table.

"It's not what you think, Tessie," she said, leaning in close now. "None of it is…" And she stopped because Jake had finally arrived.

"Come on, Tessie. We've got to go. That was Mum. She's home. She's not feeling great. We need to get some food on our way back."

Ella moved along the banquette again to stand up next to Jake.

I picked my bag up from the floor and slid myself out too. It was a relief to move.

"See you soon," Jake said to Ella, and then he put his hand on my shoulder like Dad would have done, to guide me out. He was being protective, kind.

"Yeah," Ella said. "Good to see you both."

Jake turned back.

"Don't forget, you can go and see Laura any time, yeah?"

Ella nodded, but I could see she wasn't listening, because she wasn't looking at me or Jake. She was pulling out the napkin with Kyle's name on it – looking at it again – and I wondered what it was that she knew and what the hell I had just done.

24.

I couldn't eat anything when we got home. Jake cooked pasta and slopped on some sauce from a jar and I sat with him at the table, but I was really just playing with it. All I could think about was Ella and the things she had said. And how I wanted Mum. I needed her to make things feel okay, but she was in bed and all the lights were off upstairs and Jake told me not to disturb her.

"You're not eating, Tessie?"

"Sorry," I said, pushing my plate away.

"Well you can't blame my cooking. I literally just boiled the pasta."

I smiled.

"Did Mum and Dad talk to you about what May Grover said the other day?" I asked.

"Yeah," Jake said, loading everything he had used to cook into the sink, including my bowl of uneaten pasta. I'd have to sort it all out later – before bed. I didn't want Mum to wake up and see it there in the morning. It would stress her out. "You mean about Kyle Brooks?"

I nodded.

"Yeah, never heard of him."

I looked down.

"I told Mum they should ask Ella. She's the only one who might know any of Joe's friends."

I nodded.

Jake stood with the fridge door open now, his face staring in. Even after a huge bowl of pasta he was still hungry. He was scanning the shelves looking for something more to eat.

"Do you think Ella and Joe were ever more than friends, Jake? Did Laura ever say anything to you about that?"

I'd had to ask. The question was hovering over everything right now. Laura talked to Jake about everything. They were that close. I was sure if it was true he would have known.

"What?" he said, turning to look away from the fridge towards me. "No way – that's mad, Tessie. Why would you even say that?"

"I don't know," I said, shaking my head. "It was just something…well, something Ella said, about her and Joe, about them being together before Laura started seeing Joe."

I waited a moment before I spoke again.

Jake turned back to the fridge. He didn't say anything.

"So it's not true?" I said.

"No, it's not. That would be weird, wouldn't it? Laura wouldn't do that to Ella, would she? Steal her boyfriend. You've got an overactive imagination, Tessie."

"You're probably right," I said, but I wasn't sure that Jake was right at all. There was no reason for Ella to lie and say that she and Joe had been together before Laura. Why make up a lie like that? A lie that makes you look bad, like you've been going behind your best friend's back? It must have been true. Otherwise why else would she say it?

Jake closed the fridge door – he'd found cold sausages.

"Did Ella talk to you about being questioned by the police then?" he asked.

I nodded.

"She didn't say anything to me," Jake continued. "But then I guess I didn't ask. It just felt awkward asking, you know?"

I nodded again.

"I imagine the police asked her about Kyle Brooks when they questioned her anyway." Jake leaned against the worktop, still eating.

I didn't respond. Because I knew they hadn't. I'd told Ella about Kyle. I'd written his name down for her on the napkin, and she'd looked shocked, surprised, when she'd seen it. It was like she knew Kyle, she knew who he was, but she hadn't known he was involved until then.

"I was wondering," Jake said, shifting on his feet now, looking awkward, "if you've been into Laura's room lately?"

"What?" I said.

I couldn't keep up.

My mind was still on Ella.

"I just wondered –" Jake said again – "if you'd been into her room since the police searched it?"

I shook my head. "No, but I've thought about it. Why, have you?"

Jake nodded and came over to the table to sit down with me.

"Mum wouldn't like it if she knew," I said. "She said we weren't allowed."

"Yeah, I know." Jake was clasping his hands together in front of him on the table. "I've only been in the once."

I nodded.

"I just wanted something of Laura that wasn't a hospital bed or sheet or gown. No machines, no whitewash, no sterile fucking version of her. I wanted the alive Laura. The one with a life. The one who slept in that room, you know?"

"I know," I said. "I've thought the same. The other day I just wanted to go in there and think about her. Like she was. Not like she is now."

"Exactly. For someone who doesn't talk all that much you put it loads better than me," Jake said, smiling.

"We could go up there now," I said. "Together. Mum's asleep."

"But what if she finds us in there?" Jake said. "She'd go mad. She's just so fragile right now."

"Laura's ours too. Our sister. We miss her too," I said.

"I know, Tessie. It's just – it might feel wrong. It might feel worse."

"I don't know how it can any feel worse right now," I said, and then I stopped myself from speaking because I didn't want to let myself cry.

We didn't turn on any of the lights as we went upstairs. We didn't want Mum to wake up. It already felt like we were doing something wrong.

"It shouldn't feel this wrong," I whispered to Jake as he pushed open Laura's bedroom door and we went into the room. I closed it behind me.

There was a thin layer of dust over everything. The room was dormant, like Laura.

"Can we put on a light, Jake?"

Jake leaned down and flicked a switch on the lamp above Laura's bed. The one she used to read by until she dozed her way into sleep.

I walked over to the bed. I wanted to lie down and bury my face in her pillow and smell the smell of her, but I wasn't sure I could do that with Jake there. I wondered if he felt the same. If there was something he wanted to do or touch, but felt he couldn't whilst I was there.

"It feels weird," Jake whispered.

"I know," I said. "It feels wrong to look at her stuff, but I want to."

"Yeah," Jake said, putting his hand on her desk, resting it on one of her books from school.

I walked over to the window to look out at the tree outside our house. The street light had just come on and the branches and leaves were lit up orange on one side. That tree was the reason I hadn't wanted this room when we'd moved here. It was scary. It was the sounds it made, and the shadows in the dark that frightened me. *I like the tree*, Laura had said. *I like the way it moves. I'll have this room if you don't want it, Tessie.* I remember being relieved. I wondered now, whether she'd just said that to make it better for me. And thinking that made me feel bad; Laura was a much better person than me and yet all this bad stuff had happened to her. It wasn't fair. Nothing about anything that was happening right now was fair at all.

I looked down at the bed and I ran my hand across Laura's pillow. I felt something against my fingers. There was a strand of her hair curled into a loop and I held it in my hand.

"It feels weird being in here," Jake said. "Like she's dead."

"I know," I said. "Are you alright?"

"I don't know."

"I don't know either," I said.

I reached down and opened the drawer of Laura's bedside table. There was some make-up and a hairbrush, her straighteners and a whole load of slides and clips. I smiled remembering how she had always spent ages doing her hair. She'd hate to see how it looked now. All short and wiry and growing back in different directions where her head had been shaved.

Jake had his back to me, he was looking at all the things she'd pinned up on her board – tickets to gigs and postcards from galleries and holidays and photos of her with Ella on their last day of school at the end of Year Eleven, their uniform all torn and scribbled with messages from their mates.

I sat down on the bed next to the open drawer.

Jake was touching things, feeling them too. "You know, I keep going on her Facebook page. I keep looking at it, at her photos, her comments. And all the time this room was here, and it's closer, it's more real..."

"I know," I said. "I know." I kept pulling at Laura's things all jumbled in the drawer. A mini model of the Eiffel Tower she'd brought back from her French exchange, and a phone charger, a lipstick, and a small compact mirror. I pulled out the lipstick and opened it up. It was a bright pink. I remembered when Laura wore this colour all the time. Year Ten. She never left the house without it on and Mum was always telling her to take it off.

I rolled the colour over the back of my hand, and smiled. I wondered – could I put some on? I felt a tear run down my cheek, fast, lost, like a lone runner, trying to find her way back to the race. I wiped it quickly away. I wasn't sure why that tear had come, but I knew there were more behind it jostling to start running too.

I looked over at Jake. He was engrossed in Laura's pinboard.

I pulled out the compact, and opened it up.

Something fell out onto my lap.

A photograph.

A passport-sized photograph.

Laura and Joe.

They were kissing. They couldn't have been any closer to one another. Their faces side on to the camera, filling the whole picture. Their eyes locked together, their lips so gently touching, Joe's hands cupping Laura's face, Laura's arms enveloping him, pulling him closer. I turned the photo over. Handwritten words. The writing was big, upright, bold.

ALWAYS YOURS. JOE X

He loved her. He did.

Ella was right.

When I looked at the photograph I believed it.

But if he loved her, then where was he? Why wasn't he here, now, visiting her, talking to her, holding her hand, pulling her through? Why didn't he come back and explain? Tell us all what happened?

I looked down at the photograph again – at Laura and Joe's faces – and all I could see was their love.

Can you really hurt someone you love?

I wanted to know.

I slid the photograph back into the compact. It had been tucked in there so neatly. And as I put it back I felt like I'd intruded. I'd seen something I shouldn't have seen. Something private. Something hidden.

I felt heat in my cheeks, like a blush.

And I thought again about Ella. How she was so sure that the person who hurt Laura couldn't be Joe, how Laura had loved Joe, how Joe had loved Laura, and the image of their kiss filled me up with a feeling – a feeling that was so big that I thought I might explode – like I could feel all the feeling Laura felt for Joe – and all the feeling Joe felt for Laura – and I turned to Jake.

"We should go," I whispered. "I can't look any more."

And I put the lipstick and the compact in the drawer, I put it right at the back of the drawer, and I closed it shut. And with it I put away my doubt about Joe's love for Laura. Because he loved her. I'd seen it. And it was a relief now, to know.

Tuesday

25.

Mum didn't get out of bed this morning. Jake had football training and left early. I didn't expect him to walk with me anyway. I knew Monday had been a one-off. He had no idea that things were weird between me and Max. He didn't know that Max probably wouldn't knock for me this morning. He was oblivious. Everyone at home was. I hadn't said a thing. I wasn't going to tell them what had happened… But because I couldn't assume that Max would come and walk with me, I woke with a sickness in my stomach that wouldn't go away.

I went into Mum's room with some tea, and she stirred.

"Cup of tea for you," I said. "It's seven o'clock."

I wanted her to wake up.

I wanted her to be there for me today.

I needed her.

I went in again before I left for school but she was still asleep, the tea sat on the table next to the bed, pale and cold. She hadn't touched it.

"Bye, Mum," I whispered, and I kissed her on the forehead and her hair smelled like she hadn't washed it and I wondered when she had last showered or bathed. I didn't like seeing her like this, but it's how she'd been the last time Dad went away for work. We still had three more days until he was home.

I went downstairs and picked up my bag, checking for my keys and my phone. It was my day to go to the hospital with Mum. I guessed she'd meet me at school later. I just had to walk in now. I just had to get myself into school now – on my own.

I opened the front door and stepped out onto the path. I looked around before I shut it behind me. The street was clear. There was no reason not to start walking. I took a deep breath and began putting one foot in front of the other, hoping I wouldn't see a neighbour or friend of Mum's who might start asking me how we all were, how Laura was, how Mum was coping.

And I didn't. The street was clear, and even though I crossed over several times to try and avoid people I thought I knew, it turned out they were strangers and they hadn't even seen me coming.

I turned onto the main road and looked up towards the bus stop. I searched for Kat and Holly. My heart rolled a run of beats fast in my chest. I wondered if Billy might be there again, by the wall, waiting for me. I opened my mouth to yawn, to catch a breath. It was the nerves. They did that to me sometimes. Made me tired. I looked again. The bus stop was full of people staring blankly ahead, waiting for sight of a bus. I couldn't see if Kat and Holly were there, waiting for me. Or Billy. But as I was looking for Billy, I saw him. He was walking towards me, coming to meet me. And I kept walking to meet him. And I felt myself smile and I couldn't stop myself, my stomach rolling as I walked, fast and gentle, with the rise and the fall of it.

"Tessie," he said, and I liked hearing him say it, my name.

We stood still on the street in front of one another, and I looked up at him.

"I wanted to walk you all the way," he said.

I smiled. I guessed he meant from my house. Is that what he meant?

"Maybe tomorrow, yeah? I'll come earlier."

I nodded.

And then I thought about Max, and how he would feel if Billy was walking with me, and then I let the thought go. If Billy wanted to walk with me, then that was okay... wasn't it?

"I guess we should get going," he said, and he reached out for my hand. I let him take it and the feeling of his hand in mine felt so good and right. I felt safe with him there.

And we didn't move. Not yet. We stood for a moment, just looking at each other. He looked older than me. But he wasn't. We were both in Year Eleven. But his features were sharper, stronger somehow. His face looked more lived-in than mine. I liked his face, I liked its lines, its symmetry, the gentleness that I saw when he smiled. I liked just looking at him. He was beautiful.

"I guess we should, you know, go to school?" he said, and he laughed and I realized I hadn't heard his laugh before, and I liked it. His face broke open and softened when he smiled. His eyes brightened.

And as we walked, hand in hand, past the bus stop and into school, for the first time in ages it felt like nothing and no one was in my way.

Because he liked me, and I liked him. And it was okay.

26.

And the whole day felt like that, until I picked up a text from Mum at the end of the school:

> I'm still not feeling so good. Please go and see
> Laura for us both. I've told Jake to meet you at the
> hospital. You can get a taxi home. Jake has the
> cash. Mum x

She hadn't thought about how I would deal with going to the hospital on my own. I might have known how to make my way to the cafe after school, how to walk there, but I'd only done it twice. I never went anywhere else on my own. Why didn't Mum come and get me? I needed her. I needed her to get me from school. She knew that.

"Tessie? You okay?"

I looked up, and quickly hid my phone. The classroom had emptied and there was only me and Mrs Evans in the room now. She'd been my history teacher for the last three years. She honestly cared more about the Romans than she did about anyone in her classroom. There was no way I needed her sympathy right now.

I nodded and stood up, but I wasn't sure what I was going to do, where I was going to go.

"Tessie, you look upset. Are you meeting Max?"

I nodded before thinking. All the teachers knew I walked with Max. To nod and to lie – it was the easiest thing to do.

"Let me walk you out then," Mrs Evans said, grabbing her bag. "Come on, let's go."

Mrs Evans hummed us both to the school office, her humming getting louder and faster as we went.

"There we are," she said, when we got to the gates. "I'm sure he'll be here in a minute. I'll see you tomorrow, Tessie. Be well." And there I was, out on the street, with no choice but to walk and keep walking.

I actually got to the hospital without any hassle. It was about half an hour's walk from school, which was why Mum always drove. I could have got on a bus, but I needed to walk, to be on my own, to avoid other people.

As soon as I arrived at the hospital entrance I was overwhelmed. There were people everywhere. I didn't know where to go, what to do. I just wanted to hide, be out of the way… I looked around and saw a seat on the far side of the atrium and I went over and sat down and messaged

Jake. I didn't want to make eye contact with anyone, get any attention, so once I'd messaged him I turned towards the wall, and I crossed my legs, tucking them under my chair, my phone firmly in my hand whilst I waited for a reply.

"Tessie?" a voice came from behind me.

"Tessie, have you come to see Laura?" It was Brenda, the lovely nurse from ITU. The one who'd been with Laura in the first few weeks, the one who knew me, who knew I didn't talk. "You look lost, honey. You waiting for your mum or shall I take you up?"

I stood up and nodded.

I could go with Brenda. It was safer in Laura's room than here. It was safer anywhere but here.

We went straight to the ward, straight to Laura's room.

"Here you go," Brenda said. "Much better to be here with your sis, than down there on your own." And she smiled and left.

I sat down on the chair next to the bed, and looked up at Laura. Her head looked so strange, the shape of it, her new hair so dark, darker than I ever remembered it. And I thought of the hair I'd seen on her pillow when I'd been in her room last night, her hair in my hand, and the photograph, of her and Joe and the kiss, and his words, and I took a deep breath in and I took her hand again. I wanted to say:

I saw the photograph of you and Joe, Laura. You looked so happy, so in love. The feeling of love – it came off the picture and it swallowed me whole. Does that make sense? I'm not sure that even makes sense, but I saw it. I saw the love you felt, the love Joe felt. And I never believed that would ever happen to me, but I think now maybe I do. Because there's this boy – he held my hand – and when he did it felt like everything changed. Just in that moment, in that touch. Is that how it felt for you, Laura? With Joe? If you could just wake up, Laura, then you could tell me, you could tell us all, what happened. You could tell us what we need to know. Because we need you back, Laura. Really, we do. All of us. So that we can find out what happened to you, so the police can get whoever it was who did this to you, so Mum can be better, so the family – all of us – can try and be whole again.

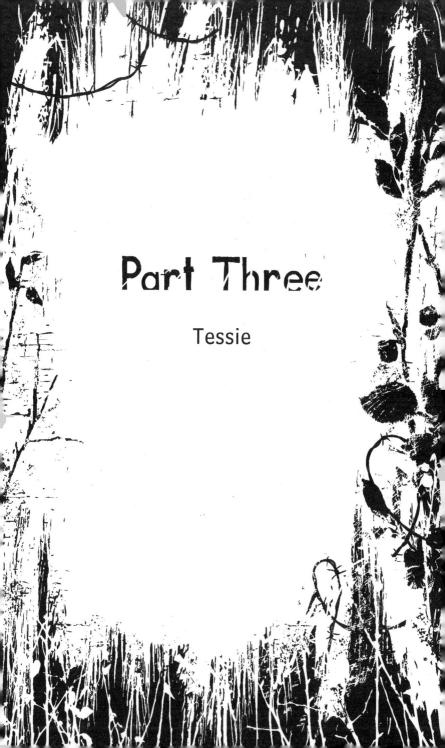

Part Three

Tessie

Wednesday

27.

I was running down the stairs stuffing my music folder into my bag when the doorbell went. I kind of froze. I honestly didn't think it could be Max, and part of me wondered if it might be Billy, even hoped it might be.

Jake came out of the kitchen, stepped in front of me, still eating his bowl of cereal, and opened the door.

"Alright, Max?" Jake said through a mouthful of cornflakes.

"You ready?" Max said. It was as if he was looking at me, but his eyes weren't actually looking in my direction. I nodded, zipped up my bag and walked towards the door.

We got to the end of the road in silence. Max didn't have his iPod out, no headphones. I was waiting for him to plug us in, but he didn't. As we turned the corner onto the main road, he spoke.

"Listen, I guess it's not really any of my business, and you could call me a coward for doing this when I know you can't answer back, but...look, there are two things I want to say. First, let's just forget about what happened on the weekend. Let's just pretend like it never happened."

I didn't look at him as we walked. I couldn't. But I was glad he'd said what he'd said. It was a relief.

"And, well…I don't think you should hang around with that new boy, Billy Johns."

I looked up at him.

"He – well, he's hardly talked to anyone. He's been kind of rude, out of order, you know? He seems like a loner, Tessie. Everyone's saying it."

I wanted to say: *Yeah, well, people are always saying stuff about me too, Max. It doesn't mean anything. You know how it is.*

"There's something not right about him," Max said again.

I wanted to shout.

Inside I was shouting, telling Max he'd got Billy wrong. No one had made me feel like Billy did before. Was Max saying that for me to like Billy, for Billy to like me, was wrong? Billy might have been different, but I was different too. In that we were the same.

"You've got friends, Tessie. You don't need him. You've…" and Max paused for a minute. "You've got me."

I looked over at Max. I didn't understand what he was saying. Suddenly it was like we were back in that awkward place he'd said we could forget about at the weekend, and I didn't want to be back there again.

"I wish we'd talked about this at yours, now," Max said. "It feels too weird not having you say anything back…"

He stopped walking and put his hand on my arm to stop me walking too, turning me towards him, so we were facing one another.

I looked at him – but as I did I saw Billy, up ahead, on the corner. He was standing in the place he'd stood before. Waiting for me. Max had his back to him. He couldn't see Billy there.

My stomach rolled.

Seeing Billy had done that.

And Max had his hand on my arm, stronger now. He wanted me to look at him, to give him my attention, but I could see Billy watching from behind Max, across the street, and I could feel the heat rising in my cheeks. I wondered if Max could see the glow – my glow – for Billy.

"Tessie?" Max said.

I looked at him but still my eyes were searching elsewhere, beyond him, for Billy.

Max turned to see what I was looking at.

He saw Billy.

"Shit, Tessie," he said, and he stuffed his hand into his pocket, pulling out his iPod and earbuds. "Did you not listen to anything I said to you just now?" And he started to walk away.

I wanted to call him back. I wanted to call his name.

I felt the tightness in my throat as if I had shouted for him to come back to me.

I didn't want me and Max to part like this, but there was nothing I could do – because Billy was walking towards us now, towards me and towards Max – and his eyes were on me, only on me – and I smiled – I couldn't help myself – as he got closer – to me.

Max had put his earbuds in now and was walking fast up the street towards Billy, towards school.

I stood still, waiting, watching Billy's worn but beautiful face as it came closer to me – and then I saw Billy pass Max – and I saw Billy barge Max – bash him – shoulder against shoulder – and Max take the blow – stumbling to the side – just recovering himself so he didn't hit the ground – grabbing the top of his arm where he was obviously in pain, before his bag fell to the floor.

My whole body jolted as I saw Max take the blow.

Max – are you okay?

Those were the words I wanted to say.

Are you okay?

My eyes started flickering, the cough started rising in my throat.

I wanted to go to Max, check him, see if he was alright, but Billy was coming towards me now, and I could see Max was leaning down, picking up his bag, stepping back, holding his shoulder, stepping back.

Could I breathe? I wasn't sure. My throat was so tight. I couldn't move.

Max turned. He started walking, not looking back, just walking away. He was okay.

And there was Billy, with me, in my space, his face close to mine, and his hands holding mine, and his lips pressing mine… And he was kissing me. And my eyes weren't flickering any more, and the cough in my throat wasn't there, and the warmth in my cheeks filled me as I let Billy hold me, just hold me, and kiss me, and I kissed him and I could breathe.

My phone started ringing in my bag.

"You should get that, no?" Billy said, stepping back.

I pulled my bag around to get the phone to see who was calling me. I wouldn't answer it. But I wanted to see who it was.

It was a number I didn't recognize. I let it ring off, and I looked again for Max. I wanted to know he was okay.

"Here, let me take your number," Billy said, reaching out for my phone. "Then I can text you, message you. Pass it over and I'll ring you. Then you'll have my number too."

I stood and let Billy take my phone and I watched him go into my contacts and get my number and call it from his, and then save it for me in the phone. I liked the way he did that, but I knew I wouldn't be able to message him in the way everyone else messaged their friends. Although for a moment I wondered if maybe I could try...

I looked over Billy's shoulder again to see if I could see Max, but he'd disappeared from sight. I hoped he was okay. Because what Billy had just done to Max – there must have been a misunderstanding. There must have been an argument or something. Was that why Max had told me to stay away? Had he fallen out with Billy? Maybe it was that. I'd have to ask Max. Ask him to tell me the whole story, because he hadn't explained it today, and there had to be some reason for it. Because to see Billy shove Max like that wasn't right. It just wasn't right.

Billy and I started to walk towards school holding hands, Billy's fingers clasped through mine, warm and tight. It was a good feeling. A simple feeling. It felt right. But as soon as we got closer to school I could feel the cough rising tight and rough in the back of my throat again. I wanted to be with Billy but I didn't want anyone to see us. Especially not Kat or Holly. And there was Max, too. Suddenly it didn't feel right to be walking with Billy like this after what he'd just done to Max. But I didn't want to think about it. My head was just too full right now.

My phone buzzed in my bag. There must be a voicemail. Whoever called must have left a message. I left it again. I didn't want to listen to the message now. I wanted to be with Billy. Take these last minutes with Billy before we got too close to school, before my panic started rising further.

"You alright?" Billy said.

I blinked. ONE BLINK. One blink for YES.

And I stood still.

I wondered if Billy would understand that as my *yes*. I hoped that he would. Because I didn't feel like I could nod...I didn't feel like I could move.

"I think that's a yes," he said, and I blinked again to let him know it was.

"I guess I'll go in, then, yeah?" Billy said looking at me, but he didn't, and suddenly there was no trace of a smile on his face to meet mine.

"I kind of..." Billy said. "Oh, I don't know..." And his face looked darker as he stepped towards me. Was he going to kiss me? I couldn't tell. And then he stepped away again running his hand over his head and he said, "Shit, this is hard...I guess I'll see you...later. I'll message you...yeah?" He turned to leave.

And I wanted to follow him and say something, anything. But I couldn't call him back to me, and I couldn't move, so he went, leaving me with the rest of the school swirling around the space we'd been standing in, like water eddying round the roughest rock in the river, and I hated it. I hated being me.

28.

Once everyone had gone into school, I found my breath and my panic slowly subsided. I headed straight for my locker to grab my science books for class. As I did I could hear someone approaching. I could feel them standing behind me. I took a small step to the side to close the locker door, to get out of the way.

"We saw you."

I heard the words before I felt the push and my face was pressed hard against the cold metal locker door.

I tried to step back, but they pushed me again. Harder. Kat and Holly.

"We saw you holding hands with him. Billy. Your lover boy," Holly said. She had her hand pressed against my back so I was flat up against the locker now, her mouth up close to my ear.

"We saw you kiss," Kat said.

"She won't talk, but she tongues," Holly said. "Who would have thought?" Holly was pressing harder into my back now.

Silence.

I could see my breath making a steam cloud on the locker…in and out, cloud, no cloud, shine, now dull… shine, now dull… Over and over… The rhythm of my breath, the repetition of it kept me still… I was used to this. I'd wait it out. I'd count my breath and wait it out. Like I'd done before.

Holly's hand fell away from my back.

I waited.

I wanted to step back and away from the locker, but I was too scared to move. I didn't want to turn and face them. I was sure they were still there, behind me, at my back. I didn't know what to do. If I bent down to grab my stuff they'd push me again. I knew they would. I swallowed hard. My throat hurt.

"Little Max isn't feeling too good today, Tessie. You know that, don't you?"

They'd seen it all then.

"We talked to him on the way in. Finding it all a bit awkward, I think, Tessie."

I hated that they had seen me with Billy. That they'd seen what Billy had done to Max.

"Left Max to come in on his own, eh? After what Billy did?" Holly said. "And I thought you two were friends."

"Left Max pretty much on the floor, to pick himself up off the pavement," Kat said.

"Dumped one friend for another. Literally. I can't believe they both like you so much, Mouse. What's your secret? We'd like to know because you've worked fast – for a mute – for a mute mouse."

I felt sick when I thought about Max.

I hadn't left him there. I just couldn't go to him – that was all. Because of Billy, because of what was happening with Billy.

"I think we should give you some advice, don't you, H?" Kat said.

"I'd say that you need to make it right with Max, Mouse, before Billy gets there first and makes it wrong," Holly said.

I looked at them both.

"You should listen to what she's saying, Mouse. Because from what I've heard, you've chosen a right bad boy in Billy Johns. A right bad boy."

I waited for them to leave.

And they did, laughing, me still holding myself against the locker, like someone had a gun to my head. And all I could feel was emptiness, and it was filling me up inside.

29.

I looked for Max all day. I looked for him in the corridors, in the canteen at lunch, but he was nowhere. I went into the loos and turned on my phone, looking for a text. There was nothing but the ring-back of the message I'd received this morning, so I listened:

Hey, Tessie. It's Ella. Just – well, trying you. I'm at the cafe – on the phone there. I – I guess I'll try you again later. It would be good to see you. I feel bad about how things were left the other day – I mean, I never really explained – about Kyle… I couldn't. But I can now. And I've had this idea… Look, I'll try you later, yeah? Okay, bye.

I deleted the message as soon as I heard it.

At the end of the day I waited in the usual place for Max, even though I kind of knew he wouldn't come, and despite the fact that I knew I shouldn't, I hoped for Billy. Billy had seen me waiting here at the end of the day before. Maybe he would come again. But I waited and he didn't. And Max didn't either.

My phone buzzed in my bag.

I pulled it out – Jake.

Meet me at the cafe? Going to see Laura on my own today. Explain later.

I looked up.

I could hear someone walking along the corridor towards me.

Mr Gardiner. He seemed to spend his life walking the corridors and chucking people out of school at the end of the day.

I picked up my bag quickly, putting my phone up my sleeve to hide it, but so I still had it partly in my hand in case there was a message. I hoped for something from Billy. It surprised me how much I wanted a message from him, even after what had happened this morning.

I headed out of the corridor into the courtyard towards the playing fields. I needed time to think. I needed somewhere to go that wasn't the cafe or home or the hospital, where I could be on my own, where no one could see me, talk to me, tell me things.

I walked quickly, quietly across the courtyard. The football team were out training. I walked over towards the trees on the left-hand side of the field so I could tuck myself away, out of sight, and pulled my coat out of my bag.

The wind was biting at my neck, making me shiver.

I sat down under a tree, putting my coat on, wrapping it around me, tucking my legs into my chest where I sat. It was cold, but this felt like a good place to be.

My phone buzzed inside my sleeve.

It made me jump.

I pulled it out.

You ok?

A message from Billy.

I looked down at it and felt a skip, inside.

Another message came within seconds.

I keep thinking about you.

I blushed. I could feel my blush like shame, but I wasn't sure why. The feeling was instant and strong.

I stretched out my legs and tried to take in a breath. I was swimming in the joy of his words, the way he felt about me, it was making me glide, but inside I was drowning. I was drowning with the need to gasp some air, open my mouth, grab some words, and reply. Because I knew he'd want a reply. And I couldn't reply to this – say what I thought or how I felt – I couldn't.

Do you think about me?

A question.

And with that question my throat locked down. Hard. And I coughed. I didn't know what to say. I didn't know how to say what I might say, or even what I wanted to say. And I wanted to breathe, to catch a breath, but it was getting harder.

Another message.

I need to know Tessie.

I stood up.

I picked up my bag and started to walk. I wasn't sure where to. I just needed to move, to get away. I put my hands inside my coat pockets and the phone buzzed again in my hand. I pulled it out.

Don't go – not yet.

I stopped.

I looked up and around me.

Could he see me?

Could Billy see me?

Where was he?

I looked around again.

I didn't like it – if he was here – watching me.
It didn't feel right.
And then I saw him.
On the other side of the field – alone.
My phone buzzed again in my hand.
I looked down.

I'm trying, Tessie. I really am. I just don't know
what I'm meant to do.

Another message.

I'm going mad…over you…wanting to talk to you.

I thought he understood.
I thought he said he would wait. He'd said that – before.
I looked up again, my fingers gripped the phone tightly
in my hand.
Why had he said that he'd wait if he hadn't meant it?
I was going mad over him too.
But I couldn't do it, I couldn't say it – I couldn't say what
he wanted me to say – what I wanted to say – none of it.
I turned my head to check whether the gate to the field
was still open. It was. I had to head out. I had to get out
that way, to move. And anyway, had Billy followed me here?
I wasn't sure. I wasn't sure that I liked it if he had…

My phone buzzed with another text.

Where are you? I'm coming to the school.

It was Jake.

And then I saw Billy move. He moved, before me, before I had the chance, and I watched him go.

He walked across the edge of the field, out of the side gate and out onto the street. He disappeared from view and he didn't look back at me – not even once. And when I saw him go suddenly all I wanted to do was follow. But my head kept my feet rooted to the ground, and despite the mad swaying in my heart, I was stuck.

30.

"What's going on? You didn't come to the cafe?"

It was Jake.

"I walked here because I was worried. Didn't you get my message, my text?" he said, as soon as he'd found me outside the school gates.

I took his hand and I squeezed it. It was my sorry. But I didn't look at him and he didn't press me any further. We walked back in the silence.

As soon as we got home and in through the front door and it was PROPER SHUT he slung down his bag and went into the kitchen.

"You hungry?" he called back as he went. I could tell from the tone of his voice he still wasn't happy with me.

"Yeah," I said, but I could already smell something cooking. I followed him into the kitchen.

Mum was there, standing at the hob making pancakes. She turned round and smiled.

"Hello," she said. "Do you fancy one?"

I was so pleased to see her, and like this, more like the mum she used to be. My heart felt like it was actually swelling with happiness. This was the mum who played games with us, took us shopping, ran around the garden, cooked our tea. The mum who smiled and laughed a lot. The mum I'd almost forgotten. I wanted to go to her, put my arms around her from behind – hug her – like I'd done so many times before – but I wasn't sure enough that she'd like it, so I hung on, hung back. I didn't try.

"Sit down," she said. "There's a mug of tea." And she came over and put the tea on the table in front of me. "Here you go," she said putting a mug in front of Jake too, as he sat at the table.

Jake raised the mug to his mouth to blow on the tea to cool it down, and he looked at me and raised his eyebrows like he noted this change in Mum too.

"Is Dad coming back today then?" he said, setting down his mug again on the table. I knew what he was thinking. He was thinking this could be the only thing that would put her in such a good mood.

"No. He may not be back until early next week. Not sure. He'll know more tomorrow. I've been trying to get hold of him all day, but I've had no luck. It's very frustrating."

I took a glug of tea. It tasted good.

"I saw Campbell and May Grover today," she said.

"That's why I wasn't around this afternoon for the hospital, Jake. Campbell wanted to see me. He had some more news."

"What did he say?" The words came quicker than I expected them to.

Jake looked up at me, like he was surprised too, at the urgency in my voice.

"They've interviewed Kyle Brooks. They're going to release the CCTV of him and the two others he was with that night now that they've confirmed identities. They've got footage of the three of them walking along the Wellbridge Road about an hour before Laura was found, and some from later that evening about a mile away in Rednor. They want to see if they can get any more witnesses to come forward, anyone else who might have seen them in the surrounding area that evening."

"So it's going to be back on the news?" Jake said.

Mum nodded. "Tonight. That's why I want to get hold of Dad – to let him know."

Jake looked at me.

It was always hell when there was stuff on the news or in the papers. You walked around knowing everyone was looking at you, feeling sorry for you, for your family, for everything you're going through, but they never said it. They just looked at you with something like pity.

I looked back at Mum.

"So do they think this Kyle did it?" I said. "Hurt Laura?"

"They're calling him a 'person of interest'," Mum said. "They seem to think he's involved – yes."

There was quiet. I looked at Mum and I looked at Jake.

"So they didn't say anything about Ella?" I asked, my voice quiet.

"Ella? No," Mum said. "Campbell seemed pretty pleased they were talking to Kyle. Kyle Brooks is saying it's got nothing to do with him, but they've been able to keep him in for further questioning under caution, and get the other two boys in for questioning too."

I nodded.

"And Joe?" Jake said. "Does this mean they don't think it's him any more?"

"Joe knows Kyle," Mum said putting a plate of pancakes in front of me on the table. "May said that they are talking to anyone and everyone associated with Kyle. She and Campbell seem sure that getting closer to Kyle will bring them closer to Joe. Something like that. She couldn't give me all the details. They're working on it. They've got leads. They definitely still want to get to Joe." Mum paused for a moment. "I told her – I told Laura from the start that he wasn't good for her. I just knew…"

"Mum, don't say that. You couldn't have known. None of us could have known this was going to happen," Jake said.

My phone buzzed in my pocket.

Billy.

Maybe it was Billy.

I pulled out my phone.

**Talk to me Tessie. I need to know you feel the
same.**

I swallowed.

It hurt.

I put my phone down on the table next to my plate.

"Help yourself to pancakes," Mum said, heading towards
the phone. "There's some syrup here too. I'm going to try
Dad again."

"Everything alright?" Jake said, motioning to my phone
as Mum left the room.

"Yeah," I said.

I stood up and pushed my plate across the table. I wasn't
sure I could eat.

I feel the same.

I feel the same.

I feel the same.

That's what I wanted to say to Billy. The words were
going around and around in my head. They were all I could
think right now. Because I did feel the same. I thought
about him all the time, and I wanted to tell him that I did.

But I could only think the words. Thinking them was all I could do.

"I'm going to go up to my room," I said and I picked up my phone and headed upstairs.

As I got to the top of the stairs I looked over at the door to Laura's room. I wished I could talk to her. I missed her so much. I knew if she was here now she'd listen, talk to me, tell me what to do about Billy.

I looked back down the stairs. Jake was still in the kitchen, Mum was on the phone. I could hear her talking. She'd got through to Dad. Maybe I had time to go into Laura's room.

I crept across the hall and gently pushed the door open and I breathed in. I could smell the smell of her, and I could see her again in my mind, as she was before, and it felt good.

I stepped inside, closing the door quietly behind me, and went over and sat on the bed. I opened the drawer again. I reached deep inside until I felt the compact. I opened it up and there she was. Her face again, smiling and happy. I loved to see her like that, see her and Joe, see how they felt about each other, see what love looked like. Because that's what it was. It was love. I had no doubt about that now.

I ran my fingers over the picture.

Somehow, if I touched Laura in the image I felt she'd be there, close to me, closer, now.

I looked at Joe – his face bent towards hers, his eyes on her, their lips touching. Was that how it looked – with Billy and me?

I lifted my gaze out through the window to the tree. It was dark and still.

If this was love, then why did it feel so bad? Mum had always said love was a gift, and looking at this photograph, this love between Laura and Joe, she was right – it was like the most beautifully wrapped gift you'd ever wish to receive. But it had been ripped open, ripped apart. And now it was like an ugly ruined thing. It didn't matter how much love I saw between Laura and Joe when I looked down at that photograph – that love was gone. It had been obliterated. And I wondered, did all love eventually, in its own way, come to this?

Thursday

31.

"Why did you ask Mum if the police had said anything about Ella yesterday?" Jake asked, grabbing the cereal. I was sitting at the table playing with my toast. It felt too dry, too chewy. I wanted to spit it out, but I didn't. I kept chewing.

"Mum said the other day that there was some evidence. She said the police had evidence that could potentially put Ella at the viaduct; that they think she's in touch with Joe. I wanted to know."

Jake shrugged, acting like he didn't think anything of it, and he carried on eating.

"Jake, are you sure Laura never talked to you about Ella? Or about Ella and Joe?"

"No – I told you, Tessie. Anyway, like what?"

"I don't know... Like had Laura and Ella ever fallen out, over Joe?"

"There was some stuff on Facebook. Ages ago. I didn't pay much attention. It happens all the time with the girls in my year. Someone makes a comment, they unfriend each other, everyone gets involved, then it dies down and they're back on with selfies, all made up again. The police asked me about it when Laura first got hurt. I told them then what I'm telling you now."

I nodded. I wasn't on Facebook. I wasn't on anything. I couldn't be.

"Do you still think Joe did it, Jake? Do you think he hurt Laura?"

"Seriously, Tessie, I don't know. I feel like I don't know anything any more."

And I was about to answer, about to tell him how sure Ella was that it wasn't Joe, and how I was beginning to feel the same, when Mum walked in. "You both okay?" she said.

I nodded, standing up to grab a glass of water, which I gulped at the sink, my back to everyone.

I wondered if Max would come this morning to walk with me. I didn't think he would after what had happened yesterday, and I didn't blame him. Really I should have texted him. If I'd been like everyone else, that's what I would have done.

"I've got to go," Jake said, slinging his bowl and spoon in the dishwasher. "I've lost my trainers. I think I left them in the changing room after PE. See you later." He left the kitchen and two minutes later the front door slammed.

It was quiet.

"It's our Laura day today, Tessie," Mum said. "I'll pick you up at the gates."

"Okay," I said, sitting back at the table and reaching for my phone, which was charging on the side.

I looked down at it for messages. There were none.

"I'm going to go," I said, standing up.

"Max not coming for you today?"

"Yeah. He should be here any minute," I lied. "I'll just grab my coat. See you later."

And I walked out of the kitchen and into the hall and stepped through the front door before she could say anything more.

And there was Max.

When I saw him, I jumped.

"Take this," he said shoving an earbud into my hand.

I wasn't expecting to see him. But I was glad that he'd come.

We walked in step down the path and onto the street.

"I'm only here because – well, put it this way – if I wasn't then I'd worry. I'm here for me really, more than for you, so I don't have the stress of worrying about you walking on your own. And because Mia told me to come," he said and he turned the volume up high and the music was loud and angry, and I guessed if Max wasn't talking it didn't matter, because this music was sending me the message that he wanted me to hear.

I looked at Max to try and catch his eye, to blink the ONE BLINK for YES but he wouldn't look back at me, so I nodded and hoped that he saw that I had. It was nice of Mia to tell him to come, but I didn't like the thought of them talking about me. I didn't like it at all.

As we walked I looked for Billy.

It was a diversion…and I couldn't help myself.

I wondered if he'd be leaning against the wall at the bus stop again, waiting for me. I hoped that he was. But then I looked over at Max and I thought about what had happened when we'd seen Billy yesterday, and I felt bad.

Max turned to me and pulled out his earbud.

"I guess I'll walk on my own from here," he said, and he nodded to the other side of the road, as if to explain. I looked over, to see what he meant, and there he was – Billy – standing, leaning against the wall on the opposite side of the street, just like I'd hoped.

Every bit of me tingled with the thought that he was close.

Max pulled out my earbud. "Looks like he's waiting for you. Thought he might be."

I nodded and suddenly the thought of Billy's fingers threaded through mine, his lips pressed to mine, was with me again.

I was suspended in the thought.

And Max was looking at me, and for a moment it was

like I had forgotten he was there, like I wasn't even seeing him at all.

Billy started walking towards me now, across the road, onto the pavement, just as Max was moving away.

"You be careful, Tessie," Max said, as I turned to go to Billy.

"What did you say?" Billy's voice broke through.

"I was talking to Tessie," Max said. "Not you."

"Yeah, but what did you say?" Billy said.

I stepped forward, towards Billy, to try and take his hand, whilst Max stepped back, away.

"See you later, Tessie," Max said, but he glanced over at Billy, when he said it, and I could feel the rise in Billy and I didn't like it. So I reached out for him – for Billy – because I had this sense that I needed to pull him back. But as I reached out, he turned and I missed his hand. And he was there, behind Max now, pushing him hard, against the wall, and Max's face was pressed against the bricks, Billy standing behind him, his arms pressed against the wall, either side of Max's head, holding him there.

Max turned round, quickly, putting his hands up in the air as if in surrender. "I'm going, Billy, okay? I'm going." And I could see that Max was alright, that he wasn't hurt, before he turned again and slipped out from under Billy's arms and walked away, fast.

Billy didn't move. He stood facing the wall where Max

had just been, and he tipped his head forward and pushed into his hands like he was pushing the wall away, pushing his anger away, his head bowed in front of him between his broad shoulders.

I waited for him to move.

I couldn't tell what he was going to do.

Was he going to follow Max? Was he going to turn and follow him, and shove him, like before? I had no idea, but I knew whatever happened next, I wanted Billy to leave Max – I wanted him to leave him alone – I didn't want Billy to go after Max again.

Billy turned his head to the side. He was watching Max now, watching him walk away, and I could see he was thinking about following.

I had to stop him. I had to. And anyway, I wanted his eyes on me – not Max. I wanted his eyes on me – I had to get his eyes on me…

I grabbed my phone out of my bag and I found the messages Billy had sent me at the field and I clicked on the last one – and I replied:

I feel the same. I feel exactly the same.

And I hit send, and I put my phone away so I could pretend like I'd never done it, written it, put myself on the line like that.

And then I waited for Billy to read the message, and to face me.

I waited.

And as soon as Billy felt his phone vibrate in his pocket, I watched him move. He turned and walked over to me and he took my hands into his, tipping his head down so our foreheads gently touched, and when he did I closed my eyes to his touch.

"I'm sorry," Billy said. "I'm just so – I like you so much – you're the only good thing – the only good thing, you know?"

And I stopped him talking. I put the tips of my fingers onto his lips to make him quiet so he would feel the moment too, and suddenly I knew that I didn't care if all the world could see me and Billy now, because I had never liked anyone like this before – never – and he – he was my one good thing – he was my one good thing too.

Friday

32.

I woke up to an early morning text from Max.

Billy told me he's walking you in now. Is that right?

Did that mean Billy was coming here, now? I wanted Billy to come. All I wanted to do was see Billy's face. But I didn't know anything about it, and I didn't want to hurt Max again. So I didn't reply. I got myself ready in super-quick time and I sat on my bed and I waited until just before 8 a.m., when Max would usually knock, and I went down the stairs and sat on the bottom step, waiting.

"What you doing?" Jake said, coming out of the kitchen.

"I'm…ready…early… I…"

And there was a knock at the door and before I could do or say anything Jake stepped forward and opened it.

"Alright? Tessie in?"

It was Billy's voice.

It was Billy.

Jake turned to me. "You know him?"

I nodded and stepped in front of Jake, towards Billy.

"Hang on, Tessie," Jake said. "Is Max not walking with you today?"

He looked worried, concerned. For a moment I thought I should have told him about Billy. There'd been no reason for me not to. If Laura had been here I'd have told her. But I hadn't. I'd kept Billy to myself. It just felt like the way I wanted it to be.

"I'm walking her, thanks," Billy said in answer. And he slipped his hand into mine and we walked out onto the street and I felt a thrill in my chest like a bird perched in a tree, ready to sing, and I didn't dare look back at Jake.

We walked up the street, but as we went I began to feel nervous. I wasn't sure what it was – the thought of him kissing me, the thought of being seen, or remembering how it had been with Max the day before.

"I liked it when you messaged me yesterday, you know? It was nice," Billy said, and he smiled.

I looked up at him and smiled, but I wondered whether my smile showed that I felt unsure. I didn't want him to think I could do that again – message him, chat – talk.

Billy stopped walking, and turned towards me. He took my other hand in his, and then he bent down so his face was close to mine, and he kissed me, slowly, gently.

It was okay. We were okay.

"You know, if it wasn't for you…" Billy said. "If it wasn't for you, I don't know what I'd do… Things are shit, you know. Stuff has happened, and it's shit. It's always been shit. Everyone leaves. And I don't know why. And whatever I do, it goes wrong. I mean, like really wrong. But now I've got you… It feels different. It feels okay. And I know that's because of you."

He kissed me again, even slower this time and he stroked my face. I couldn't believe how gentle he was, but the look in his eyes when he'd stopped kissing me – it was like something was dying inside.

I pulled back, away.

I wanted to say something.

I needed to say something.

I wanted to make that sadness in his eyes go away.

You make it all okay for me too. I don't know why. But you do, Billy. You really do. Please – don't be sad, Billy. Don't be so sad. That's what I wanted to say.

"Do you think you could talk to me, Tessie?" Billy said, quickly. "I mean, one day, soon, will you talk to me? I can wait. I think I can wait. But…I've kind of got to know…"

His voice was a whisper, but it wasn't gentle like a whisper. It was urgent. I could feel his urgency and when I did my neck stiffened and my shoulders tightened and there was a pain at the top of my back like someone was burning me, branding me.

"It's just there's so much stuff I want to tell you, to talk to you about, but I can't tell you if you won't talk to me…"

You can still tell me, Billy. You can.

Billy leaned in to kiss me again, and I let him, but I felt nothing because my lips were holding in all the words I couldn't say and suddenly I was cold – completely cold – I started to shiver – and then a voice – out of nowhere.

"You're brave, Billy Johns."

Another voice.

"Kissing the mute."

It was Kat.

Billy lifted his head and I turned to see Kat and Holly walking towards us.

"She's cursed, you know. The whole family's cursed. That's what my mum says."

That was Holly.

"You do know that don't you, Billy Johns?" Kat said, following Holly's lead.

"Her mum's depressed, her sister was attacked, been in a coma…her boyfriend's the main suspect…and he's missing…"

"No wonder her dad's never there," Kat said.

Billy turned towards them.

They were circling us now.

"She'll never talk, you know. *Never.*"

Billy turned and he looked at me. I could see the confusion on his face.

"You happy snogging a cursed mute, eh, Billy?"

"You happy having a cursed mute for a girlfriend?"

"Never heard of Selective Mutism then, Billy? SM? She not told you what she's got? Not explained it?"

I looked back at Billy, and all I could see was anger – his anger. It was all over him. All over his face. I hadn't wanted him to find out this way. I'd wanted to find a way to tell him myself – tell him that I might talk, one day, if he came to my house, to my home. I didn't want him to know about the SM now. Not the extent of it. He couldn't know that now. Because he liked me and I liked him, and I didn't want that to end. I couldn't risk that. I hadn't told him about Laura, about Joe, about anything, because I couldn't. How could I? And anyway, I didn't want him to know. He was the one good thing. He was the good in amongst all my bad. He was separate, different. And so was I. I was his one good thing too. That's what he'd said.

"It's your sister? The one in the reconstruction this week on the news?"

Billy spoke.

I nodded.

"You mean, the one from the viaduct? That's your sister?"

I looked at him and blinked.

ONE BLINK. One blink for YES.

"Are you serious?"

I could feel tears, the tightening of my eyelids. I waited for the tears to come. I blinked again.

"Fuck, Tessie… Fuck. Why didn't you fucking say anything?" he said, his face close to mine, his voice rising all the time. "Why didn't you fucking say?"

My eyes filled like a spring well.

Because I couldn't.

I couldn't.

"Fuck!" he said again, stroking his head with his hands, turning this way and that. "Fuck, Tessie! Fuck!"

Why was he talking to me like this? Why? I didn't like it.

"She didn't say anything about her sister because she doesn't talk, Billy. Like *ever*," Holly said. "You only just realized that?"

"Ah, bless!" Kat said. "He cares! Look at him – he really cares. About Mouse, and her dying sister!" And she laughed, and went towards Holly, so they could link arms, enjoy the scene.

I stepped forward to go to Billy, to touch him, to let him touch me, hold me, so I could hold him. But he turned. He stepped around me, away from me.

"Is that right – what they're saying? About you? About your sister? I need to fucking know if that's the truth…"

And that's when I saw it again – the look in his eyes, in his face – and it was rage this time – burning putrid rage.

I swallowed and I gagged.

Kat laughed. "Ah, she's going to be sick. Look at her, she's actually going to be sick!"

"We did tell you she was shy, lover boy!" Holly said stepping towards Billy, almost leering, Kat following, still hanging from her arm.

"We thought she liked you enough to speak – to tell you herself about her messed-up life – but maybe she doesn't like you that much after all, Billy Johns."

"What do you say to that, eh, Mouse?" Holly said, turning to look at me now. "Do you like him enough to speak? To say something, now?"

I stood still. Completely still. I closed my eyes.

"Ah – still can't speak!" Holly said, laughing. "Disappointing for your lover boy, Mouse! Look at him! Open your eyes! Look at his face, Mouse! He looks really sad!"

And they turned to start walking away, laughing.

I waited.

I waited until I could hear that they had gone and I opened my eyes and I looked at Billy.

He was staring at me like he was going to burn a hole in my brain with the looking.

We were alone now.

And all I wanted him to do was hold me. All I wanted him to do was take my hands, like he'd done the day before and the day before that, and hold me and kiss me like he had before.

But he didn't.

He took a step forward and he put his face really close to mine and he said, "I don't know what I'm fucking meant to do now, Tessie. Because you've ruined it, and it's fucked," and he turned and he walked away from me.

And if I could have called out his name – if I could have called for him to come back to me – then I would. I would have screamed for him to come back. Screamed and screamed. Because I didn't understand, and I hated myself for letting him go, and all I wanted was for him to explain.

33.

I just about got through the day. I went to registration and I attended most of my lessons. A couple of times I made the sign to my teachers that I wasn't feeling well and I went and sat in a cubicle in the toilets and rested my head on my knees. My teachers probably thought I was upset after seeing the reconstruction; I could sense that everyone had been looking at me slightly differently the last couple of days. But it wasn't that. I hadn't even watched the news on Wednesday night. It made me feel too weird. Your own life on the news – not someone else's – it was too hard to see.

No, it was Billy that was making me feel this way…

I'd tried not to replay what had happened with him this morning, but it was almost impossible to get it all out of my head. I hated Kat and Holly for what they'd done. I'd thought me and Billy were okay. But now they'd ruined everything. Billy had said it was fucked. He'd said everything was ruined and fucked. I hated that word – I never used that word – but he was right. It felt like it was now. I hadn't wanted it to turn out this way. I'd wanted to find a way to talk to Billy, in my own time. To tell him, to explain. It's just – I hadn't worked out how, yet. And now he knew about Laura. And that mattered too. Because I hadn't told him. And he cared. He cared even more than I realized. That look on his face – when I remembered it – it almost frightened me – the strength of his feeling – it was all over his face. What was it? I'd thought it was anger, but was it disgust? It felt like it was. And I didn't like it. Did he look that way because of me?

At the end of the day I hung back and looked for Max. I knew I couldn't ask him to walk with me, I knew I couldn't do that. But I figured I could follow him, walk just behind him, and that would give me something – some kind of safety, some kind of comfort. I knew he wouldn't be in our usual place, so I went through the office and stood just outside the gate and waited by the school sign.

He was with Mia, when I saw him. I followed them out of school. They were heading in the direction of the cafe. It was Friday. Me and Max often used to go to the cafe on a Friday. I'd almost forgotten how much time we used to spend together last year. Everything had changed since we'd gone back to school this year, and the term was still so new. Since we'd been back it felt like I'd been swept up into a river, across a border and into a country where I didn't belong. And I knew there was no way I could get back again, however much I tried.

Max didn't see me as I followed them down the street to the cafe, but Mia did. She turned around and looked and just smiled when she saw me, and I hung back further after that, my eyes to the floor, still following. I was glad she'd seen me, acknowledged me, because it made me feel safe. To follow Max and Mia to the cafe was the safest thing for me to do. It took me away from Kat and Holly, and away from Billy too.

I gave it about five minutes before I followed them in. Max and Mia had already sat down at a table by the window, and ordered. When I pushed the door open, everyone looked at me. I knew they did, and I felt the heat rise in my cheeks as I went in, but I didn't look in Max's direction at all. I couldn't. I walked straight towards the booth at the back and as I did I felt a hand on my shoulder – gentle. It was Ella.

"Tessie, hi! Go and sit down. I'll bring us over a drink. Coke alright?" She turned to the front of the cafe to head to the fridge and shouted across to Leila, "I'm going on my break now!" Leila was serving and nodded.

I sat down in the booth and checked my phone. No messages. That was probably a good thing, except I wanted to hear from Billy. I wanted to know we were okay. I still hoped somehow that we could be, that we could fix things, make them good again.

Ella came and sat down with two Cokes.

"I saw the news, Tessie. I saw Kyle on the CCTV." Ella clicked open her Coke as she talked.

"The footage shows them really close to where Laura was, you know, when they found her. It's got to be Kyle who did this to her. It's got to be."

Ella seemed pumped up. Excited.

I wanted to ask her when she'd met him – Kyle – how she knew him, recognized him.

I twisted the unopened can in my hands. It was cold.

"Have the police said anything about Kyle? They must think it's him if they've released the footage. What have they said? Do you know?" As Ella spoke she looked around her, around the cafe, nervously.

I followed her gaze around the room. It was like she was looking for someone, or waiting for someone.

She looked back at me, and leaned in, her voice quieter now.

"It wasn't Joe, Tessie," she said. "All this with Kyle just confirms it, you must see that now?"

I thought about the look I'd seen on Joe's face in the photograph – his eyes holding Laura's. I hadn't seen Laura's eyes for so long. I longed to see them. And I thought about Billy, and his eyes on me, and then I stopped. I stopped the thought and I tried to see Laura's eyes – her deep brown eyes. They were closed to the world now, but behind them was everything; all that had happened, all that she saw, all that she knew. I just wanted her to wake up and tell us what happened so we could go back to how things were before.

"I didn't say anything to you about Kyle before, because…well, you know…I don't know him," Ella said. "And I wanted to explain…the other day…I really did, when you wrote his name on the napkin…"

I didn't understand.

I don't understand.

That's what I wanted to say.

"Joe told me all about Kyle, Tessie. They knew each other. There's history. Their dads worked together. Scaffolders. In Wellbridge. But they did stuff on the side, for cash. And Joe said it worked. It kept them all afloat. But then Kyle's dad accused Joe's dad of stealing. They were out, in the pub, and he told Joe's dad he'd… Are you listening, Tessie?"

I nodded. I was listening but I was thinking about how Joe had told Ella all this. How she knew so much about Kyle. And I wondered – did Laura know about this too?

"Anyway, they were in the pub, they were drunk. They argued," Ella said. "They went back to the yard, you know, where they worked, and Kyle's dad said that Joe's dad had stitched him up, and he wanted his cash. And I don't know what happened, but Joe's dad picked up a hammer and smashed Kyle's dad in the legs. He floored him. Cracked his knees. Both knees. And when he was on the ground he went at him again. Harder. Kyle's dad is in a wheelchair. Blind in one eye. Doesn't leave the house. Can't. Disabled."

I pulled in some air. To breathe.

Joe.

Laura's Joe.

That was his dad.

That was his life.

"Joe and Kyle weren't mates. But they knew each other, you know. Same school, but a different set. Kyle was in a gang. Always. But after this, it was like Kyle had one person in his sights and it was Joe, and that was all he cared about."

I nodded. I could see Ella was going to tell me more.

"Joe's dad had been in prison before all this with Kyle's dad, you know? He'd been in for GBH. That was when Joe was about four. Joe said his dad had always been violent, always in a fight with someone. He said he remembered that, even though he was so young. And he said life was calm when his dad was in prison. His mum was happier. She met this other bloke, Al, and they had a son together, Joe's brother. They were a family – for a bit. But then Joe's dad came back, out the blue, five years ago. Al left, his dad moved back in, and it all turned to shit. His words. Not mine."

And suddenly I thought about Mum. If Mum knew this, if she knew even half of this…

"After Kyle's dad was attacked, he never said who hurt him. Never told the police. He had a stash of cash from all the previous jobs that he needed to protect. That's what Joe said, anyway. And Joe's dad just left – went underground. Joe said he guessed he couldn't face prison again. There were plenty of other people who would have been happy to go to the police and see his dad put away again, so he had to go. Get away. He couldn't risk that. And Joe and his mum and little brother moved away, you know? There was other stuff going on at home anyway. His mum drinks and they owed rent. They moved on a few times. Eventually ended up over here, in Ford Green. Joe said he thought they'd be safe. Away from all the landlords chasing them for rent, from all the connections to his dad, away from Kyle."

Safe. There was nothing safe about any of this. And now it was in my world, Laura's world, it was part of our world. And Ella was saying that the police didn't know about any of it. None of it.

I swallowed but there was a lump in my throat like a rock.

If Joe's dad could do that to Kyle's dad, then what was Joe capable of?

Ella moved in closer to me, and she whispered, "Tessie, me and Joe are in touch. We have been all along, one way or another. There have been some gaps in between, some weeks when I didn't know where he was. But this week we've talked. We've actually talked. And he's desperate to know how Laura is. He's as desperate as the rest of us."

Pain radiated down my throat like heat.

Ella was desperate now, but she'd never been that desperate before.

"Tessie, listen. I called you and left that message the other day because I know what we have to do now. We have to help Joe see Laura. We have to do that, before the police question me again, or arrest me, because they know if they get to me, they'll find Joe. I think they're pretty sure of that now."

I looked across at the napkins on the table. Could I write something? I wondered. Like I'd done before when I'd written Kyle's name. Could I do it again?

I had to find a way to speak.

I reached across for a napkin.

"Don't you see, Tessie? It's what we have to do."

I picked up my bag quickly from the floor, and grabbed a pen, and I opened the napkin up in front of me and I wrote:

Tell the police. Not me. Tell them everything.

And I pushed it over to Ella. She looked down and then

up at me again, and then she bit her lip before she spoke again.

"I had to tell you, Tessie," Ella said, and she looked like she was going to cry. "I'm sorry, Tessie. I'm so sorry. You're the only one I can tell. The police won't get it. They won't understand. But if we can get Joe in to see Laura, he might get through to her. She might wake up, and then she can tell everyone what really happened."

I picked up the pen and I scribbled hard under the words I'd already written. I underlined them all. If I could have spoken them I would have. Again and again and again. Loud. Fast.

I pushed the napkin forward a second time, and Ella took it, folding it in half, making my words disappear. She was ignoring me.

I felt a pressure in my head.

I needed to scream, but I couldn't.

A silent howl filled all the spaces between the words I could only think in my head.

What was I meant to do with all that I knew?

What was I meant to do?

I looked up at Ella for some answers and as soon as I did I almost couldn't see for the chaos I was thinking, feeling inside.

"Kyle did this to get back at Joe, Tessie. You see that now, don't you?" Ella said, leaning across the table towards me.

"That's the truth of it. Kyle did what he did to Laura to get back at Joe, for what Joe's dad had done."

I needed to stop the noise, the howling in my head, see if I could stand up, if I could get away, to get some air, to breathe, because I couldn't be there any more, in the booth. I couldn't think, and I couldn't take in everything Ella was saying… But I couldn't move. My body was heavy. It didn't want to move.

I pushed my hands flat on the table and pressed them down, hard, to help me stand up. I looked over towards the door. I could see Max – he was paying at the counter. Mia had gone. I didn't want to have to pass him when I left. I tried to swallow but I couldn't. Ella was calling my name from behind, her voice was faint, but I could still hear it. It was there.

I started to walk, to move.

My phone buzzed in my bag.

I got to the counter. Max was still paying. He was almost gone.

I reached into my bag to find my phone – to give me a minute.

Left hospital. Be at the cafe in 2 mins. You still there? J

It was Jake.

I texted quickly:

Yes.

I wanted him to come. I needed him now. But I could stand there for two minutes. I could. I could wait for him. I just had to block out Ella. Surely it was the end of her break now? It had to be. I looked across at Leila. She was taking her apron off and, almost on cue, she leaned across the counter and motioned for Ella to come back to the till.

I watched Max go to the door, and there was Jake. Max was passing Jake in the doorway as he left. Jake gave Max a friendly nudge on the arm as they passed one another. A jab. A jibe. Like they were brothers.

"Alright, mate?" Jake said, and Max nodded and smiled.

Jake came in and went straight to Ella as she slipped back behind the counter.

Didn't he see me standing here? Was I invisible? Had I been sucked into the horror inside my head?

"Hey, how are you doing?"

I heard Jake's voice.

He was smiling at Ella.

I was invisible.

I was.

"Alright, Tessie," Jake's voice again. He'd turned round, towards me.

I stepped forward.

I had to stop him ordering. We had to go. We had to leave. Now. We had to leave.

And that's when I heard it. The sound –

A smash.

An almighty crash.

Like thunder.

In the room.

And then a sharp tight hollow cry.

I turned, quickly –

It was Max.

His body thrown against the cafe window and a crack in the glass like a fault line opening up before me, his body slipping down it, a mass of bloody injured shifting ground.

34.

"Shit," Ella said. "What's happening?"

Max was on the floor, and the person who'd thrown him against the cafe window was kicking him now.

Jake looked up, his phone in his hand. He was dialling. "Ambulance and police…" he said.

Max was holding his arms in front of his chest and his legs were tucked into his tummy, and he juddered with every kick, and with every kick I felt it – like an axe splintering my own rigid bones.

I stepped forward towards the door – without thinking – to go to him.

"Don't go out there, Tessie!" Jake said.

I looked at Jake. He carried on talking into the phone.

"No, he's wearing a hoody, I can't see his face… Jeans, trainers…all black… I can't see… There's no one else out there… Should I go and help?"

"Someone's got to stop this!" Ella said and she started to walk towards me, towards the door.

"No, Ella!" Jake said. "Hang on… They're saying we should stay here, inside… That everyone should stay inside."

I looked around.

Five or six people had stood up, watching. One woman had her hand over her mouth.

I wanted to cry, but nothing came.

"What are they saying, Jake?" Ella said. "It looks so bad, it's so bad…"

Is this what had happened to Laura?

Is this what it would have been like to see Laura hurt? In pain?

The world slowed.

Everything was distorted.

I was distorted.

I could feel myself going – I was going to faint…

I must have been out for a split second. When I came round, Max was still on the ground, still taking the kicks.

I felt Ella's arms around me, and she was looking at Jake, talking to him.

"We have to do something, Jake… We can't just stand here… Maybe if I went out there he wouldn't hurt me… I'm not a bloke…not a threat… I could just go out there and…"

"There's an ambulance and a police car less than two minutes away, Ella. They've said we should wait. They'll be here any minute…"

And that's when the kicking stopped.

Max lay on the ground like roadkill.

And the person who'd done it – who'd mowed him down – looked up – and I saw his face – before he turned and ran –

Billy.

And somehow I'd known it was him all along.

Saturday

35.

I woke up and remembered.

When I remembered I wanted to disappear.

I held my eyes closed.

I wanted to sleep and block it all out, but now I'd woken and remembered Max lying on the ground, and the look on Billy's face before he ran, there was no way I could go back to sleep.

I looked at the clock.

11.06 a.m.

I hadn't slept this late in ages.

I pulled myself up and out of bed and went downstairs.

The television was on in the sitting room, so I went straight in. I saw Mum before she saw me. She was sitting upright, dressed, staring out of the window not at the screen – a cooking programme blaring on, people talking over the hiss and steam of a hob, cracking jokes.

"Mum?"

She jumped.

Depression.

That's what Kat and Holly said.

Her mum's depressed, her sister was attacked, been in a coma, still pretty much is…

No one had ever said that Mum was depressed before. No one had ever used that word. But now that Holly had said it, it made total sense.

"You made me jump, Tessie."

"Sorry."

She looked at the television.

I waited for her to say something, to look at me, but she didn't.

"Where's Jake?" I asked.

"He's gone for a run."

"Will he be back soon?"

"I think so…"

I waited for her to ask me something, like if I'd slept okay, or if I'd like breakfast, but she didn't say anything.

"Is there any word on Max?"

"Yes," she said, and then she looked at me and I saw a blankness in her eyes that I guess I'd always seen before, but I'd never really recognized. The sense that I'd had that she was somehow removed, a step away, like whatever I tried to do to get to her, she'd always be just out of reach… It was like we were constantly playing a game of tag, a game of tag I could never win…because I could never get to her, to touch her, bring her close to me... It was depression. I just didn't know why I'd never realized it before.

"Is he...okay?"

There was silence.

"Mum?" I said again, prompting her to speak.

She turned to me, slowly.

"He has cuts and bruising to his face and body, a fractured collarbone, two broken ribs. But there's no internal bleeding. That's what Janice said. Yes... I think that's what she said."

He wasn't going to be on a machine like Laura. He was conscious, breathing. No internal bleeding. He would heal. That was certain. That was some kind of strange relief. He wasn't going to be like Laura. But he'd been kicked until his skin had been cut and his bones had broken – and he must have been in pain. It almost hurt just thinking about that.

"Did you see Janice then?" I said.

"No. Jake called to speak to her. She wasn't there, but he left a message. He was out running when she called back. I talked to her."

"Is Max back at home?"

"He should be discharged this afternoon. Janice said you can pop round and see him later. Apparently he isn't saying much. He hasn't really talked to anyone since it happened. He won't talk to the police. Janice is keen you go over, see him. She thinks he might talk to you."

I nodded, but I wasn't sure if it was a good idea for me to go over. I didn't know if Max would even allow me to be his friend any more. And I was frightened at the thought of seeing him, seeing his pain… I didn't want to think about the fact that Billy had hurt him, that it might in some way have been my fault. I really didn't want to think about it at all.

Mum turned and looked back out of the window.

"I'm going to go and have a bath," I said, and I walked up the stairs and into the bathroom and turned on the taps to fill the bath, deep. I took off my clothes and stepped in, closing my eyes and taking a long breath in, sitting down, lying down, letting my whole body sink under the water.

And Billy's face was there with me as I sank.

And Max's body, in a heap on the floor, too.

Billy's face.

Max's body.

I hadn't done anything to stop it happening.

I brought myself up and out of the water.

I hadn't given a statement when the police had arrived at the cafe.

All the adults had sat down with an officer in turn, all those who were there, who'd witnessed the assault. I had taken myself off to the booth at the back and no one asked me to talk. Eventually Jake came over and said that one of the officers was ready to take us to the station. We couldn't be questioned without Mum, and Ella couldn't be questioned without Heather, and Jake had called them both and they were on their way to meet us at the station. Jake told me that he had explained to whoever was in charge that I had SM, that I was fifteen, and he'd said that they'd come back to us if they felt they needed to talk to me, once Mum had arrived at the station, once they'd gathered all the statements. And as it turned out no one asked me a thing. They took me and Mum into a room, and they asked Mum a whole load of stuff about me and then they said they'd be in touch again over the weekend if they needed to be. They said I could make a written statement. Mum suggested a voice recorder…I wasn't sure I could do either.

I sank my head under the water again.

"Oi, Tessie – you in there?"

It was Jake, back from his run, his voice muffled in my watery ears. I sat up again.

"Yeah," I said.

"How long you gonna be? I'm minging. Need a shower."

I plunged my hand down into the bathwater and pulled out the plug.

"Just getting out," I said and I shook my head to try and shake away the images of Max from last night because they were there again.

I stood up and stepped out of the bath, wrapping my towel around me, and I turned to look at myself in the mirror.

A sob heaved out of my chest.

"You alright, Tessie?" Jake was still there, outside the door.

It's fucked now.

Billy was right.

It was all fucked now.

I thought about Max again.

Had I done this?

Made things this way?

"Yeah, I'm okay," I said.

But I wasn't okay.

Just be careful, Tessie.

That's what Max had said. And all the time it was Max who needed to be careful. Not me.

She's cursed, you know. The whole family's cursed.

And they'd been right.

Kat and Holly were right.

I was cursed.

We all were.

36.

Jake came into my room after his shower. He looked clean, fresh. I'd got back into bed with a book after my bath, because it was Saturday, and I could do that. But I wasn't reading. I was thinking about Joe and Laura, and then Max, on the floor again and seeing Billy's face before he ran…and then remembering how he kissed me in the street, how he held my hand, how amazing that had felt… Had I seen him by mistake outside the cafe? Had I imagined him there? Had I thought it was him because he was always there, filling my head right now? I wished for that to be true, but however much I tried, I knew deep down that it was Billy who had attacked Max. I knew it because he'd looked at me before he'd run away. He'd locked his eyes into mine, like he was trying to show me something, tell me, prove something. And then he'd run.

"You sure you're alright?" Jake said as he came over to the bed. "I couldn't really tell through the bathroom door. You sounded like you were crying."

"I'm okay," I said.

Jake sat down on the bed next to me. "Do you keep thinking about yesterday?"

I nodded.

"Yeah, me too," he said.

"Are you going to go over and see Max later?"

"I don't know," I said, shaking my head.

"I could come with you, if you wanted."

I didn't say anything.

"Did you see anything, Tessie? You know, when I was calling 999? Because I didn't. I'm not sure why. I was distracted by the call. I keep going through it in my mind. I just saw the black hoody, black jeans. And even now, when I think about it, I'm not sure I completely remember even that. It's like a big jumble in my head."

"I know what you mean," I said, looking down.

"I don't understand any of it. And I mean, why Max? He's the nicest guy. It's like the world's got all messed up and it's all happening here. Right here. First Laura, and now Max."

I closed my eyes.

I wanted Jake to stop talking now.

He was making it worse.

"It's just the police are going to keep asking us questions…"

"I know!" I said. "I do know that!" I said it louder than

I meant to because I wanted him to stop. Because there was still everything that Ella had told me about Kyle, about Joe, and my head was too full. There wasn't any room to think clearly about any of it. Joe was in touch with Ella. She'd been in touch with him all along. He was around. He had history with Kyle. And no one knew. No one but Ella. The police didn't know, but Ella knew. And now I knew. And I wished I didn't.

"Tessie, listen, I'm not trying to stress you out. It's just we've got to help them find who did this. I know it's not easy for you – but I'll help if I can – so you can make a statement – if you saw anything – you were looking out of the window all the time—"

"I don't know whether I can do it, Jake," I said and my voice cracked and I started to cry.

"Write it down, Tessie. Surely that's easier? Just write down what you saw."

I nodded, but I wasn't sure I could write down Billy's name on the forms when the police came. Jake knew that even to write wasn't something I could easily do. And anyway once I gave them a name, there'd only be more questions I couldn't answer. More things I couldn't say. And what might Billy do when he found out it was me? That I'd given his name to the police? I liked him so much – but he'd done this…this terrible thing… And I couldn't pretend that the thought of giving the police his name didn't frighten me. If I gave the police his name, would he get angry again? Hurt me? Hurt someone else? I didn't want to think about that. The thought scared me... The Billy I thought I knew would never have done this to Max... Never. It just wasn't him. It wasn't... The police said I didn't have to make a statement, and I didn't want to. I wouldn't.

"Everyone's doing their best, Tessie," Jake said. "You just do your best too."

I nodded again, and Jake grabbed me a tissue from the bedside table and passed it over. I wondered for a moment if anyone else had seen Billy – recognized him.

I looked up at Jake.

"When's Dad back anyway?"

I wanted to change the subject.

"Early next week. He'll find out exactly when on Monday morning. He'll call as soon as he knows. That's what Mum said. See, Tessie? It's not all bad. Dad'll be back soon," Jake said, smiling and trying to pinch me on the thigh to make me smile too. "And anyway, who's the secret boyfriend, eh? You haven't told me about him!"

I swallowed.

I blushed.

And then I panicked.

Did Jake see Billy after all?

"I saw him hold your hand, Tessie, when he came to

pick you up for school, remember? So what's his name?" Jake said, smiling the whole time, like he found it funny, like the thought of anyone liking me was funny. And I thought about Billy and his eyes in mine, and my eyes in his, and the way it made me feel, and nothing about it was in any way like the way Jake thought it was. Me and Billy had kissed. We'd kissed, such gentle kisses… And Jake, he didn't have a clue.

"I – I—" No words quite formed in my mouth.

"Tongue-tied, eh? 'Cos you got yourself a secret boyfriend?"

"Secrets? Who said anything about secrets?" I said, swinging my legs over the side of the bed and standing up now, but in my head I knew I was full of them and it didn't matter if I stood up and left the room, if I left the house, if I left the country – because they would still be with me. There was nowhere I could go without them now.

"No one," Jake answered. "I just meant he was secret because you hadn't told me…"

"Well then I wish you'd shut up because you don't know anything, Jake!"

I started to head towards the door, to get out of my room, but Jake stood up and grabbed my hand before I could.

"Woah, hang on. I didn't mean anything about anything, Tessie. Seriously. Slow down."

I looked at the floor, and I waited to let him step in and say something first, to make it right, and he did.

"Come on. Let's go downstairs. I'll make us a snack. Just forget what I said. Okay? Forget it."

"Okay," I said, but the thought that somehow Jake might have seen Billy, might have recognized Billy at the cafe, that anyone might have, it was eating away at me fast, like a parasite. Because suddenly I knew I didn't want anyone to know it was Billy. No one could know. Not yet. Whilst it was just me and him who knew, and Max wasn't saying what had happened, we were safe. And I wanted us to be safe. Because I wanted to find a way to listen to Billy, to let him tell me what he had to say. Billy had to have had a reason to do what he did. He had to. What he'd done was wrong. I knew that. I just so wanted him to explain.

Sunday

37.

I woke early and lay staring at the ceiling. When the police had come yesterday I'd signed the piece of paper saying I didn't want to make a statement, and Mum asked me if I was sure, and I nodded, and then the officers left. It bought me time. And that was all I wanted. Some time – to talk to Billy. I could always change my mind, give a statement later on. The police had said I could.

I'd managed to avoid going to see Max yesterday. In the end Janice called and said he was home, but too tired for visitors. When Mum told me, I felt bad to admit it, but I was relieved.

Go tomorrow, Tessie. Jake has said he'll come with you, Mum had said that three times, maybe more.

I would go today. I had to. But the thought of seeing Max's smashed-up body still made me feel sick with nerves. I didn't want to see what Billy had done to him… I couldn't face him, talk to him, sit with him, wondering if the pain was down to me. And I didn't want to hate Billy.

Once I saw Max I knew I'd hate Billy for what he'd done, and I didn't want the way I felt about Billy to change at all. It was wrong, I knew, to feel this way, to try to hang on to the Billy I thought I knew. But it was how I felt, and it was all that I wanted to try and do.

My phone buzzed with a text.

I'm sorry.

I sat up and I felt a kick in my stomach.

Billy.

I stared again at the phone.

What did that mean? Was he sorry for me, for Max?

I looked out of my bedroom window.

If I said sorry too, if I could, I wondered, would Billy go back to being the boy with the sparkling eyes who held my hand and made me feel so good? Could *sorry* take us all the way back there?

My phone buzzed again.

Meet me tomorrow after school.

I wanted to meet him. I really did.

Jake was calling for me up the stairs.

"Tessie! Come and have some breakfast. I've said we'll go over to see Max in half an hour!"

To see Billy.

That was all I wanted.

There was only one way to reply.

So I did.

With a *yes*.

38.

I almost didn't recognize Janice when she opened the front door to me and Jake. She looked like she was the one who'd been beaten up. Her face was red and her eyes were puffed out. She'd been crying.

"Come on in," she said. "He's been sleeping but I think he'll be awake now. He knows you're coming."

I felt an empty sickness inside as we climbed the stairs up to Max's room. I wondered if he'd have music on. He always had music on. Maybe music would help. But when we pushed open the door it was completely quiet in his room, and Max was lying on his back staring up at the ceiling, his face, his body, a motionless mess on top of the covers.

"Alright, Max," Jake said. "You okay if we come in?"

Max's eyes flicked over to where we stood, but he didn't say anything.

This was where I was meant to say something – say hello – say sorry – say something – but I couldn't with

Janice stood behind me and Jake in the room. Only Max knew I talked here. Only Max.

"Well, I'll leave you to it," Janice said. "Let me know if you want anything, Maxie, eh?"

Max blinked and his eyes looked back up to the ceiling.

"Max?" she said. "If you feel you can talk to Tessie and Jake about what happened then you should. I won't be hurt. I'll understand." She turned to me and Jake. "He's not saying anything about who it was. But you were there, weren't you? All of you. Maybe between you, you'll remember something. If you talk about it, if you can get Max to talk, then I think it would help. Help him, help the police," and she nodded. "Okay – I'll leave you to it," and she stepped out of the room closing the door behind her.

"How are you feeling, mate?" Jake asked.

"How do you think?" Max said, his eyes still on the ceiling.

"Right, yeah. Sorry. It looks sore," Jake said.

"It's worse than that."

Jake nodded and looked up at me, beckoning for me to come over. I was still standing by the door.

I shook my head, but I took a couple of steps closer, into the room. I knew I had to.

Max's face was bloody and raw. It was hard to see how it would ever be like it was before, how it would ever heal. How any of this would.

Max coughed and without thinking I stepped forward to put my arm out and touch him, to check he was okay. He flinched, and then let out a short gasp of air. I guessed he was in pain. I could almost feel it myself – across my skin – crawling there. My eyes started to burn as I tried to hold in my tears.

"You want some water?" Jake said, leaning towards an empty glass by the bed. "I'll go and get some," and he left the room.

I followed Jake and closed the door, PROPER SHUT, and went back to Max. I stood by the bed.

"So did you see him, Tessie?" Max said, still not looking at me.

I didn't move. I didn't say anything.

"I told *you* to be careful. Ironic, eh."

I bowed my head.

Max knew.

He knew it was Billy.

He knew.

"I didn't know…" I said. "I didn't know he would do this…could do this…"

Max didn't reply.

"He's texted," I said, "he says he's—"

"What?" Max turning his head towards me. "Sorry? Have you looked at me, Tessie? Properly? Have you seen my face? He did this to me – him. And do you know why?"

I lifted my eyes to Max's face and scanned it. The right side of his face had been split open, like a ripe piece of fruit. The stitches and the glue made a pattern over the swelling like a quilt. I blinked but I couldn't blink away my tears.

"Because he says he loves you and he wants you all to himself. Told me I was in the way. He must have followed me home, after school, on Wednesday, after band practice – that day he shoved me in the street. He told me to leave you alone. I guess when he saw me with you after that, the following day, he didn't like it…and this was his answer, right? I wasn't going to tell you, but I have now, because you need to know he's not right, Tessie. He's not right in the head. Do you see that now?"

I nodded, but I couldn't stop thinking about how Billy had told Max that he loved me.

That's what Max had said.

That Billy loved me.

I wanted to stop thinking the thought, but Max had said it now, and it was there, and I couldn't stop thinking it.

I looked at Max, and wiped the tears from my cheeks with the back of my hands. I took a deep breath in.

"Are you going to say anything? To the police?" I said.

As soon as I said it, I knew I shouldn't have. It made it sound like I didn't care at all, and I did care. I did. It was just everything was just so messed up in my head right now and I was grasping for the words – any words – the right words – to say.

"I think you should go, Tessie. Please. Just go." Max turned his head to face the wall and I heard the air in his lungs rattle as he tried to turn his chest, his whole body in the bed, to move away, to move completely away from me.

"I'm sorry, Max," I said. "I'm so, so sorry." And I left and went back downstairs and found Jake in the kitchen talking to Janice.

"Is he tired?" she said.

I nodded, and felt my throat tense. It went hard in my ears.

"I'll take the water up, Jake. Thanks for coming over. I'm sure seeing you will have helped. Mia's popping over later too. Max doesn't want her to see him like this, but she's coming. She said she doesn't care if she just ends up sitting down here with me. Maybe he'll change his mind when he knows she's here. That's what I'm hoping anyway."

"I'm sure he will," Jake said to Janice as we left, but when we got to the end of the path, having said our goodbyes, he turned to me and said, "Shit, I wouldn't want Mia seeing me like that either. She can't see his face like that. No way."

Monday

39.

Mum drove me to the hospital after school in complete silence. I was glad of the time to think. The atmosphere had been strange at school today. Everyone knew what had happened to Max, and they let me know in quiet ways with the odd smile or kind look. The whole school was a quieter place. And no one came near me. Not even Kat and Holly. What had happened to Max was too horrible even for them to put into words. And Billy wasn't in. I guessed that meant I wasn't going to see him after school today after all, and that was okay – I was going to see Laura. And anyway, when I'd woken up I'd felt nervous about seeing Billy, unsure. I knew I couldn't like him any more – I mean I couldn't let myself. Not after what he'd done to Max. But still, now it was the end of school, and I was here with Mum not him, I couldn't pretend that I didn't feel a whole heap of disappointment that I wasn't going to see him, touch him, look into his face. And I knew that was wrong, but still, it was there.

When we got to the hospital Mum nodded to indicate that I should go straight in to see Laura.

"I want to find the sister," she said. "I'll only be a minute."

I was pleased to hear her voice. It made things feel more normal, and I went into Laura's room.

As soon as I opened the door I knew something was different. Something felt different. I stood at the door and looked at the bed. Laura looked the same – the lines, the drips – it was all the same, but something didn't feel right. I stepped inside and slowly closed the door behind me, and as I did I looked to my side. There was someone in the room. There was someone standing behind the door and they'd been there the whole time.

It was Ella.

"Tessie, I—"

I guessed my face showed what I was feeling. The confusion and distress I felt was instant, strong.

"Tessie, are you okay? You don't look okay..." Ella whispered, stepping closer to me now.

I stepped back.

Why was she here? I didn't want her here. I wanted to see Laura by myself, on my own. I wanted her to go.

"I thought I'd come. I mean I wanted to come before, you know? But it's all just been so...busy." She looked past me, through the glass in the door. "Is your mum here?" she said, craning her neck to look out along the corridor.

She was looking for Mum, to see if she had time to talk to me, to tell me something more, I could see that she wanted to, but I didn't want to know any more. There was no room in my head for more.

I took a step back again, and nearly fell, tripping over my own feet. Ella reached out to grab me so I didn't fall, and she held on to my hand and I thought she wasn't going to let it go. She pulled me close to her.

"Listen," she whispered. "I gave Joe your number. We've spoken on the cafe phone, just a couple of times. I told him that you know everything. He's good with that. He just wants to know how Laura is. He and I – we can't see each other, we can't really do that. The police are watching me. I'm sure they are. But the thing is he's desperate to be in touch, you know? Get closer to Laura," and she looked over to the bed.

I looked over at Laura too. I wondered, could she hear us? Ella was talking so quietly, her voice low, but could Laura hear what she was saying? Could she hear Ella's voice, know that she was here, that she was talking about Joe? And was that a good thing if she could? I wasn't sure.

My heart started beating hard in my chest.

"I don't think I can come again, Tessie... I don't think I can face it. I mean, to see Laura like this... I knew I'd find it hard, but… It's even worse than I thought." I realized Ella was squeezing my hand now, and I didn't like it. "God, Tessie, it's like she's just gone. My best friend, and she's here, in the room, but she's gone." She started to cry.

I pulled my hand away from Ella's. We both loved Laura. And coming here – no matter what – we felt the same. But I didn't want to feel trapped by Ella again, not here, not like this.

Ella looked up at me, and she looked me straight in the eyes, and she whispered, "Tessie – Joe might be the one who can bring her back, you know? He could bring Laura back. You could get him in here, to see her, to talk to her and…"

Ella wiped the tears from her eyes, and took in a deep breath.

"Didn't you say that the nurses said she can hear, feel, touch maybe? That it was a good thing to bring in the people she loves?"

I nodded.

"We could get Joe here. We could do it. We could make things better, Tessie. I'm sure of it."

Ella looked at me for a response. I couldn't move or make a signal. I knew Ella thought Joe was innocent, and I thought I believed it too, because I believed that he loved Laura, truly I did. And there was Kyle Brooks, and that made sense now. He'd been there, at the viaduct. The police said he was close by at the time of Laura's attack. And Joe loved Laura. He did. But still I wasn't sure I could trust Ella, trust the things she was saying to me. She'd been withholding information from the police, and I didn't understand why.

"Look, I know how bad all this looks – on me. It's a mess. I know that. But I swear I haven't done anything wrong. I've kept quiet about a few things – that's all. But the police know about me and Joe, or at least they think they do. They've got a whole lot of stuff wrong, about him and me, but well, yeah, I've been in touch with Joe... And I should have told them. But I've told *you*, I've been honest with *you*, so it's not...it's not completely hidden... Is it? You can trust me, Tessie. I promise. You can."

I nodded, but all I kept thinking was how I didn't want to know the things that I knew. And it was Ella who'd put me here. It was Ella who'd done this to me.

"I just wanted Joe to myself, you know. Just for a bit. That's all. I never got that before. And I was going to tell the police that he was in touch – I really was. But then Joe said if he could get in to see Laura, if he could do that, then maybe he could fix it all, maybe then we wouldn't have to go to the police at all..." Ella paused. "Don't you want to help, Tessie? Help make things better for Laura? For Joe?"

I wanted to make things better for Laura. Of course I did.

I wanted Laura back. But bringing Joe here? Being the one who made that happen? I didn't think I could do that.

"When the police find out I've been in touch with Joe – when they find out for sure, when they have the evidence to prove it – well, it's over for me," Ella said. "You realize that don't you, Tessie? They'll arrest me. I know they will. For withholding evidence, obstructing the law. Something like that. Joe told me. So I have to be careful. I'm in all of this too deep now. I can't bring him here. I can't let the police know what I know about Kyle, about where Joe is, about how we are in touch, because if they find out they'll arrest me. And then they'll arrest Joe – and then we'll have no chance of getting him in to see Laura and changing this around for the better – for Laura."

Ella had put all her trust in Joe. She trusted Joe. She was prepared to take risks – for Joe.

"Tessie, if you can just get him in to the hospital to see her. Let him see Laura. Let Laura know that he is there. Let her feel him – his hand in hers. Let her hear his voice. Then, when she wakes up, she can tell everyone what happened. She can tell everyone that it wasn't him who did this to her. Don't you see? It really is that simple. But you have to help me make it happen. You. Because you know when your mum is visiting, you know the nurses, you know the best time to get him in. You know all that stuff."

I stood looking at Ella. I didn't move. I was still.

"And after that, after Joe's seen her, we can go to the police. I promise we'll do that. And I'll tell them everything I know – about Kyle and about Joe. I promise, Tessie. But right now we have to stay silent. Both of us. We can't say a thing. You do understand why, don't you Tessie?"

I didn't move. I couldn't.

Ella walked over to the door, and put her hand on the door handle, peering out into the corridor. She was ready to leave, but before she did she turned back to me.

"Will you at least think about it, Tessie? Promise me that you will. Because it's the only chance we have now."

And without thinking I blinked ONE BLINK. One blink for YES.

Because I could think about it.

I could do that.

And I'd do anything for Laura.

Anything at all.

40.

When me and Mum got home I dumped my bag in the hall. I followed her into the kitchen. She was checking the home phone for messages. I knew she was checking to see if there was a call from Dad, but there wasn't, so she turned and headed towards the stairs. "I'm going to lie down," she said. "Just for a bit."

I nodded, pulling my phone out of my pocket.

There was a text – from Billy.

I'm at the end of your street.
I'm waiting for you.
You home?

I texted straight back.

Yes.

I had to see him.

And despite everything, I was so glad that I would see him – that I could.

I walked to the bottom of the stairs and waited to hear Mum close her bedroom door. The house was almost completely dark where I stood. Only the landing light was on where Mum had passed through. I could hear the clock ticking in the hall. Nothing else. I looked at my phone again, and then I grabbed my coat, and I went out to meet Billy.

I saw him before he saw me. His profile dark and strong in the shadow of the wall at the end of our street. I walked up to him and touched him on the arm, and he turned towards me.

"Alright, Tessie," he said. But it wasn't a question, and he didn't smile.

I wanted him to smile.

I needed him to.

I waited for him to speak.

"Let's walk," he said, and he took my hand, firmly, and we headed off, down the street, his pace leading me, fast, and for a moment I wondered whether I should be doing this – going with him like this – suddenly I was unsure.

I slowed down, but as I did Billy pulled me, a little harder, by the hand, to keep up, to walk along, until we were at the park. The gates were closed, but Billy stopped and hopped up onto the railings, leaning back and turning towards me to take my hand again, and pull me up.

I wanted to say: *No.*

I wanted to say: *I can't do this.*

But he took my hand and before I knew it I was following, climbing, jumping down onto the path inside the park on the other side, grazing my thigh against the bars as I landed in a gasp.

I looked back at where we'd just come over the railings and wondered how I'd ever get back over.

"Come on," Billy said taking my hand again. "There's a hut I've found, hidden in the bushes. I want to take you there."

I looked at the sky ahead of us. I knew it wouldn't be too long before it was completely dark. I didn't like it. I wanted to go.

We were approaching a bench on the path, and as we went to pass it I sat down. It was the only thing I could think to do to make him stop, stop walking.

Billy turned, feeling the tug of my hand in his as I sat.

"What are you doing? We're nearly there. Come on!" His voice was loud, too loud.

I didn't respond.

He bent down, so his face was close to mine and he let go of my hand, putting both his hands on my knees where I sat, and his touch – like a warmth – spread over me.

"I'm sorry," he said. "I shouldn't have shouted. It's just, I found this place, and I want to show you…"

I put my hands on top of his, without thinking. They felt rough. I rubbed my thumbs over his knuckles and I felt the scabs – the marks he'd made on his hand when he'd beaten Max – and suddenly I pulled away. It was real. What he'd done to Max was real. The consequences of it were right there – his hands in mine. I couldn't pretend it wasn't.

"Look, I'm sorry," he said, looking down at his hands. "I didn't mean to hurt him like that. It's just…you don't know what it's like, being like this, feeling like this, it's like everything's out of control and there's nothing." He looked away from his hands, over his shoulder, quickly, like he thought someone was watching him.

He turned back to me.

"But then there isn't nothing, is there? Because there's you…" He ran his hands over his head and he closed his eyes, and I looked at him, at his beautiful face, and I wanted to kiss him for a moment, but I didn't. I held myself back.

And then he opened his eyes and he spoke again.

"There isn't nothing, Tessie, because there's you."

His eyes were wide now, and his voice loud again.

"And now I know that – now that I know you – it makes everything so much fucking worse – don't you see?"

I looked back at him. I didn't understand.

"Why won't you talk to me, Tessie?" he said, grabbing my hand again, but stronger this time, in his. "It would make it so much better if you'd just fucking talk to me— "

I tried to pull away, but I couldn't. My throat tightened, and the pain ran like a shard, a splinter through to my neck, my shoulders. I couldn't swallow. I couldn't breathe.

"Don't do this, Tessie. Please… Don't be like this. There's stuff I've got to tell you. There's just so much stuff and…I have to tell you… And that's why I brought you here… To tell you, because I have to tell someone, and it has to be you."

I pulled in a breath. I didn't know what to do, how to move, or even if I could, but I wanted to get away. So I squeezed his hand, hard, and I saw him wince with the pain, where he was bruised, and he let go, sighing, tipping his head down, still crouched in front of me, in front of the bench.

There was silence.

It seemed like he was taking a moment.

I wanted to move, but I was frightened. I couldn't see his face. I didn't know what he was going to do. I didn't want him to hurt me, like he'd hurt Max. I didn't think he'd do that. Because he liked me. Max had said that he loved me – that Billy loved me – he wouldn't hurt me, would he? Not if he loved me.

He stood up.

"It fucks me off, Tessie. It totally fucks me off that you won't talk to me."

His anger.

It was still there.

In his eyes, in his voice, in everything now, controlled.

"I mean, I thought you were shy, nervous... I don't know... Something like that. Kat and Holly totally played me, you know? Told me you had something to say to me. Told me you were really shy. Told me it would take time but it would be worth waiting for. Told me that that was just what you were like. You needed to take your time. And you looked shy. I mean I totally believed them. And when I looked into your eyes I – I didn't care – I was lost in them – in you... I thought it would be worth the wait...to hear you speak, to hear your voice, hear what you were going to say. Do you know what it's like for me not knowing what you sound like? And I imagined what you might say... And I thought that was all part of it, you know? The waiting. That's why I said I'd wait. But it's not what's happening here. It turns out you don't talk – and – and it's just the way it is... You don't speak. It's who you are. And it's really fucking me off. Because how was I meant to know? How? And it's too late for me to do anything about it now..."

I couldn't swallow. There was no saliva in my mouth. I opened my lips to try and take in some air.

Billy was pacing now, back and forth, like a tiger in a cage.

"I know I should be grateful. I know that. You didn't tell on me. I know you saw me outside the cafe with Max. I'm grateful for that," he said, and he stopped for a moment and lifted up his hand and stroked my cheek, and he was soft again, almost tender, standing there in front of me, looking at me, and I was his again, just for a moment.

And then he stepped back again, to walk, pace.

"I really am grateful, Tessie," he said. "And I'm sorry. I didn't mean to frighten you. That's why I texted to say sorry. Honest. To frighten you, that's the last thing I wanted to do."

But he was frightening me now, and he couldn't see it, and I couldn't say it.

Did he not care about what he'd done to Max? Did he only care that I'd not spoken out? I tried again to swallow, but there was no moisture in my mouth, just cold air hitting sharp against my teeth as I opened my mouth to breathe.

"I shouldn't be having a go at you, Tessie. I know that. You're good. You've been good to me. Keeping quiet. Not saying stuff… And Max deserved it, you know. I couldn't get near you. I needed to get near you. I was going mad not being the one to see you, in the mornings, after school, waiting to see you, hear you. And him, always him, walking with you, talking to you… I wanted that to be me. I warned him. I told him to leave you alone, leave you to me, when I left you at the playing field, I saw him, and I told him. But he didn't give up. He didn't back off. So I had to do it, to get to you, to be with you."

A tear ran from my eye, hot and quick, down my cheek. Max had walked with me to protect me from Billy, from Billy's jealousy. He'd done that for me. And Billy had beaten him. It was all so wrong.

I wiped the tear away with my hand before Billy could see.

"But you know, after all the shit that's happened – all the shit – to not know that it was your sister who got hurt, that it was your sister in the coma. It was a shock. Because I didn't know. Because you didn't tell me – and you know, your sister being in a coma? That's big shit to know. And if we're going to be together, Tessie, like properly together, I needed to fucking know!"

His voice had turned again, to anger.

"But it turns out you couldn't tell me. You couldn't fucking tell me. You'd *never* have fucking told me. And it's like all the things we need to say are the hardest ones, you know?" And he started moving again, in front of me.

"Shit, shit, shit," he said, running both his hands across

his smooth head and pacing, pacing, pacing in front of the bench.

"If you knew, Tessie. If you knew what I've seen…"

I coughed. It sounded more like a grunt. It was a sound. I'd made a sound.

Billy turned, and he looked at me – like he was waiting – like he thought I would speak.

I grabbed a breath whilst I could, and I swallowed. My throat was thick with tears but I could swallow and I could breathe and I could cry.

"And I don't even know what you're thinking now," he said. "Do you know how hard this is, Tessie? For me? For the other person? I mean I've got all this stuff inside of me, all this stuff I've got to say and there's no one who'll listen. No one. It's like it's piling up and it's shit on shit on shit and now it's so high it's coming out of my mouth…it's got nowhere else to go…it's filling me up, Tessie, you know? It's totally filling me up."

And I wanted to say:

That's how it feels.

That's how it is for me.

And it's all the time.

And I wanted to go to him. With every muscle in my body I wanted to go over to him and hold him, put my touch in the place of my words, but I was scared. I was scared of how big he seemed now, how loud, how angry.

I was scared of what he might do.

He was still pacing, stroking his head with his hands, his fingers, shaking his head this way and that when he swore, like he had flies to swat around his head. But he wasn't looking at me – not all the time. He was moving, he was still pacing, crying out – for me – to do something – to do the one thing that I knew I couldn't do – the one thing…

"Fuck, Tessie! I need you to talk! I really do. So we can talk about stuff, like your sister, Laura, and what's happening with us. Because I need to do that, I really do…" he said, and then he rubbed his whole face with his hands. "But I can't do it. I just can't. Not if you can't say anything back to me." And he ran off, leaving me in the darkness, with no sense of how I might get out, and a feeling so huge inside me I thought I might explode.

41.

I followed the path Billy and I had come down to get myself back to the park gate, but when I got to the gates I was stuck. Without a pull up from Billy I just couldn't get myself high enough on the railings to climb over and back onto the street. I tried several times, but I just didn't have the strength.

I walked along the railings, following the path again, looking for any gaps in the bushes that might show me another way out. And then I found one – a gap in the hedge that led me to some broken fencing behind it. I almost cried again when I saw it. I told myself that however small the gap, I'd get myself through it. And I did, grazing my back as I bent myself round to pull my legs through.

When I made it out onto the street I started to walk. I could feel my panic hovering. I was conscious of it there, waiting. A group of people were walking towards me – at first I couldn't tell if they were boys or girls – and as they got closer my heart sped up. Two kids. Kids maybe a bit older than me, with their mum. They were talking, all talking to each other, laughing, and I soon realized that they weren't interested in me, but still my heart sped up as I walked towards them, like I was standing at the edge of a cliff and being asked to look down, jump off. With each person I passed it was the same. And these words in my head...Billy's words...

I need you to talk... So we can talk about stuff like your sister, Laura, and what's happening with us... But I can't do it. I just can't. Not if you can't say anything back to me.

I hated myself because I couldn't do the one thing that he wanted me to do. The one thing that *I* wanted to do.

When I got home all the lights were still off, apart from the one on the landing. Jake wasn't in yet. Mum must have still been asleep.

I made my way up the stairs as quietly as I could. I didn't want to wake Mum. All I wanted to do was run a bath, have a soak.

I turned on the taps and began to undress. My clothes were damp, the fresh smell of the park still lingered on them as I pulled my school jumper over my head.

I stuffed all my clothes into the wash basket. It was already overflowing. I'd need a clean shirt for tomorrow. I'd put some washing on before I went to bed.

I stepped into the bath and immediately felt the warmth envelop me. As I stretched out and lay back I felt my toes tingle. They'd got cold. They were thawing through. This was a nice feeling. But then the graze on my back stung and it hurt. I turned to try and look over my shoulder, to see where it hurt, but I couldn't quite turn far enough. I curled my hand and put it behind my back and felt the roughness of my skin where it was grazed. There was a flap of skin, I could feel it now, floating in the water like a fin. I didn't like it. I didn't like the feeling, the hurt, the tinge of pain. It made me think about Max, and how he must be feeling with the cuts and bruises all over his body, and how much better it was for Laura that she was unconscious, protected from the pain.

I sank down so my head went right under, my eyes closed, my ears filled with water. I could hear the water in my head, like shingle washing up along the beach of my brain. Was this what it was like for Laura, with the words she was thinking, trapped, floating, like a nightmare, in her head?

I sat up lifting my head out of the water and took a gasp of air.

Could she wake up and tell us what happened, I wondered, like Ella had said? Could it really be that simple?

I closed my eyes again and breathed out.

I thought about Billy's touch.

His hands today, on top of mine, his fingers soft against my face… Despite everything, I still wanted that – the way he made me feel – I didn't want to let that go – and yet I knew it was wrong – to think it, want it, to feel that way.

I wondered if Laura had known about Joe's dad? That he'd been violent? Had she known that Joe hung around with kids like Kyle Brooks? Did she fall for him anyway? Did she decide to ignore those things because she just liked him so much? I understood now how you could like someone enough not to see the things you didn't want to see. Not to let them matter. Not to care. If Joe's touch had made Laura feel anything like the way Billy's touch made me feel, then I guessed it was the same. And maybe Ella was right. Getting Joe in to see Laura was worth a try, a chance – the risk. Right now I couldn't think of anything else we could all do to change things – and it was so frustrating – waiting – not being able to do anything to help. Maybe it was worth taking the risk, getting Joe into the hospital, keeping him away from the police, if it meant we could have Laura again – our Laura – the old Laura – and hear her voice – and what she had to say. If his touch could do that, it would be worth the risk, wouldn't it?

I lay back down in the bath one final time, dipping my head right under the water and I thought about the photograph of Laura and Joe in the compact.

He loved her. If there was only one thing that I believed out of all the things Ella had told me, it was that. And if I heard from Joe now, I'd reply. I decided that. I'd find a way to reply.

Tuesday

42.

I slept through my alarm.

When I woke it was gone 7.30 a.m. and the house was completely still. I turned over in bed and felt an ache in my limbs. I remembered the park, and how I'd climbed through the fence and it reminded me why my body felt this way. The park. Billy. I let myself dwell on the thought of Billy's eyes, his face, his kiss…and then I remembered what he'd said, how he'd been, and Max – his face again – the sound of his cry outside the cafe – it was all there – and I pulled the duvet up over my head.

Jake must have gone early or he'd have woken me up, I was sure. Mum was probably in bed. I hadn't seen her last night at all. I wondered whether I should check on her. See if she was okay.

I picked up my phone to see if he'd sent me a message. There was nothing.

Maybe I wouldn't go into school today. Maybe I'd stay here a little longer. Tell Mum I was sick. And then I could go and see Laura. That's all I really wanted to do. To see her, to be there, to make sure she knew that I was there for her. And I wondered if maybe one day soon Joe could do the same thing too.

"Tessie?"

Mum's voice was just outside my bedroom door.

"Are you still here?"

"I don't feel well," I said.

Mum came in and sat on the bed. I could see her blurred outline if I opened my eyes just a little. My curtains were closed and the room was still dark. She was in her dressing gown. Her hair was a mess. She'd just got out of bed.

"What's wrong?" she said.

"Headache."

It was the first thing that came to mind.

"Anything else hurt?"

"I ache. I feel bad."

"Okay," she said. "I'll call the school." And she got up and went downstairs.

It had never been this easy to get a day off school before. I guessed Mum had run out of all her fight.

I lay in bed and drifted back into sleep and when I woke Mum was in the room, standing over me with a mug of tea.

"Here." She passed me the mug as I sat up and propped myself against the pillows. I took a sip of the tea and looked at her. She was dressed, and her hair was brushed. I wasn't sure but I thought she had make-up on. "I left you to sleep," she said.

"What time is it?" I asked. I had no idea how long I'd been lying there. It could have been twenty minutes. It could have been three hours.

"It's almost ten thirty," Mum said. "Now listen, Dad's back today."

That was why she was up and dressed. Somehow I'd forgotten he was coming home today.

"I'm going to pick him up from the airport now. I'll be a couple of hours," she said. 'You'll be okay, won't you? Here on your own?" But she didn't wait for my reply before she stood up and left the room.

As soon as I heard the front door close I got up and got dressed.

I ran downstairs and pulled on my shoes, scooping up my bag from a hook in the hall.

I stood at the front door and looked at it.

I had to get better at walking on my own.

I had to.

I took a deep breath and grabbed my phone, putting my headphones in so I could listen to some music as I walked, and I opened the door. The day was cool. Cooler than it had been for ages. I stepped out and started walking down our path with my head down. I didn't want anyone to come near. I just wanted to get to the hospital.

I looked back at Max's house as I went down the street. The blind on his Velux was down. It had been down for days now. Ever since he'd come home from the hospital.

I wondered how he was, whether he was still in bed, whether he'd ever forgive me, and I felt a lump in my throat as I walked. I missed him.

Once I'd sorted this mess out with Laura I told myself I'd make it right with Max. I'd find a way. Find the words. The right words. I'd do that.

When I got to the hospital I went into the lift and up and onto the ward and straight to Laura's room. I pushed open the door and walked in.

I wanted to say: *Hey, Laura. I'm here.*

I wanted her to know I was here, that I was going to help her. I was going to try.

I walked over to the bed and carefully lifted up her right hand. It was so heavy, so limp. I slipped my hand, gently, under her palm.

I'm here, Laura. I'm here.

Those were the words I would have said, if I could have said them.

And I'm going to help you. I'm going to try. I really am.

I squeezed her hand as I thought the words, as I said

them in my head. And I tipped my head down and looked at our hands, together, and that's when I saw it – saw her hand move – it contracted in and then out, gripping mine – squeezing me back as if in answer – I felt it – her hold – her touch –

Laura?

I looked up.

I thought I heard my voice in the room.

I went hot.

Had I spoken?

My neck was hard.

That wasn't me, was it?

I looked around.

Was there anyone else in the room?

No.

Just me.

I swallowed down the thought, the word that I'd spoken. I swallowed it away.

And I looked down at Laura's face, immobile, her hand still in mine.

I looked over at the door.

It was PROPER SHUT.

But I couldn't speak.

I couldn't.

I stood up, and I pulled my hand away from Laura's, and I bent down towards her and I kissed her on the cheek.

I had to go.

I had to tell Mum and Dad what had happened. I couldn't tell anyone here. I couldn't phone. I had to get home now. I had to. And I had to tell them all what Laura had done.

43.

As soon as I stepped through the front door I saw Dad and I threw myself at him.

"Tessie!" he said, and he pulled me into his arms and he held me so tight that I buried my face into his chest and I squeezed him so hard I thought I might never let him go.

"Pleased to see me?" he said, laughing, and I laughed back and looked up at him. "We just got in," he said, looking over to Mum. I hadn't seen her standing there, just behind him.

"Where have you been?" she said.

"To see Laura," I said, without thinking. "You won't believe—"

"But you're ill," she said. "You can't go and see Laura when you're ill. She can't handle a virus or an infection…"

I could hear the panic rising in Mum's voice.

"I…"

"What were you thinking, Tessie?" she said.

"I wanted to see her," I said. "I felt better and—"

"Well then you should have gone to school!" she said, and she started to walk away from me.

"Mum—" I said, trying to call her back, to explain, but I looked at Dad as I said it because I could just see her moving further away, and I wanted his help to bring her back.

She turned.

"You don't think, Tessie!" Mum said. "Do you? You never think!" And she went into the kitchen and she slammed the door behind her.

"She hates me," I said to Dad. "She's always hated me. And I hate her too!" I pulled away from him and I ran upstairs.

"Tessie!" Dad called after me. "Come back, darling."

And I heard his feet on the stairs following me up, and I threw myself face down onto my bed and buried my face in my pillow, hoping to push back the tears pricking at my eyes.

"Tessie?" Dad's voice was softer now, and he was looking at me from around the door. "Can I come in?"

I turned onto my side so I could see him, and I nodded.

He came over and sat on my bed.

"You've still got your coat on, Dad," I said. "I'm sorry. You've just got back – and to this."

He stroked the hair off my face. "You know how much I love this coat," he said, and he smiled. He'd always hated it.

Always. But Mum had bought it for him and told him it was expensive and every autumn she'd get it out and tell him that he had to wear it for one more winter, at least.

I smiled. "I'm glad you're back," I said.

"Me too," he said.

"I bet you aren't," I said.

"Well, I have had better homecomings," he said, and laughed.

There was a silence.

"Are you okay, Tessie?"

I looked up at him.

"Dad, something amazing happened at the hospital just now. Laura moved – she squeezed my hand. I came back here so fast to tell you, to tell Mum—"

"Did you tell anyone at the hospital, Tessie? While you were there?"

"No, Dad. I couldn't. You know I couldn't. That's why I came straight home."

Dad stood up. "I'm going to ring the hospital, speak to them," but as he said it he looked worried.

"Surely it's a good thing, Dad? That she moved?"

He nodded and started walking towards the door, turning back to speak to me.

"Well, yes. I think so. I don't know, Tessie. That's the thing. If it was just a twitch or a spasm, it doesn't mean that she'll wake up... She's had those before. You know that.

But, I'll go and talk to Mum now. Let's call the hospital. Let's see what they say. We can go down there if you like, all together."

I nodded.

It was a good thing. I didn't care what the hospital had to say, or what Mum had to say. It was a good thing that she moved. It was.

"Dad?"

I called him back and he turned.

"I know Mum's not well, depressed. I sort of...well, I worked it out."

I could see he didn't know what to say.

"You know she's been in bed most of the time, while you were away?"

Dad shook his head and wiped his face with his hand, wiping away all the stress that was showing on it. He looked back at me.

"No. I didn't know that," he said. "That must have been...hard."

Dad looked tired. Smaller. Like my words had knocked all the air out of him.

"Call the hospital, Dad," I said. "I'll be down in a minute so you can tell me what they say." I smiled.

"Sounds good," he said. "Don't be long." And he went, closing my bedroom door behind him.

I sighed and heard my phone buzz in my pocket.

I wondered if it was Billy.

Or Joe. It could be Joe.

I wanted to look and at the same time I didn't.

It buzzed again.

Two texts.

I pulled it out.

Both from Max.

Mia said you weren't in school.

You okay?

I texted straight back. Without thinking.

Yes. You?

I waited a minute. Then another. And then my phone buzzed again.

I'm speaking to the police in the morning. I thought you should know.

I stuffed my phone into the back pocket of my jeans, and I turned round to face the window. Everything was about to come crashing down. All of it was. And there was nothing I could do. The police would want a statement from me now, and that was right. I saw what Billy did. I had to tell them what I'd seen. Max was right to talk now, to say what had happened to him. I knew he was. So why did I feel like I somehow wanted to protect Billy so much? Was it just because I wanted to protect myself from losing him? Everything was so messed up right now, and I wanted to hear, to know, what he had to say. And I didn't want to lose him… Not yet. Not with everything else that was going on.

Wednesday

44.

Dad dropped me at school the next morning. As soon as he knew that Max was still off, and there was no one to walk me in, he offered to take me. It wasn't on his way to work or anything, but he knew that the walk was painful for me and well…he just knew how it was. We didn't need to talk about it. Dropping me at school was a massive favour, and he knew that, and it made me remember why I needed him. He might not have been able to talk to me about Mum, but he did other stuff, and him being there made things better. Always.

"Have a great day then," he said. "I'll see you tonight." And he leaned across and kissed me on the cheek before I grabbed my bag and got out of the car.

As soon as I got through the gates I saw Kat and Holly, and my heart started to kick. It beat louder, fiercer in my chest.

They began to walk towards me.

I stood still, my legs weak. Fear was in my body. Fear

was running up and down my legs, my back, my chest now, like a radar from my brain. I should have been ringing like an alarm, the way I was feeling.

"So you're back, Mouse," Kat said.

"Nice day off with lover boy?" Holly said.

They meant Billy. They were talking about Billy. He must have been off yesterday too.

"Where d'you go? His house or yours? Probably hard to do it at yours with your mum moping around. Would she notice though, Mouse? I mean does she even know you're there?" Kat said.

I thought about the hut. How Billy had tried to take me to the hut. What would have happened if he'd got me there? He'd wanted to talk, hadn't he? That's what he'd said.

"My mum saw your mum in the supermarket on the weekend. She said your mum looked straight through her. Like a zombie. Like there was nothing behind the eyes."

"Little Mouse and her zombie mum..." Holly said. "Poor little Mouse."

"Not a virgin any more though, eh, Mouse?" Kat said.

"Did you squeak when he put it inside you, Mouse?" Holly said, stepping closer to me now.

"Did you?" Kat said, laughing now, pushing me.

I opened up my mouth to pull in the breath that was stuck in my chest. The inside of my nose was burning with the air that I couldn't get to my lungs, the pain like fury – burning me fast – making my heart pound and my throat lock – holding the scream – my scream – the only defence I had – that I couldn't let out whilst they stood around me, too close, prodding me, poking me until I heard someone say my name...

"Tessie!"

It was coming from the other side of the playground.

Kat and Holly turned round too, to see who it was.

"Ah – Mia. She's coming to save you. See ya then, Mouse," Holly said.

"Yeah, laters, Mouse," Kat said.

And then Mia, her voice still calling my name one more time, came and put her arm through mine, scooping me up as she went, leading me into school and towards the lockers.

I grabbed a breath when I saw her. I was panting like a dog as we walked.

"Just keep breathing, Tessie. Nice long breaths, yeah?" she said, and when we got to our lockers she guided me to lean against them and she stood close, in front of me.

"You alright?"

I blinked back an answer. It wasn't a yes or a no. I didn't know what I was feeling in that moment, other than light-headed – and sick. Sick to remember the stuff Kat and Holly had said, about Mum, about Billy, about me.

"Listen, I know this isn't the best time, but the bell's about to go and I have to ask – have you seen Max?"

I looked up.

"He won't let me see him. I keep going round there and having cups of tea with his mum because he won't let me go up and see him. How is he? How does he look?"

I bent my head.

I was ashamed.

About everything.

Mia grabbed my hands.

"Out of ten, Tessie," she said, holding my fingers up. "Ten is good, one is bad. Tell me."

I took a moment, and I remembered Max's face and how he'd turned away from me in the bed.

I held up six fingers, but in my head I knew it should have been four, no – it should have been three.

"Shit, Tessie. He's pretty bad then?"

She didn't know the half of it. Max was so good to protect her. He didn't deserve any of this.

"You know he's going to talk to the police today? His mum said he's ready to talk."

I nodded.

"Of course you know," Mia said. "You've been to see him."

I looked up at her. I could see she was trying to hold in her anger, her tears. She must have hated me for seeing him.

I wanted to explain. I wanted to tell her I'd only been once. I wasn't in the privileged position she thought I was. I didn't deserve to be. I wanted to tell her that. I could see the tears welling in her eyes as she looked at me. I wanted to make it better for her, but I couldn't. I couldn't do it without the words.

I grabbed her hand.

"What, Tessie?"

She was so pretty, and kind. I didn't know why Max had said he didn't like her. She liked him so much. And he deserved someone better – better than me.

"You can't say. I know. I'm sorry," she said. "I should never have asked. Listen, I should go to lessons. You should too," and she took her hand out of mine and she left.

I heard the bell go, and I stood up. I felt weak.

I walked out onto the main corridor and began to head towards my tutor room for registration. The corridors were mostly empty. I would probably be marked late if I didn't speed up. I didn't care. I carried on walking, slowly, until I turned to pass the office. I glanced in, through the glass in the door. There were two policemen at the desk, signing in. They were here already. Had they spoken to Max? They must have done.

I stopped walking. I leaned against the radiator and felt the hot metal on the backs of my legs and I tried to breathe. Long and slow.

The police were here for Billy. They had to be. And if they were here for Billy then they'd want to talk to me too. I was sure of it.

I swallowed and it hurt.

But would Billy even be in today? I hadn't seen him on the corner when Dad had driven me in. I'd looked for him. I couldn't help myself – I still wanted to see him. I didn't want the park to be the last time I spent time with him. I wanted to listen to what he had to tell me, what he needed to say. I wanted to understand.

I braced myself to try and swallow once more. There was no saliva in my mouth and my head was pumping now.

I heard the door of the office open and voices, men's voices, in the corridor.

I started to walk in the opposite direction. I headed for the toilets. I'd wait in there and then I'd leave. I'd go out of school, and then I'd wait for them to come to me at home with their forms and their reports and their sympathetic talk, whilst Mum explained my needs.

I heard the voices pass the toilet door. I counted to sixty and then I walked through the corridor and out of the building. I slipped through the gates before they closed for the morning, and I went to see Laura. Because she needed me more than I needed school. And right now I felt like I needed her too.

45.

When I got to the hospital entrance, I stood outside and texted Dad.

> Didn't feel well. Left before registration. Heading home. See you later.

I hit send, and I didn't text Mum.

My phone buzzed as I went to put it away.

I looked down, and hoped Dad wasn't going to suggest he'd come and collect me, take me home.

> Who are you texting?

It was from Billy.

I looked up, and around me. Was he here? Was he watching me? He must have been. He must have followed me here.

I swallowed and felt a scratch in my throat like glass,

and my face flushed red with heat.

I couldn't see him.

My phone buzzed again.

I miss you.

The heat in my cheeks was burning now. I didn't like the feeling that Billy was here, watching me, seeing me, and I couldn't see him. But I liked the words – I liked what he said – because somehow I missed him too.

I looked down at my phone, and waited. Would there be another message?

I waited.

There was nothing.

So I put my phone in my bag, taking a final look around me, and went into the hospital.

Laura looked the same as she'd looked the last time I was here. As I went over and sat on the bed I wondered if I'd imagined her hand squeezing mine. Dad had phoned the hospital after I'd told him yesterday and they'd explained that it didn't necessarily mean Laura was waking up. When he got off the phone, he sat down with me and explained that, as time went on, it was less and less likely that Laura would wake up. I shook my head when he told me that.

I shook it over and over. I told him again how Laura had squeezed my hand – that if he'd been there – he'd have seen it. And he said that he believed me, that everyone believed me, but that we needed to have realistic expectations about how this was all going to turn out. He'd given up hope. That much seemed clear to me.

I picked up Laura's hand again now and clasped both of my own around it.

Squeeze my hand again, Laura. Prove me right. Prove them wrong.

That's what I wanted to say.

I looked around at the door. It was PROPER SHUT. No one could hear us in here.

I looked back down at Laura. Her head was less swollen, less bruised, less damaged than before. But what was happening inside? Were there just the sounds: the sighing of her lungs, and the lapping of her blood into and out of the shore of her heart. I guessed maybe that was all there was.

Something has to happen.

Something has to change.

Something, Laura, something…

said a whisper of a voice.

Laura –

it was there again –

a whisper of a voice –

was it mine?

46.

When I left Laura's room it was busy in the corridors. I went down the stairs and walked out into the cool air. There were people in wheelchairs smoking, and families standing in huddles all speaking into their phones, and the wind, so cold.

I wondered where Billy had been standing, before, when he'd seen me.

I looked around for him.

There were a couple of trees over by the entrance to the hospital from the road, and a long wall that ran alongside the pavement to A&E. I was sure I would have seen him if he'd been standing there. I looked to the right. There was a bench and a bus stop – and there he was. Looking at me. His hood up, his eyes only on me. I felt for my phone in my bag. I pulled it out and I looked down at the screen to see if there were any messages, any texts that had come through, but my eyes wouldn't keep still and I couldn't focus.

I looked up again towards him, but when I looked, he wasn't there. He had gone.

I couldn't see him.

I wanted to see him.

I wanted to know where he was.

Suddenly, I was scared.

If I started walking, would he follow me?

I swallowed hard, to push down the coughing that I could feel trying to break through at the back of my throat. I needed water, I needed space, I needed to be in a place where I wasn't so hot and then so cold and the wind wasn't distracting me, making it difficult to think.

But there was nowhere to go, nowhere, except back into the hospital. I could go there. I could sit there. And I could wait. I walked inside to the cafe and grabbed a cup and filled it from the water fountain and I sat in the corner, tucking my legs under my chair and folding my arms across my chest, holding the cup to my lips, pretending to sip water, until the feeling of needing to cough subsided.

I pulled out my phone again, once I was calm, and held it in my lap, keeping my eyes on the phone or to the floor, so no one could catch my attention and speak to me.

But it didn't work.

"Do you mind if I sit here?"

I looked up to the voice. Someone was pulling out a

chair from the table next to mine, and sitting down, close, next to me.

I wanted to say: *No.*

I felt my neck go stiff and my shoulders followed.

It was a face that I knew.

Green eyes, dark hair beneath a hoody, a smile that I recognized, a look in his eyes that I knew.

And there was nothing I could say and there was nothing I could do.

Because there, sitting next to me, was Joe.

It was Laura's Joe.

47.

"You don't have to say anything," Joe said. "I know you can't. But do you have your phone?"

I lifted my hand up from my lap and showed Joe that my phone was in my hand.

"Great," he said. "We can text. I figure no one will notice us if we just sit here quietly and I don't speak either." He smiled and it was the kindest smile I'd seen in days and I kept looking at his face but I couldn't quite believe he was here, sitting here, in front of me – Joe.

My phone beeped in my hand. A text. I opened it.

Hi Tessie. I'm Joe.

I looked at my phone in my hand, and I didn't do anything. I waited for a moment, and then I typed.

Yes. I know.

I looked up after I'd hit send. I could feel the blush in my cheeks, and I quickly looked back down at my phone. Joe was even more gorgeous than Laura had said. More gorgeous than in the photograph, and I could see why Laura liked him – no, why she was mad about him. Because he was different. He was different from us and our friends – Laura's friends. He was different from the boys in school – I mean I'd always known he was older, but he seemed older even than twenty. I wanted to hear more of his voice, hear the way he spoke, but he didn't speak. He texted again.

I'm not here to stress you out. I just want to see Laura.

There were so many things I wanted to ask him, so many things I wanted to say. But the thought of speaking made my heart thump loud and fast and I put my phone down to pull off my hoody, because suddenly I was so hot. I could feel the back of my neck was wet with the fear.

Joe was looking around the cafe, his eyes moving quickly from one corner to the other. He hadn't seemed nervous before. He was nervous now. He typed again.

Will you help me?

I didn't reply.
Another text.

I shouldn't be here.

I knew he shouldn't be here. But I shouldn't either. Neither of us should have been there. But we were.

Tessie – please.

I remembered what Ella had said about withholding evidence or obstructing justice – something like that – and I thought about how me sitting here now was the same. It was exactly the same. The police were looking for Joe, and he was here, with me, inside the hospital, where Laura lay.

I looked at him.

Did you do it, Joe? Was it you?

That's what I wanted to ask him. And I needed to hear his answer. I needed to look into his face and hear his voice – hear him say it – that he hadn't hurt her – but I couldn't make that happen without words of my own.

Joe looked behind him and, still clutching his phone, he ran his hands over the top of his head and put them behind his neck before bringing them down onto the table and leaning forward, towards me again.

"I didn't do it, Tessie," he said in the softest voice.

"You have to believe me. I would never hurt Laura. Never. I ran because I was drunk. I wasn't thinking straight. I made a lot of bad choices that night," and then he stood up. "Seriously. I know I did. But the police seemed to have pretty much decided it was me from the start…" He turned to look behind him before he went to leave.

"You've got my number now, Tessie. I'll have to dump the sim in this phone tonight. It's safest if I do that, because of the police, you know? I'm in touch with Ella a bit. But I have to be careful. I don't want the police to find me, follow me. Not yet. So text me tonight, if you change your mind about taking me in to see Laura. If you can help me see her, show me where her room is…maybe make sure I don't bump into anyone who might recognize me." He paused. "It's just until they arrest Kyle, you know? That's why I've come back. Because I won't give up on Laura, Tessie. I'll never give up," he said, and he turned and left me with my phone in my hand and a ticking time bomb in my heart.

48.

I walked home with my headphones plugged in but I didn't put any music on. If I could have walked with my eyes closed I would have done. I didn't want to see anyone, and I didn't want anyone to see me. I didn't want to hear any sound. I just wanted to escape.

When I got home the lights were all on and the kitchen door was closed. I could hear voices. Mum and Dad were talking. They hadn't heard me come in. I was glad. I dumped my stuff in the hall and crept upstairs to see if Jake was around, but he wasn't. The voices were raised in the kitchen now. Mum was shouting, Dad was placating. Were they arguing about me? I crept to the top of the stairs. It always used to be about me, but more recently it had been about Laura seeing Joe. And now…now there weren't any arguments. There was just this constant underlying hum – a hum that emanated from Mum – that engulfed everyone and everything – her sadness. And it was always there.

I could hear Mum crying.

I crept all the way down the stairs, slipped off my shoes at the bottom, and tiptoed over to the kitchen door.

"It's not a decision we can make today, that's all I'm saying," Dad said. "It's not a decision we can make in one conversation."

"You're not listening to me, Michael. You never listen."

"That's not fair. I've listened. I *always* do."

"Oh, and now you won't any more? Is that what you're saying?" Mum said.

"No. That's not what I meant. I meant I'm trying. I'm trying my hardest. I'm always trying."

"Well it doesn't feel like that," Mum said.

I could feel Dad's despondency through the kitchen door in the gaping silence.

He really was trying. We all were.

"I'm not ready," Dad said, after the silence.

"And you think *I'm* ready?" Mum said.

What were they talking about? Ready for what?

"I'm not judging you," Dad said.

"It's not about judgement!" Mum answered. "It's about taking advice, it's about living like this. It's about Laura, and us all living like this."

What were they saying?

I pressed my body closer to the door, so I could listen better.

"I can't make the decision," Dad said, and I heard a cry that sounded a wounded dog – not like my dad at all.

"And you think I can?" Mum said, in a voice so quiet it sounded like a whisper.

"No!" Dad said. "That's not what I'm saying. You know that."

"Then what *are* you saying? That you want *me* to do it, to call it? That you want *me* to decide? I can't do it on my own. Surely you must see that?"

My mind was scrambling to understand. What did they mean? What were they talking about? Was it about Laura? The future? Was that the decision? What happened to Laura now? Was that the decision that Dad couldn't make in one conversation, that Mum couldn't make on her own...? But I'd felt Laura's hand squeeze mine – I'd felt her hand moving in mine. And Joe was back now. She loved him, and he loved her. She'd squeeze his hand back too – if he was there – I was sure she would. Joe said he'd never give up on her. I felt the same. Mum and Dad couldn't give up. They couldn't. I had to stop them.

I stepped away from the door.

I walked into the hall.

I pulled my phone out of my bag.

And I texted Joe.

I'll help you. For Laura.

Thursday

49.

Dad was sitting at the kitchen table staring into his cup of coffee. He didn't move when I came into the room.

"Morning," I said.

He looked up, and spoke, his solemn face breaking into a smile – a fake one.

"Tessie," he said. "How you doing?" As if he was almost surprised to see me there.

"I don't feel that well, Dad."

"Come here," he said, lifting his hand to my forehead.

"I'm hot," I said.

"You don't feel hot."

I didn't say anything. I let him rest his warm palm on my forehead. It felt nice.

"Do you want to go back to bed? See how you feel in an hour or so?"

I nodded.

"I'm going into work a bit later – I've got a meeting.

Heading straight there. I can drop you on my way, if you feel better."

"Okay," I said.

"Hop back into bed. I'll check in on you in an hour. I'll call the school now, and let them know."

I nodded. "What if I don't feel better later?"

"Then I'll go to my meeting, and I'll come straight back." As he spoke, he looked so tired.

I turned and walked towards the kitchen door.

"Where's Mum?" I said.

"She's sleeping," Dad said, standing up and taking his cup to the open dishwasher.

I didn't answer.

I just walked straight on up the stairs and into bed, and I prayed that Mum kept sleeping and Dad would let me stay in bed when he came to check on me.

I waited the hour, with my eyes gently closed, and I thought about seeing Laura, and Joe seeing Laura, and when Dad came in I kept my eyes closed and Dad kissed me on the forehead and he whispered, *Sleep tight* – and inside my head I was smiling. Inside my head I was on my way to the hospital to save Laura. Because I knew that Joe had to see her. I had to give him a chance to see her. He loved her. I was sure of that. And Laura needed that chance too. The chance to have him there, feel his hand in hers – like she'd felt mine – the chance to put it right. I had to let him try. I had to.

As soon as the front door closed I shoved off my duvet and got out of bed. I felt light-headed as I sat up. I was nervous. Joe had texted back last night and we'd agreed to meet at 11 a.m. this morning. It was actually happening. He was going to see Laura. He was going to make her better. He was going to make everything better.

I crept downstairs and pulled my shoes out of the basket. I didn't want to wake Mum up. I had to get out of the house silently, like I was still in bed, like nothing was amiss. My stomach rumbled loudly. I hadn't eaten. I was starving, but I felt sick – excited sick. I wasn't sure I could eat. I went into the kitchen to see what I could find in the cupboard to take with me. There was a note on the table for Mum from Dad, telling her that I was ill. Telling her to check on me in case I did have a temperature. Telling her he hadn't given me any medicine, that he'd be back, that she should call him if need be. He knew she needed all this information. He was trying to prove to her that he was there for her, solid as a rock for her, but what he didn't realize was that she probably wouldn't get up to read this note until after he'd got back.

I didn't look in the cupboard for food.

There was no way I could eat now. I was too nervous.

I slipped out of the kitchen and into the hall. I picked

up my bag and my phone and I let myself out of the house and I walked quickly, quietly up our garden path and out into the street, my earbuds in, my eyes down, all the way.

50.

I saw Joe up ahead as soon as I got close to the hospital. He was standing near the entrance with his hood up, turned slightly inwards, leaning against the wall by the automatic doors. I couldn't see his face, but I could tell it was him from the way he stood. He looked strong.

I wondered, for a moment about Billy.

He'd been here the other day. Was he here today?

I stopped and looked around me, over to the bus stop, the bushes, the wall by A&E.

I couldn't see him. I looked across to the parking bays, but it was hard to see for all the cars and the ambulances coming round, parking and then going. I started walking again. Maybe he was in school. Maybe he was with the police. I didn't want to think about that, about the police.

I walked straight up to Joe, and put my hand on his arm. As soon as he saw me he straightened up to standing and looked about him.

"Hey, Tessie," he said. "It was so good to get your text last night. Made me so happy, you know?"

He was looking around again, his hood still up, his phone in his hand. He was nervous. I could tell he was. For a moment I wondered whether I'd done the wrong thing.

"Shall we go in, then?" he said, and he stepped closer to me and he smiled and it instantly made me feel better, because his face sort of lit up with the smile, the same smile I'd seen yesterday. He looked like the Joe in the photo – Laura's Joe – and as he smiled, he squeezed my arm so gently, that I didn't believe he could ever hurt anyone. Not a soul.

I nodded and walked into the hospital entrance, and Joe walked with me through the endless corridors towards the lift.

"Not sure I'd ever have worked out how to find her in here without asking someone," he said.

I nodded.

"No one can know I'm here. You get that, don't you, Tessie?"

He spoke fast.

I looked at him and nodded again as we got towards the lift. I understood. Only I could know he was here. But he was going to make things better. That was why he was here. I blinked at him. ONE BLINK. One blink for YES. But I'm not sure he really understood.

"I'm a bit nervous, if I'm honest. Just seeing her, seeing how she looks," he said as we waited for the lift.

I looked at my feet. I couldn't tell him how she looked. I couldn't explain. And even if I could I knew nothing was going to prepare him. Not really.

We stood in silence as the lift went up to the ward.

"This is all kind of surreal, you know?"

I nodded, although I wasn't quite sure what he meant.

He leaned his hand against the inside of the lift and started tapping his fingers, fast, loud, over and over. The lift was still going up and Joe's tapping was getting faster and louder.

"Christ, I'm nervous," he said, shifting on his feet.

For a minute I wondered if it was seeing Laura that was making him so nervous, or whether it was the possibility of being seen. It was the way he kept looking around him, checking. It actually made him look suspicious. It wasn't normal.

The lift door opened. I stepped out, but Joe stood still. He didn't follow.

I motioned with my head as if to say: *This is it. This is our floor.*

Joe stood in the lift, pushing his hands together and rubbing them. "Christ, Tessie – there won't be any police here, will there?"

I shook my head, quickly. I wanted to get him out of the

lift before the doors closed again, but his nerves, his behaviour, the thing he was doing with his hands, it made me wonder whether I should have brought him here at all.

I looked up at the ward, walking towards the desk, looking up and down the corridor as I went. There were no police. It was clear. And I knew it would be. There had been a policeman in ITU those first few days after the attack, but after that, they never came.

I turned back to Joe and took a few steps towards him. He'd stepped out of the lift now. He looked shifty, nervous. I looked behind me again. It struck me that if Brenda or Magda were here they might recognize him. They'd been briefed about Joe when Laura was in ITU. I scanned the corridors again. It was safe.

I looked back to Joe. He'd pulled his hoody up over his head. He was tightening the strings so it closed around his face.

I wanted to say: *Take your hood down. Pull it down.*

But I couldn't.

So I started to walk. I walked quickly towards Laura's room, and I hoped that he would just follow, and if he didn't, then I wasn't sure what I would do. When we reached the door I stopped and I could feel Joe right there behind me. I looked through the door and into the room to check no one else was there. No nurses, no one. Just Laura. And then I stepped to the side and nodded to let him go in, handing him an apron and pointing at the hand sanitizer on the wall as I did.

He looked at me.

"Shall I go in on my own?" he asked. He looked like a child.

I nodded again, and I watched him push the door open, and then I turned to walk away. I wasn't sure where I would go. I didn't want to go far, but I knew I didn't want to be there when he saw her for the first time. I wanted to give him some time, some space, to see her.

I walked through the main corridor towards the vending machines and the turquoise chairs stained with tears and hot chocolate and I didn't like to think what else, and I sat down. I bent forward and looked down the corridor I'd just come down. There weren't many people about. The ward was quiet today. I leaned back and looked out of the window.

Joe was here. He was with Laura. He was here.

I looked down the corridor again.

Suddenly I felt nervous.

Nervous like Joe had been nervous.

I crossed my legs and bent forward, looking down the corridor again, checking.

What if the police came now and found him here?

What if Mum came?

He shouldn't have been there. But he was. Because of me.

I sat up straight to try and calm myself down, but I could feel my panic rising.

What if it was Joe all along? What if the police were right and he did hurt Laura, and he was in there with her now, hurting her again? Pulling out the lines, covering her mouth, finishing off what he started? What if that was why he was so nervous, asking about the police? Because he knew all along what he was going to do, and he knew all along I was the only person who could help him do it? Because I'd led him through the hospital, I'd taken him to the room that he could never have found on his own, when no one else was visiting, when no one else was around. Me, the stupid cursed mute. He could rely on me to help him. Both he and Ella could. It made sense now. They were in this together. They had to be.

I stood up.

I was shaking all over. I felt cold. I looked at my hands and they were pale, so pale. I had to get to Laura. I had to go to her and I had to stop Joe. I had to stop him.

I walked and I walked and the world seemed to slow around me. I pushed open the door to Laura's room, and still I didn't feel like I was present, like I was in the room, like I could see properly. And I was looking, looking, looking to see – what did I expect to see? Joe gone? Laura dead? I stopped suddenly, because time caught up – and there he was – Joe – sitting on the side of the bed, holding

Laura's hand, one earbud in his ear, one earbud in hers, and he was singing. He was softly, gently, singing. And he hadn't gone and she wasn't dead. She was there. And she was with Joe.

Joe turned to me. His face was soft, his eyes so clear.

"She loves this song," he said.

I nodded.

He was stroking Laura's hand now, humming.

I looked up at her face. It was so peaceful, so still. And then it wasn't –

She made a move – like a jolt – sitting up – reaching out –

Her eyes opened wide –

They flickered – opened again – wide –

and her mouth now – open –

"Laura!"

There was a voice, in the room.

My voice.

"What's happening?"

That was Joe, and he stood up and all the time he still had hold of her hand.

"Get someone!" he said.

I looked behind me, and a nurse was there, already, in the room.

"It's okay, it's okay," she said. She'd got here so quickly. How had she got here so fast?

She went to Laura's side and started looking at the machines, the lines, reading data, pushing buttons, and other people arrived, whose faces I didn't recognize in that moment. "Can you move please, son? Just move away so I can get to her."

I stepped back, and so did Joe.

"I have to go," Joe whispered.

"It's okay," the nurse said. "It's okay. Move into the hall. We'll get her stable. Give us a minute here. We won't be long. We'll get her settled."

I nodded and Joe came towards me and took my hand. It was as cold and shaky as my own, and he squeezed it and he smiled and in that moment of kindness I knew I'd done the right thing bringing him here. In that moment I knew that no matter what anyone said, he'd helped. He'd got Laura to react, to move. He'd done that, here, with me. And that had to be a good thing. It had to be.

And then he let go of my hand and he leaned in towards me.

"I have to go, I can't be here any more," he said. "Tell Laura I was here. Tell her."

And I opened my mouth to call out to him, but no sound came.

And I watched him as he disappeared down the stairwell, pulling his hood up, breaking into a jog, as he went. And he didn't look back. Not even once.

51.

I turned to go back to Laura's room.

The ward sister was walking towards me as I approached.

"She's okay, Tessie. I'm sure that was a shock – seeing her move like that. But it's good. These types of movement, they indicate she might be coming through, becoming more conscious. She's settled now. I'm going to ring your parents. You can go back in and see her if you want."

I nodded and I smiled, but I knew my smile didn't show anything like the amount of joy I was feeling inside. I should have been screaming with the joy I felt.

The sister moved towards the desk, stretching her arm out to stroke my head as she went. "You're a sweet girl, Tessie," she said, and she smiled as she walked away.

I went back in to see Laura. It looked like the nurses and doctors had moved her slightly higher up the bed, but otherwise she seemed the same. I felt kind of disappointed. But I told myself not to. I grabbed her hand, and I squeezed it gently in my own.

I think it's going to be okay, Laura. I think everything is going to be okay.

And then I bent down, and I kissed her hand. It was warm.

I sat up.

I thought about Mum and Dad. About seeing their faces when they got the news. I wanted to see the joy I'd felt lighting up their faces too. But right now I needed some fresh air and I reckoned I had a few minutes to go down to reception, and check my phone, be ready for when they might text.

As I walked out of the lift, I wondered how I would explain being there. I was meant to be ill at home, and there'd been no good reason for me to come into the hospital today. Mum had gone mad at me before for visiting Laura when I was supposed to be ill. I just hoped that, once they knew what had happened with Laura, they wouldn't be angry. Maybe with all the joy of what was happening I wouldn't need to explain.

The reception at the main entrance of the hospital was busy again. There were people everywhere. I scanned the atrium for a seat but there were none. I couldn't stand there and wait for Mum and Dad. I didn't know how long they'd even be. It was about a ten-minute drive from home to the hospital. I had to get out, get away from all the people... I stepped through the automatic doors and into the cold air, but I was still in the way... There were just so many people coming and going. I started to walk away from the entrance, and I pulled out my phone. There was some grass, a bench, just on the other side of the car park. I'd head for the bench. I'd sit down. Wait for Mum and Dad. I guessed they'd get the call from the hospital and they'd wonder where I was and they'd text me, and then they'd come in, and we'd see Laura, together.

I walked between the final row of cars and hopped up onto the low wall to get over to the bench. I felt a hand on my upper arm. It grabbed me and pulled me back hard. I almost fell, but the person behind me steadied me, pulling me harder, further back.

A panic filled me.

There was a gasp trapped in my throat that I couldn't let out...

My mouth opened and I gagged as I was pulled back again between the cars in the car park and pushed up against a van.

I was out of sight now. I knew I was.

Another hand grabbed my waist and turned me around.

Billy.

He had me in his grip.

"For fuck's sake, Tessie," he said. "I mean, what the FUCK is going on?"

I shook my head. I shook it because I didn't know what

he meant, what he was going to do, what he was saying. I didn't understand.

"Are you trying to fuck with my head? Are you trying to completely fuck with me? Are you?"

I tried to swallow but my throat was locked.

Billy brought his face up close, closer again, to mine and his voice was lower now, calmer. "Have you got something you want to tell me, Tessie? Is there something you want to tell me?"

I closed my eyes, gently. I blinked TWO BLINKS. Two blinks for NO. Because my head wouldn't move. None of me could move. And I hoped that Billy might remember, from before, how I blinked, and what it meant and that he'd understand now what I meant.

But he didn't. He can't have. Because his hands came up to my neck and he grabbed me, hard, one hand wrapped around the left side of my neck and the other around the right. And he was strong, like I'd always known he was strong, and he pressed his thumbs into my throat like I was putty and he was moulding me, and all I could feel was the burning and the fear where my breath should have been.

And the words in my head were:

You can't make me speak.

You can't make me speak.

You can't make me speak.

And the words that lay between us, in the spaces between our faces, were:

I don't understand.

I don't understand.

I don't understand.

I knew that those were the words, because whilst I was suffocating in his hold I looked into his eyes – the boy with the sparkling eyes – and I read them there.

I saw the words. I saw the pain. And I knew them.

And once I saw them in his eyes, I saw them all over him. The lines on his face were filled with them, the deep contours of his hollow cheeks cradled them, and the scars on his head ached with them. And I wondered, why hadn't I seen it before? Why had I been so blind before, to his pain? And now I was facing it. I could do nothing but see it, feel it, live it.

I had to do something. Or he was going to hurt me – even more than he was already hurting me now.

I lifted up my right knee, and I flicked out my foot and I kicked him. I didn't think about what I was doing – I didn't question it – I just did it. To get away...

I kicked Billy, front on, hard. I kicked him again. His shin. And when he didn't immediately let go of my neck, I kicked and I kicked and I carried on kicking until he loosened his grip and let me go. And I didn't allow myself to collapse. I pulled in a breath, because I knew I could, and I ran. And as I ran I was sure I could hear Billy crying. Crying, like a baby, but I didn't look back. Not even once. And I didn't stop running until I was all the way home. Because I hadn't got a message from Mum or Dad, and I couldn't wait any longer. I had to get safe. I had to get home.

52.

I went straight into the kitchen. All I wanted to do was see Mum and Dad – were they there? I needed to see their faces… I needed to talk to them about Laura. I'd pushed all the pain of Billy away as I'd run home. I'd pounded it out of my feet and smashed it flat on the pavement, because I wasn't going to let him take away what had happened with Laura. I wasn't going to let him do that. And I burst into the kitchen breathing heavy and loud, looking for Mum and Dad.

They were there, standing up. Mum had the phone in her hand. They both turned when they saw me.

"Tessie!" Mum said. "Where have you been? The hospital have called. About Laura."

"Tessie, are you okay?" Dad said. "I left you in bed this morning. I thought you had a headache. What's going on?"

"I'm fine," I said. "I just went…out. I needed some air."

It seemed easier to pretend I hadn't been at the hospital at all right now than to explain.

"I ran back here. I've got to have some water," I said. "So what's happened? What did the hospital say?"

Dad walked over to the sink and grabbed a glass from the drainer, turning the tap to get me the water.

"There's been a change," Mum said. "Laura's responded. I'm not clear exactly what happened, but the sister called. She's asked me and Dad to go in. We need to go and see her."

Dad passed me the water and I took a huge gulp. It was cold. It felt good.

"So go," I said. "Don't worry about me. I feel better anyway now I've had this water."

I couldn't stop myself smiling. I'd done this. I'd helped.

Dad looked at me. He saw my smile.

"Don't get your hopes up too high, Tessie. Remember, if she becomes conscious again it will probably be gradual."

"I know, but if this is a response, then it might be the beginning of something," I said. "It might be."

Dad nodded. He looked at Mum.

I didn't need to tell them I was even there. Not yet, anyway.

I felt a tinge of excitement in my belly.

I'd tell them everything when this was over. I'd tell them about Joe, and how I'd taken him in to see her, and how that had made her move, sit up, reach out. When Laura was awake, properly awake, and everything was okay again, I'd tell them. If I told them now, they'd freak. I knew they would. And I'd made it clear to Joe I wouldn't tell anyone he was back. In my own way I'd promised him that.

"Look, we should go," Mum said. "I need to speak to the doctor, see Laura for myself." And she picked up her keys from the hooks.

"You stay here, Tessie," Dad said. "Rest, and we'll call later on, when we've seen her. We couldn't get hold of Jake. You tell him what's going on when he gets in. We were hanging on for you both."

"Okay," I said, and I smiled again.

As soon as the front door shut I put my hands to my neck, almost instinctively, where Billy had held me. It hurt.

I went to the mirror in the hall. I wanted to see if there was a mark or a bruise – if it showed.

There was nothing there. No mark on my skin. But Billy had hurt me. He'd really hurt me. I couldn't even begin to imagine what it must have felt like for Max, to be beaten like he had.

I thought about Max.

I hadn't seen him. I hadn't heard from him. Not since he'd spoken to the police. I didn't feel good about that. I wanted to see him. I wanted to know he was okay. But there was just so much going on... I wondered for a moment, did I sound like Ella? Was I making excuses not to see Max, like Ella did about not seeing Laura? I was. I knew I was. I didn't want to be that person – not being there for my best friend when he needed me most…

There was a noise – a key in the door – it opened – a voice…

"Tessie?"

It made me jump.

I turned, quickly.

It was Jake. Of course it was. But I realized I was nervous. I didn't feel safe. Billy had made me feel that way.

"What's going on? You still not well?" Jake said, dumping his bag on the floor.

"No, I'm okay," I said, but as I spoke, I burst into tears.

Jake came over and put his arms around me.

"What is it? What's going on?"

I pulled away from him, wiping my eyes with my hands. I didn't know what I could and couldn't tell him, but I wanted to tell him everything.

"Did Mum ring you?" I said.

"I got a missed call. I was almost home…"

"The hospital called. Laura's made a response. They've asked Mum and Dad to go in. They left a few minutes ago…" I smiled through my tears.

"Shit," Jake said. "Shit, Tessie. When you started crying I thought it was something really bad, but that's great, isn't it? That's good news?"

I nodded and laughed but the tears came again. "Yes, it is."

Jake bent his face down towards me.

"Why the tears? You still look so sad?"

I so wanted to say something, to tell him everything that had been going on.

"Tessie, is there something else?"

I thought about Billy for a moment, but I didn't want to talk about Billy. I couldn't.

"Seriously, Tessie?" Joe said again.

I wanted to tell him about Joe. I wondered…if I could…

"I was there, at the hospital, when Laura moved…"

Jake took my hand. "God, Tessie," he said. "Was it bad?"

I shook my head and carried on.

"I didn't go to school today, Jake. I kind of…I kind of pretended I had a headache. And I went to the hospital."

"Well, that's not the worst thing in the world, Tessie. Don't feel so bad about that – about bunking – is that why you're upset?"

"It's not that."

"Okay," Jake said. "I'm not sure I understand what's going on then."

"Seeing Laura respond was amazing. And scary," I said. "I didn't know exactly what was happening but one minute she was there, like always, still in the bed, and then the next she was sitting up and her eyes were opening and closing and – it was everything I wanted to happen, everything I'd hoped for when Ella had said we should try and do something to change things—" and I looked at him to gauge his reaction to what I was saying before I carried on, but I wanted to carry on and I was about to, when he interrupted me.

"What do you mean? When Ella said what? I don't understand what you mean..."

"I mean," I paused and looked down, "look, don't be angry, Jake. Just hear me out, okay?"

"Okay," Jake said, more slowly.

I took a deep breath.

"I took Joe to see Laura today. It was seeing him that made Laura respond – he played her music, he sang to her – it was—"

"What?" Jake said, dropping my hand. "Did you just say what I think you said? That you've seen Joe? That you took *Joe* to see Laura? Are you serious, Tessie?"

I nodded.

"What the hell!" He raised both his hands and put them on top of his head and turned his back on me.

I stepped forward to grab his arm and turn him round again. He let me.

"It's not bad, Jake. It turned out well. It turned out just like Ella said it would."

"So this happened because of Ella? Ella made this happen?" he said.

"Well, yes, no – I mean, she suggested it. But I took him there. *I* did this, Jake. And I—"

I wanted to tell him how happy I was, how good I felt, that I'd made things better. I was the person who usually made things worse, but I'd done something good today. Something really good.

"What the hell's been going on? I don't understand…"

"Ella's been in touch with Joe," I said. And I said it slowly because I wanted my slow, steady words to slow him right down too.

"Since when?"

"I don't know exactly," I said.

I fudged it. Ella had said they'd been in touch all along, but I didn't know what that meant. I didn't know for how long.

"And she's not told the police?"

I shook my head.

"Christ, Tessie. This is all so messed up. Joe's wanted by the police – have you forgotten that? They still want to find him, you know? Just because they're talking about this Kyle Brooks now doesn't mean they don't still want to find Joe. You heard what Mum said. They're interested in Kyle so they can get to Joe."

He started pacing.

I watched him, pacing, up and down the hall.

"So what's Ella saying about Joe?" Jake was looking

at me now, his voice was slightly raised, as he continued to pace.

"She says Joe loves Laura. That he really loves her. She says he would never hurt her."

"And you believe that?" Jake said.

I nodded.

"And you think that makes all this okay? That it makes it safe for you to take Joe in to see Laura? She couldn't be any more vulnerable than she is right now, Tessie. And you've taken Joe in to see her, someone who's wanted by the police in connection with her attack. Are you mad, Tessie? Seriously, have you lost your mind or something? What were you thinking?"

"She responded, Jake! I did it for her – for Laura – and it worked!"

"And Ella told you to do this?"

"Yes. She said it might work, and Joe thought so too, and we should try it. She gave Joe my number. But then he was there at the hospital – by chance, I think – I'm not sure – he was outside the hospital when I was visiting Laura – and well, he talked to me and he told me he didn't do it, and I believed him. I totally believed him."

"So where is Joe now? Do you know?"

I shook my head. "He left the hospital. He ran."

"After Laura woke up?"

I nodded.

"And you think that's the action of an innocent person?" Jake said.

"He didn't want anyone to see him. He didn't want anyone to know he was back. Not yet. But I'm telling you now, aren't I?"

"Ella should know better," Jake said. "Way better."

"I thought you'd be happy about Laura responding, and I thought you'd be proud of me, Jake. I thought you'd be proud of me being a part of making this happen."

Jake came up close to me and took both my hands.

"I don't understand why you didn't tell me before. I don't understand why Ella talked to you about all this – not me – when you…you…you shouldn't have to deal with all this. You've got enough going on, Tessie, with the SM and Max, and…"

And Jake didn't even know about Billy. He knew nothing about Billy.

"Ella told me not to tell anyone, Jake. But then I heard Mum and Dad talking last night. They were talking about decisions, and the future and Laura and I swear Mum's giving up on her. Dad said he wouldn't make the decision on his own, that it wasn't a decision you could make in one conversation, and I swear they were talking about Laura and what happens now, if she never comes round, if she never wakes up, but she will wake up, Jake – she will…"

"Tessie, I think you've got confused. They wouldn't have been talking like that—"

"So why were they saying those things last night? It was like they'd given up on her, Jake. They were talking like there was a decision to make. I heard them. If it wasn't that then what was it? You tell me."

"Well, I don't know. I wasn't there and I didn't hear what they said—"

"When I heard Mum and Dad talking like that I just knew that I had to give Joe a chance. I had to. I can't talk to Laura, you know? I can't tell her about my day or talk about the things we used to do or any of the stuff that you and Mum and Dad can talk to her about. I can't. I'm useless to her. I can't do anything. But I put my hand in hers the other day and she squeezed it. She actually squeezed it back and—"

"That's amazing, Tessie. Did you tell anyone?"

"I told Dad, but he said not to get my hopes up. He said that again today when the hospital called and asked him and Mum to come in. They've both given up. I swear it. They don't want to make the decision, but they don't believe she's ever going to come back. But I knew, when Laura squeezed my hand the other day, I knew then that stuff like that works – touch and sound. And Ella was right. She was totally right. Joe came and he held Laura's hand and he talked to her, and—"

"You make it sound like it's goddam Sleeping Beauty, Tessie. Grow up! What if he *was* the one who hurt her? The one who put her in hospital in the first place? The police haven't eliminated him from their investigation. Did you think about that when you showed him where she was on the ward? Did you think about that at all?"

"Yes, I did!" I said. "But you don't know all the stuff Ella told me about Kyle, about Joe and Kyle Brooks. And I met Joe and he loves her. I swear to God he does, Jake. He totally loves her."

Jake put his hands on his head again, like he was moving them into a position of safety, to stop himself punching something, punching the wall.

"I'm going to kill Ella. I'm going to bloody kill her," he said, and I could see a tightness around his eyes, on his face, that I'd never seen before. He brought his hands back down from his head and clasped them together in front of him, like he was holding himself together.

"Don't be angry with Ella, Jake. She was trying to help. That's all she was trying to do." But even as I spoke, I suddenly felt unsure.

"Just what the hell has she been doing being in touch with Joe in the first place, Tessie? She knew the police wanted to find him. She knew that… I'm calling her," Jake said. "I'm calling her now. And I'm going to get her over here. She needs to explain," he said and he walked into the kitchen to go to the phone while I stayed in the hall, and I stood still, completely still, as he went. "And when I've got her here I'm going to get her to call the police. I'm going to watch her do it."

It was suddenly quiet.

I turned to the mirror and I lifted my hands to my neck again and I felt an ache under my fingertips where Billy had had me in his grasp. It was a rising bruise. I knew it was. Soon it would show.

Had I done the wrong thing today?

I thought I'd done the right thing.

I closed my eyes.

Mum will call in a minute, I told myself. She'll call and she'll tell us that Laura is awake, that she's well, that she's talking. And Laura will tell us that Joe didn't hurt her, that I didn't put her life in danger again by taking Joe into the hospital to see her. She'll tell Mum and Dad that I've done the right thing. And she'll tell us all that it was Kyle who hurt her, just like Ella said it was. And the police will arrest him. And we'll be a family again. All of us. We'll be together again. That's what is going to happen. It has to now. It has to.

53.

Jake didn't come back into the hall after he'd phoned Ella. I heard his voice, talking to her, and then it went silent.

I went upstairs to the bathroom and washed my face and tied my hair back. I looked washed out. Tired. Because I was.

I wondered what Jake would say to Ella when she got here. I wished he wasn't so angry. I hoped that he'd hear her out. And I didn't know what she'd say back to him, or if she'd be angry with me. She'd told me not to tell anyone about Joe. Would she lie now to protect him, to protect herself? I didn't know which way this would go.

I went downstairs and stood in the kitchen doorway. Jake was sitting at the table, looking at his phone, his head in his hands.

"I'm sorry if I messed up," I said.

Jake didn't reply.

"I was trying to do my best," I said. "For Laura."

The doorbell went.

Jake stood up fast, scooping his phone off the table, and into his pocket and walked towards me. "Come on," he said, and I let him pass me and then I followed him into the hall.

I could hear voices on the other side of the door.

Jake looked back at me, his hand on the door, his face like an open question. Who was Ella talking to? Who had she brought? Was it the police? We must have been thinking the same thing, because Jake hesitated, still looking at me. Maybe the police had found Joe, or Billy, now that Max had talked to them. Either way they would be coming to find me. They would want to talk to me. I didn't have time to say to Jake that I didn't want him to open the door – to tell him, not to open it.

"Hey, Jake," Ella said.

There was a silence.

"Can we come in?"

And there, standing beside her, was Joe.

Jake nodded and they stepped into the hall.

"Alright, Tessie?" Joe said when he saw me.

I couldn't talk now.

I couldn't talk in my house.

Joe was here. A stranger. And now he was here, I couldn't say a thing.

Jake closed the door.

"You better come in," he said and he walked into the sitting room, and they followed. Jake stayed standing up but I heard him tell Ella and Joe to sit down when they came in, and they did.

I stood in the hall.

"Tessie!" Jake called out. "You need to come in here too!"

I wasn't sure I could move, but I took a breath to steady myself, and then I took one step and then another until I was there with them in the room.

"So you must be Jake," Joe said. "I'm Joe."

"Yeah," Jake said. "I'm kind of catching up here, but I guessed you were."

Jake's voice was low, tight, like he was controlling it, controlling his anger.

There was a silence.

"Listen," Ella said. "I brought Joe because—"

"I don't care why you did it, Ella," Jake said, his voice rising. "Just tell me straight. What the hell has been going on?"

"Well, I'm guessing you called and ordered me around here like you did just now because Tessie has told you some of it already, right?"

Ella looked round at me. She shot me a look that said she wished I hadn't said a thing.

"You should never have involved Tessie. Never. This

should never ever have had anything to do with her, Ella. She's got enough going on without—"

"Look, I understand you're upset," Ella said. "I understand that. But if you want to talk, you need to calm down."

"Calm down?" Jake said. "Are you joking, Ella? Are you fucking joking?"

I looked at the floor. I kept my eyes on the floor. I didn't like hearing Jake talk like this. He was losing it. He was losing it like Billy. And there was nothing I could do.

"Did you hurt my sister?" Jake said, turning to Joe. "Was it you? Did you do that? Put her in a coma, put her in the hospital? Was it you?"

"I didn't hurt her. I swear," Joe said.

"He didn't," Ella said.

"Shut up, Ella. I want to hear it from Joe, not you," Jake said. "So tell me, Joe, tell me what happened."

I kept my eyes on the floor and I pretended I was somewhere else. And I listened.

"I don't know what happened. That's the truth. I was drunk. Totally drunk. I walked with Laura under the viaduct. I wanted to...be there, with her, you know? But I'd drunk too much. I went over to the pillars to be sick, and she waited for me. That's the last thing I remember."

He paused.

"Go on!" Jake said.

I closed my eyes. I screwed them shut.

"I guess I must have passed out, because I don't remember anything until I was coming round and it was darker. I don't know what time it was. I looked around for Laura. But I couldn't see her. It was really dark, you know? And I called out for her but she didn't come. And I really wanted to find her. But when I didn't, well then I looked for my phone, so that I could call her. I thought it was in my pocket, but it wasn't. I felt around on the ground for it and I couldn't find it. I couldn't see anything. It was raining and it was just so dark and wet... I just wanted to find my phone so I could call her, and say sorry, you know? I knew I'd messed up. I'd got so drunk – too drunk."

I thought about Laura. How she was, before. I tried to remember her. I tried to make a picture in my head.

"And Kyle and his mates had turned up before and they got...they got kind of...pushy."

"So you *do* know Kyle Brooks?" Jake said.

I opened my eyes and looked at Joe.

He nodded.

"Yeah. Kyle hit me, you know? Him and his mates had a go on the bike...I'd kind of borrowed this motorbike from work...and...he threatened me, hit me... I was so relieved Laura didn't see them. And I kept thinking how I had to get the bike back to the garage, because I shouldn't have had it. It had to be back that night. And I know I

shouldn't have got back on the bike in the state I was in…
It was a mess – my mess. But when I couldn't find Laura or
my phone, I left. I knew I had to get out of there, sober up,
get the bike back, get to a phone, call Laura. I had to sort
it all out. So I went back to the road bridge, off the path. I
cut through the bushes so I could get out of there fast –
and I got the bike and I went."

"He crashed the bike…" Ella said.

"Let him tell me," Jake said, holding his hand up to stop
Ella talking, and she looked over at Joe, and he looked back
at her, and there was something between them that I
couldn't read – a world of unspoken feeling. And most of
it was in Ella's eyes.

Joe turned to Jake.

"So I got on the bike, and I was still pissed. I shouldn't
have, but I did. And yeah, I crashed. This idiot stepped off
the pavement in front of me and I swerved and went
straight into a lamp post – it fucking hurt—"

"Go on," Jake said.

"Well, I got up and ran, you know? My leg was bashed
in but I had my helmet and, well, I don't remember.
But I got up and I ran and I knew then I couldn't go home.
I didn't want the police to find me. When they found the
bike I knew they'd trace it back to the garage, and they'd
want to talk to me. So I went to the flats on the West Way
and I slept behind the bins. I used to sleep rough when my

dad came home raging – when I couldn't be at home – so I kind of knew what I needed to do, where I needed to be."

I looked at Ella and she looked back at me, and she blinked, a slow blink, in acknowledgement. Because everything she'd told me about Joe's dad was true. I'd been right to believe her. It was true.

"Did you even think about Laura?" Jake said. "About what had happened to Laura? Where she was?"

"Of course I did, but I didn't know she'd been hurt. I thought she'd just got fed up with me, that she'd gone home. I told you – I wasn't thinking straight. I'd had a shit night, you know? Crashed a bike that wasn't mine – I didn't have insurance or anything. I'd seen Kyle, and yeah, I'd lost Laura…but I swear I thought she'd just got pissed off with me and gone. I knew she wasn't happy. She'd wanted to go, to find her shoes – she kept telling me she wanted to go – but well, I kind of ignored her… Started being sick. I just guessed she'd gone and I needed to sleep and I told myself I'd sort it all out in the morning, you know? I felt so bad, but I couldn't have done anything else. I had to just sleep it off. I wasn't in any fit state to sort anything then."

I wondered, did Laura know this Joe? The Joe who drank too much. The Joe who slept rough. The Joe with a raging dad. Ella seemed to know this Joe really well.

"So what happened in the morning?" Jake said. "I mean, did you try and call Laura, try and find out how she was?"

"I didn't have my phone, Jake. Her number was on my phone. When it got light I headed towards the bus station, to get away. I had to get away. I wanted to call Laura, but I didn't know how and… I just needed to get away for a bit. But that's when I heard the news. The coach driver had the radio on as we boarded. Girl attacked. Found in the meadow by the viaduct. I didn't need to hear any more. That's when I knew. I just knew it was Laura…"

Joe stopped. He leaned forward, his elbows on his knees, his head bowed down in his hands.

"I knew they'd think it was me. I had even more reason to get away then, so I just kept going."

Ella moved up on the sofa and put her hand on Joe's shoulder, before looking up at Jake and speaking.

"Kyle was there at the viaduct. You heard what Joe said. He gave Joe a hard time. It's got to be him, Jake. It's got to be."

"What? Just because he was there, Ella? Just because Joe told you he was there!"

"No, Jake. It's not just because of that—"

Joe looked up and interrupted. "Look, I can't say it was Kyle for sure. I didn't see anything. But he's got it in for me, and his mate Marky took Laura's wallet, her phone.

He wasn't on his own. Another mate, Kris, was there too. And…well, Kyle threatened me, punched me around. He's done it before. We've got history – our families. It's complicated, you know?"

"No," Jake said. "I don't know."

But I knew.

I knew it all.

"My dad, his dad. I won't go into it. But yeah – it could be him that did this to Laura. To get back at me, for what my dad did."

Jake turned to Ella.

"Did you know all this?"

Ella nodded.

"And you told the police, right?" Jake said. "You told them what you knew about Kyle?"

"No," Ella said. "I didn't. I didn't know all this when they questioned me at the station. Joe filled me in after that. Jake, when they questioned me I hadn't seen Joe, I didn't know about Kyle. I hadn't seen Joe, I swear."

But Ella had said they'd been in touch all along. That's what she'd said. They might not have seen each other, but she'd said they were in touch. She wasn't telling the whole truth. She wasn't.

"I admit I really did want to hear from Joe – and I tried calling him a lot – but his phone was dead. All the time I was worrying about him. Tessie knows that – don't you, Tessie?"

Ella looked at me, but I didn't move. I didn't want to be brought into the conversation, asked what I did and didn't know. I couldn't be. And I wasn't sure that she was telling the truth now.

"And when the police questioned me they kept asking me about Joe and the viaduct and this receipt they found, and they just wouldn't give up. They thought I'd been seeing Joe, that me and Joe had been seeing each other, behind Laura's back, that I was jealous – involved."

Jake looked at me, and then back at Ella.

"And had you been seeing Joe?"

"No," Ella said. "We were friends. As soon as Joe started seeing Laura that's all we were. Friends."

Jake nodded, and sighed. "And before?"

Ella looked at Joe.

He didn't look at her.

"Well, we never really got started, me and Joe. Not really."

Jake looked at Joe, and Joe looked back at him and nodded.

"So go on," Jake said to Ella.

"Well, when the police took my phone I knew they'd see all the messages I'd sent and all the calls I'd made to Joe, and well, there was nothing I could do about that. That's how it was. But then Joe called me at the cafe, and we were in touch in other ways, you know? And he told me about Kyle and—"

"Christ, Ella, what were you thinking? It doesn't matter if you found out about Kyle after the police questioned you. You were in touch with Joe and you never said. Why didn't you go to them when you found out? You'll be done for withholding information now or worse," Jake said.

"Not if Laura wakes up, properly," Ella said. "Not if she wakes up and she tells everyone what happened."

"You don't know that's ever going to happen," Jake said. "It may never happen!"

I looked at Jake.

That's not what he'd said to me earlier. That's not what he'd said before when I'd told him about Mum and Dad and the conversation they'd been having. Why was he saying that now?

The phone started ringing in the kitchen.

I looked at Jake.

"So what am I meant to do now, Ella? I mean now I know all this stuff too? I don't want to be in this situation and it's you – you've put us all here. You've put Tessie in it too. You've made it worse, for everyone."

Jake was right. It wasn't just me now. It was Jake too.

The phone was still ringing.

"We have to go to the police," he said. "We have to."

"No, Jake!" Ella said. "Not yet, please."

"Well, when? I mean, shit – Joe's here. He's here in the house. The police want him. Christ, Joe. How are you even here without them knowing? They're looking for you. The police are looking for you right now—"

"I've been careful, Jake. I've kept changing my sim. I've been sleeping rough. I don't talk to anyone when I'm on the street. My hood's up – I'm quick, I avoid the CCTV. Ella's been saving me food from the cafe, leaving it out…"

The phone stopped ringing.

Jake rubbed his head with his hands and looked up again at Ella. I could see he was struggling to take it all in.

"You've lied, Ella. You've lied to us all, to the police, to everyone – to me, to Mum and Dad. I thought you were Laura's friend. I mean, I really thought—"

I could hear a phone ringing. A more muted ring. A mobile. Jake looked up. So did I. It was his ring, his phone, in his pocket.

"I *am* her friend," Ella said. "You know that…"

Whoever was ringing needed to get through.

Maybe it was Mum.

From the hospital.

Maybe she had news about Laura.

I couldn't move.

I couldn't speak.

I wanted Jake to get the phone.

Get the phone.

Jake, get your phone.

"Should you get that?" Ella said, pointing to Jake's pocket where the phone was ringing.

"Yeah," Jake said, like he'd been in some kind of momentary trance, and he pulled the phone out of his pocket and walked into the hall as he answered it.

Ella looked at Joe. "You okay?"

Joe nodded. "We should have told the police about Kyle, about my dad. Jake's right."

"How? How could we have done that?" Ella whispered, and as she spoke to him she bent down and put her face next to his. "How? If they'd have known we were in touch they would have arrested you, Joe. And you didn't do this to Laura. You didn't."

She loved him.

Ella still loved him.

That world of feeling I saw when she looked at him – it was love.

I waited for Jake to come back into the room.

I could hear him talking, his voice low, calm again, in the next room. He hung up and came back in.

"That was Mum. Laura's made some more responses. She may be coming round – they think, they don't know, but she may be coming round."

Joe, his head in his hands, started to cry.

"I told you, Joe. Didn't I tell you? It's going to be okay. It is. It's going to be okay," Ella said, and she was rubbing his back, as she spoke. "Laura can tell the police now. She can tell them what happened. That it wasn't you."

I looked at Jake and he looked back at me.

"We should go," he said. "I said we'd meet Mum and Dad at the hospital. I said we'd leave now."

Ella stood up, and Joe lifted his head, wiping his face with his hands.

"What happens now, Jake?" Joe said. "I mean, you should say what happens now." But before Jake had a chance to open his mouth to answer there was a voice, shouting, in the street, at the door, there was a hammering on the front door, and a voice, shouting.

"Open up, Tessie! Open the fucking door! I know you're in there!"

I knew the voice.

It was Billy.

54.

Jake walked over to the window to look out onto the street.

He turned back into the room and looked at me.

"It's that kid you've been seeing, Tessie – what's his name?"

I went hot all over. I felt like my whole body was alight.

I swallowed.

Tight.

"Come on! Open up!"

Billy's voice again, shouting.

Jake started walking to the front door.

I wanted to say:

Don't let him in.

Don't do it.

Don't let him in.

But I couldn't move. Not one single part of my body would move to signal or sign to Jake to stop.

Joe stood up, and followed Jake into the hall. I watched through the doorway.

"What boy have you been seeing, Tessie?" Ella said. She looked intrigued. She was almost smiling.

Shut up, Ella.

Shut up.

Jake turned back from the hall, and looked at me, like he hoped I'd answer, like he wanted me to answer, and when I didn't, he opened the door and Billy burst into the hall.

"Oi! Hang on!" Jake said, but it was too late to stop Billy from coming in. He was in the house now. He was in.

"I fucking knew it!" Billy said. "I fucking knew it was you!" And he went to Joe and he pushed his forehead against Joe's, hard, backing Joe up against the wall, while Joe held his hands at his sides in submission.

"What the hell is going on?" Jake said, but he didn't move either. He stayed back, close to the front door.

"I saw you at the hospital with her," Billy said, pointing at me. "With Tessie. Is that why you've been hiding from me, because you've been seeing her? She's my girl, Joe. Mine!"

"Calm down, Bill," Joe said. "Calm down and we'll talk."

I grasped at the words they were saying – Joe to Billy – Billy to Joe – and I didn't understand.

"I didn't understand why you just disappeared. You just fucking went and you left me. And then I saw you with her at the hospital. Sitting all cosy with her at the hospital.

Exchanging numbers, texting, were you? Where the fuck have you been?"

"Take a step back, Bill. Take a step back, away from me, and we'll talk," Joe said.

I didn't understand.

Joe knew Billy.

He knew him.

Billy took a step back, and as he did he looked into the sitting room at me. And when he looked at me, my head went light, like I might float or faint or fly with the fear I was feeling.

Billy knew Joe.

He knew his name.

"Are you going to fucking talk to me, Joe, or what?"

Ella came and stood next to me, and quietly put her hand in mine.

She steadied me.

"Come and sit down, Bill. Come and sit down," Joe said, and he walked into the sitting room and Billy followed. "Sit down," Joe said again and then Joe sat, and Billy sat too.

Jake closed the front door and went slowly into the room. Ella pulled my hand, and we followed.

Joe looked up at us all.

"This is my brother, my brother, Bill," he said.

A tightness rose in my throat like a twisted rope.

I held Ella's hand so tight I could feel my nails digging into her skin.

I started to shake.

Ella pulled her hand away and turned me to face her.

"Tessie, do you need to sit down? Shall we sit down?" and she led me over to a chair by the window.

"So what's going on, Bill. Tell me what's going on?" Joe said.

The boy with the sparkling eyes – the boy who beat Max to a pulp – the boy who kissed me – the boy with his hands around my neck – the boy I liked – the boy who told Max that he loved me – who I'd thought maybe I could love – he was Joe's brother.

I took a breath to try and open my throat and I looked at him.

He was rubbing his face with his hands over and over, and then pushing one hand over his scalp and then another. Fast. Like he was smoothing something down, softening his pain.

I looked over at Jake. He was leaning against the table by the doorway.

Lost.

We were lost.

We were all lost.

"Why didn't you come back, Joe? Where've you been?" Billy said.

"I had to go, Bill. You heard what happened to Laura," and he paused before he spoke again. "I didn't know you knew Tessie."

"But why did you go? You left me with Mum. I needed you," Billy said.

"I had to go, Bill. I had to. I was in trouble. I had to get out."

"You could have taken me with you, you know? I'd have come. We could have started again."

"We've done that too many times, Bill. Haven't we? This was meant to be our new start. This was meant to be the one."

"Yeah, I know, and then you went, and you made it bad. You ruined it."

"That wasn't my fault, Bill. It wasn't my fault. I wanted you to have a chance. New area, new school, new flat, new everything. I wanted you to have a chance because I fucking blew my chance. I blew it when I took Laura out on that bike, you know, and I drank too much beer. I think about that all the time. I really do. So I left, to give you a chance…"

"But then you came back, right? And you went after Tessie. No more Laura, so you went for her sister? That right? That what's happening here?" Billy's voice was getting louder again.

"No, Bill. No," Joe said, quickly. "That's not what's happening."

"But you didn't come and see me!"

"Joe's not with Tessie," Ella said. "He's not. I promise you. He's not."

Ella was shaking her head as she said the words.

"He with you then, is he?" Billy said and he laughed, when he said it. "Don't think so. You're not his type."

Ella looked hurt, scorned.

I looked over at Jake.

Say something, Jake.

Say something.

For me.

Say something, for me.

"Anyway," Billy said. "I saw them, at the hospital – together. And I worked it out. Because the girls have always liked Joe. He could always pick and choose."

Jake looked at Ella.

I looked at Ella too.

She blushed.

"Nothing's going on with me and Joe," Ella said. "Nothing."

"Yeah, right," Billy said. "I can see you like him though. And I know how this goes. How it always goes. It always goes the same. The girls always like him, and it always ends up bad. Always. Everything always does with me and Joe. It's like it's written in the fucking stars, you know?"

"Well this isn't written in the fucking stars," Ella said.

"I'm Laura's friend. I like Joe – I like him a lot – I'll admit. But I'd never do that to Laura. Never. No matter how I feel about him."

And I was relieved to hear Ella say those words – but I wanted to say my own. I wanted to say:

I'm not with Joe.

Billy – I'm not with him.

Because I didn't want Billy to lose it.

I didn't want him to hurt me or anyone else here again.

Joe spoke.

"I was at the hospital because I wanted to see Laura. That's why I was there, Bill. I was waiting for Tessie so I could talk to her, and she could help get me in to see Laura. And she did. She helped me see her."

I wanted to go to the hospital now.

Jake had said to Mum that we'd go in. Mum and Dad would think that we were on our way. I wanted to see Laura now. I had to see her, as she woke up. That was all that mattered now. It was all that mattered.

"She not dead yet, then?" Billy said.

Jake stood up.

"Get out, Bill. Get out right now," he said, strongly, calmly.

Billy stood up to meet Jake's stance.

"You're the brother, aren't you?" Billy said to Jake. "Tessie's brother."

Jake didn't move.

"You gonna let Joe do this, then?" Billy said. "Mess around with your sister Laura, and her best friend? And now your little sister too?"

Joe took a step forward, towards Billy.

"Saw you when I came to walk Tessie to school," Billy said. "Saw you in the cafe when I was working on Max, didn't I?"

"You? That was you?" Ella said.

"Yeah, that was me," Billy said, looking at Ella before turning back to look at me. "Because Max didn't get the message. I told him to stay away from you, Tessie, but he didn't listen. So I had to make him listen."

I looked away.

I looked through everyone in the room and into the hall.

I didn't want to see Jake's face – I didn't want to see any of their faces.

I didn't want them to know that I'd known all along. That I'd known what Billy had done to Max.

"And Tessie didn't talk. I wanted her to talk. That's all I wanted her to do. To listen to me, and to talk to me, but she didn't."

"What are you talking about, Bill?" Ella said.

I could see that Jake was poised to fight. He was poised to protect himself, protect me. He was on alert. And Joe was the same. He stood in silence next to Billy and he was exactly the same.

"I'm talking about all the things I wanted to tell Tessie, all the things that are going on, fucked up, inside me, that she needs to know. All the shit, all the stuff she didn't tell me, all the stuff she needed to tell me, all the stuff I needed to tell her, all the stuff she needed to know."

"I—" Ella tried to speak but Billy ignored her.

"You fucking should have told me, Tessie. You fucking should have told me what happened to your sister."

I couldn't tell you, Billy.

I couldn't tell you.

"I didn't know you couldn't talk, like never, not ever. I thought you'd talk to me in time. And I decided I'd give you time because everything about you made me feel like it would be worth the wait. I liked you so much, you know? From the minute I saw you I liked you. I liked seeing you in school, your eyes in mine, mine in yours. I liked just walking next to you. Most of the time we didn't need to say anything. But then I'd want to ask you something, tell you something, and you'd look at me, and all I could see was fear. And there was just all this stuff between us. All this stuff we couldn't say, and it wasn't just about you and me and these feelings you were making me feel – it was about how no one made me feel like this before. No one. I wanted to hold you, take you some place where I could just hold you, and kiss you, and let you speak, because I knew we both had so much to say... You were this one good thing, Tessie. In amongst all the shit you were my one good thing..."

And Billy looked at me and I looked at him and just for a moment all I could think about was him and how I'd felt the same.

"But where's the bad in that, Bill?" Ella said. "Tessie being this one good thing?" I could hear the fear in her voice as she said it, but she said it anyway.

"Because she never told me it was her sister who got hurt, that it was her sister in the coma!" he said. "I only found out the other day, from someone else, from those girls, who hate her and tease her, who told me she was just shy. And it turns out she never told me because she couldn't, but what was I meant to do with that, eh? What was I meant to do with it? Now that I knew? Now that I feel like I feel about her?"

"I don't know what you mean," Ella said. "I don't understand what you mean."

"It was never going to work, was it? Me and love. Never. I mean, I never thought it would, it could. I never thought it would happen. I never thought anyone would love me. But then it happened, and it was her – but it just fucking had to be her, didn't it? It had to be her." Billy was pointing at me and the pain on his face was palpable.

I wanted to reach out and touch his face. I wanted to hold him and wipe the pain away.

"You can't love someone you've hurt, can you? You can't love someone you've really, really hurt. I know that better than anyone. I know that better than any of you in this fucking room, you know?" and Billy turned and he looked at Ella and Jake and then he stopped, and he looked at Joe.

"Because I've seen it – love turn to hate turn to more hate. I've seen your dad kick our mum in the face. I've seen worse. You never saw it, Joe, did you? You never saw it because you never came home. You left me there with your dad, with the big man – Kev McGrath. Some kind of stepdad he's turned out to be… And I saw it. I saw it all."

"No, Bill, no—" Joe tried to butt in, to speak, but Billy kept talking.

"And I always told the police what happened when they came, and they'd talk to Mum, and she'd always say it was okay. Always. Broken ribs, fractured skull. It's okay. That's what she'd say. So they'd go away. They'd leave her alone. And she'd drink it away. All the bad stuff. And you were trying, Joe. I know you were. You got us moved, you got a job, you bought me stuff – food, stuff I liked to eat. Like those noodles in the packet. And those sour chews. Why d'you get those things for me, Joe? Was it the guilt? Because no one had done that for me before. I know you were trying to make it right when we moved here. And I was trying too. I was really trying. But then you met Laura – and you were gone."

"I wasn't gone, Bill. I wasn't," Joe said, shaking his head over and over.

"Yes, you fucking were, Joe. You were gone. Five weeks I had you in this new place, this place where I knew no one, had no friends. Five weeks, and then you were hers. Not mine. I needed you, you know? I needed you to look after me, not leave me with Mum and the crying and the bottles and the crying. I needed you. I know Kev's gone away and it feels like he can't hurt us now, but it doesn't take it away – the fear and the hurt and the pain. He's going to come back one day. You know that. I know that. Like he always does. But you went. And you left me."

"What are you saying, Bill? That I shouldn't have had a life? I was trying to make us one, Bill. That's all I was trying to do."

"Yeah, well, it looked to me like you were going off and having a party all on your own, Joe. You didn't invite me, did you? You left me in the new place with Mum to rot and die and you went with Laura. It was all about Laura."

"That's not fair, Bill," Joe said.

"Yeah, well, that's why I went to the viaduct that night."

The room felt like all the air had been sucked out of it. I heaved for a breath I couldn't breathe.

"I fucking knew you'd take her there on that bike.

That's where we used to hang out, Joe – you and me. That was our place. And you were taking *her* there. So I went too. I got on the bus and I got there after you. I saw Kyle and his mates. I saw them running circles round you on that bike. I saw Kyle punch you full on in the face. And you didn't see me. I made sure you didn't. And I went to the viaduct. I climbed up onto it. High. Onto one of those platforms under the arches where the pigeons sit and shit. And I looked down on you and Laura as you walked by on the path because I knew you'd want to take her there, under those arches. Look for the bats, like we used to do. And I saw you, but you didn't see me. You walked straight past me."

"What are you saying, Bill?" Joe said. "That you were there?"

I looked up at Billy, and I thought I was going to scream, but all I could do was catch the scream in my throat like an insect in a web.

"Yeah, I was there," Billy said.

Joe stepped back, away from Billy, running his hand through his hair, looking at Jake, looking at Jake, like if Jake hadn't been standing by the door he'd have run, he'd totally have run.

"What are you saying, Bill?" Ella said.

"I'm saying it was me. I'm saying it was me who hurt Laura. I did it. It was me," and Billy stared at Joe. He didn't take his eyes off Joe. "I didn't plan it. But I saw you taking her under the viaduct, to our place. And I was so angry – I was so fucking angry that you'd taken her there. There was this big lump of stone, a piece of the viaduct, crumbling out the walls. It was just sitting there, on the ledge, and I picked it up. And you were puking. Seriously puking. I couldn't see you, but I could hear you. The retching echoes, you know. And she was walking off – Laura. And she was heading along the path, and she was calling for you all the time. And you'd gone quiet. And I could see her, in my eyeline, she was right in front of me, and the stone was in my hand and her voice was calling out for you and I threw it. I just threw it – the stone – at her head. I just did it. With everything I had inside of me. And it felt good – just in that moment – because I hated you, Joe – for bringing her there—"

I gagged.

The boy I'd kissed, the boy I'd held, the boy who'd held me – he'd been the one who'd nearly killed Laura.

And then Billy turned to Joe.

"And you fucking ran, didn't you? You passed out, and then you got back up and you ran through the bushes. And you still don't know what it feels like to be me. You still don't fucking know."

"Bill, slow down. Do you even know what you're saying?" Joe said, looking across at Jake, and then at me.

"And you know what?" Billy said, ignoring him, carrying on. "I blame you for her lying there in that hospital bed. It's not on me – it's on you. Because you didn't face it, did you? You left me, and you made me do this thing, to show you how it feels to be me, to show you what it's like to lose the person you love, to always lose them, but it didn't work. You didn't see it. Because you did what you always do, you avoided it and you ran. And now I'm walking around with this feeling like I'm going to explode with the shit I feel inside, like it's all going to come pouring out of me, and there's nowhere I can go, there's nothing I can do and it's shit and pain and rage and what the fuck am I meant to do, Joe? Tell me, what the fuck am I meant to do now?"

Joe opened his mouth to speak, but Billy stepped towards him, closer, his voice louder, and he moved, closer again, and Joe stayed where he was, ready to receive a punch, a blow.

"And you made me lose the one good thing!" Billy screamed in Joe's face. "Tessie was my one good thing, Joe – and I've lost her now – because of what I've done – because of you!"

And Billy turned around to face me.

I looked up.

"I didn't know she was your sister, Tessie. You have to believe me – when I threw that stone – I didn't know – maybe if I'd have known or if I'd met you before,

I could have loved you better, I could have been better, I could have done better. But I see now I was fucked from the start."

And my heart was bleeding out for him, like I was opened up. A river of feeling rising up and over the banks of me, and the words would have been:

I'm so sorry, Billy.

For you, for me, for Laura.

For the silence.

No one spoke for a moment.

"I'm not sure what we do now," Jake said.

"Me and Bill should go," Joe said. "We should just go."

"But where?" Ella said. "Don't go," she said. "Please, Joe."

Billy sat down on the sofa.

His face was white, washed out, like there was nothing left inside of him.

I walked over and I knelt down next to him and I took his hands in mine and rested them on his knees.

Billy bowed his head and he started to cry.

I wanted to love you, Billy. I thought I could. But in amongst all this wrong, I can't.

That's what I wanted to say.

But for the first time I was glad I couldn't say it.

Because Billy couldn't hear those words.

It wouldn't help him to hear those words.

And someone so needed to help him, but it wasn't, it couldn't, be me.

The doorbell rang.

Once.

Twice.

Three times.

No one moved in the room.

I counted in my head, the seconds, into a minute and then two, and then the front door burst open, smashed in, and there were police everywhere in the room. Uniforms, and Campbell and May Grover in the hall, and behind them, Max. He'd brought them all there. He must have heard Billy shouting, seen him arrive. And he was leaning against the doorframe, his arms across his chest, protecting his bruised body, and he looked at me, and he mouthed the words – *Are you okay, Tessie? Are you okay?*

I blinked back. ONE BLINK. One blink for YES.

And Max nodded because he understood me. And I was glad.

May took my hands from Billy's and two officers lifted him to standing and cuffed him. They did the same to Joe. I didn't hear the words they said. I just watched, as they took Billy and they took Joe, and they left me, standing, in the silent spaces of the room.

Jake came over and stood next to me, and he took my hand, as more police filled the room.

"We'll be okay now, Tessie, you know that, don't you? We'll be okay."

And somehow I knew he was right.

Somehow I knew that all of us, we'd be okay now.

Because those were the words I'd been waiting for someone to say in a way that actually made sense. Those were the words I'd been waiting to hear in a way that made me feel safe. And those were the words I knew now I wanted to say to Laura, when she woke. Those words, I decided, would be the first that I'd say to her, the first she would hear. Because we weren't ever going to be perfect – we weren't ever before – and we all still had to recover. But now, at least, it felt like we had a chance.

We'll be okay now, Laura. We'll be okay.

That is what I wanted to say.

Part Four

Six months later

LAURA GREEN

Laura came home. She had a slow and painful recovery, but aside from the scar on her head and intermittent headaches, the doctors all agreed that, given the nature of her injury, she had made steady progress back to a good level of health.

Laura remained friends with Ella, but she didn't see Joe McGrath again. She couldn't. When she saw him it made her remember, and all she wanted to do was to move on with her life, and forget.

But one thing she will never forget is what Tessie did to help her. How brave Tessie was in the face of everything that happened, is something that she will never forget.

JOE McGRATH

When considering the available evidence the police decided to drop all possible charges against Joe in relation to taking a vehicle without the owner's consent. This was in agreement with the owner of the motorbike. Joe offered to repair and restore the bike in his own time, at his own cost, in recompense for the damage done, and the owner of the bike was satisfied with this in the light of the other events that had occurred on the day in question.

Joe didn't give up on Billy. He continued to spend time with him, whenever he was able.

Joe still loves Laura. If you asked him now, he'd tell you she is still the love of his life. He hopes that in time they may get a chance to somehow try and start again, when Laura is better. He's waiting for the day.

BILLY JOHNS

The police filed two separate charges against Billy – GBH for his assault of Max and Attempted Murder for his attack on Laura. His case is due to be heard in court next month. His lawyer expects him to serve a custodial sentence given the serious nature of his crimes. She is keen to ensure that the judge and jury fully understand the extreme and persistent stress he had been under at home over a number of years whilst living with Kevin McGrath. Billy remains in custody as he waits for his trial.

When Billy thinks about what happened, what he did, he recognizes the pain he caused, and the damage that he has done. He regrets it. But still he cannot forgive Joe for not being there when he needed him most.

If you asked Billy about Tessie now, he would say she is still his one good thing. Because he's pretty sure she's the only one he'll ever have.

He knows he's lost her. He knows he's lost everything now.

TESSIE GREEN

Tessie spoke to Laura when she woke, just as she had planned, and Laura smiled and squeezed her hand back in reply. It was in Laura's room at the hospital, one week after Billy's arrest, and the door was PROPER SHUT. After that Tessie agreed to go back to speech therapy, and Mum supported Tessie in this both at home and at school. Tessie's progress is slow, but there is progress. She is aiming to be able to answer the register in front of the whole class by the end of the summer term. She thinks maybe, after everything that happened, she can be that brave. Laura tells her to believe that she can.

Tessie and Max walk to school and back together most days. Tessie knows that the way Max looked out for her, helped her, forgave her…the way he's always been, is no small thing. She knows she let him down. But she's making it up to him every day. And love? Well, Tessie and Max agree that right now, love is not for them.

When Tessie thinks of Billy she has just one hope. That if he ever thinks of her, he remembers the time when she was his one good thing. She'd like to be able to give him that. Because she knows he needs it. She knows everyone does. And if Billy doesn't have that, the memory at least of that, then she wonders, what does he have?

Acknowledgements

I'd like to give a huge and heartfelt thank you to the following people:

Hilary Delamere for reading the very beginnings of this book, when it was just a series of monologues. Despite that rather shaky beginning you encouraged me to keep going until I found this story, and I am very grateful for that.

Anne Finnis, my editor, for your belief, care and understanding of these characters. This was always an ambitious story to tell, and there are many reasons why I don't think I could have done it without you. And of course to the rest of the brilliant team at Usborne for all their hard work in bringing the book to publication, with a particularly special thank you to Sarah Stewart.

For giving me the generosity of their time in relation to my research: Brenda Wilson, Tracey Puri, Alys Stephens, Bob Allon and Giles Newell. I have done my utmost to use the knowledge you all passed on to me well. Should there be any errors then I claim them all wholeheartedly as my own.

Lindsay Whittington, the Co-ordinator and Founding Member of the charity for Selective Mutism, SMIRA (Selective Mutism Information & Research Association), for reading my book when you were so very busy, and for supporting it so generously with your review.

And to Sheri Pitman, without whose bravery in going on the radio and talking about her experiences of SM I would not have found the inspiration to write this story, a very special thank you indeed.

Emma Higham, Michelle Wood, Gita Ralleigh, Caroline Gerard, Maria Waldron, Beverley D'Silva, Barbara Rustin, Allison Ouvry and Daniel Wright for reading work in progress and being so generally brilliant all year round. So happy our writing gang is still going strong! And to Anthony McGowan, who brought us all together at the start, for his continued guidance and inspiration.

And last but in no way least, to my closest friends and family who have all supported me in a myriad of other ways this past year. In particular I want to thank my mum Lyn Dougherty, my best friend Zanna Hall and my family, Robert, Reuben and Rosa. Amongst them all, however, the biggest thank you must go to my husband, Robert; you've been my rock. So, truly, thank you.

Q & A with Faye Bird

Where did the idea for the story come from?

I happened to listen to a young woman, Sheri Pitman, speaking on the radio about her past experience of suffering from Selective Mutism (SM). Her mother was speaking on the programme with her, and they talked about how the condition had affected them both. I was moved by their experiences, and as I hadn't heard of SM before I was also, I admit, intrigued to find out more. It struck me almost immediately after I'd listened to Sheri talking, that a story in the first person could be a really powerful way of giving a teenage girl, who was suffering with SM, a voice in a way she wouldn't otherwise have in the outside world. This is really where the story started – with an idea for a character. The crime story and the love story followed on from there.

Did you do any research for Tessie?

It was important to me that the representation of SM was both accurate and realistic within the demands of my story, and so I did research the condition thoroughly. And as part of my research I met a teacher who had worked with two SM children in school. There is a huge amount of misunderstanding around a child who does not speak, and of course the cruelty of the condition is that a child or young person cannot easily explain the reasons for their silence, adding to the suffering they already feel.

You have an amazing ear for dialogue. Where do you think this comes from?

I spent years reading screenplays when I worked as a literary agent in film and television. In fact during that time screenplays were pretty much all I was reading. And I am beginning to see now how this experience has influenced my writing. I love writing dialogue, and I have to admit I tend to struggle when it comes to the detail of description sometimes. As a result the style of my prose is probably rather spare and the dialogue probably does rather punch through!

There seems to be a theme in your novels which explores "living life well". Do you have any thoughts on that?

In both my novels I write about a period of time in the main characters' lives that is undoubtedly extremely traumatic, and I admit I am interested in exploring how difficult times in our lives can push and challenge us. But that doesn't mean I see life as a bleak or persistently unhappy place to be.

In both my novels there are no quick fix happy endings, because I felt strongly that for both Ana in *My Second Life* and Tessie in *What I Couldn't Tell You*, given what they have both gone through, an immediate happy ending just didn't exist in any realistic way. But at the end of both books there is a sense of hope, a sense of greater understanding, and there is always, in its many forms, love. In these things it seems to me Ana and Tessie have a more real chance at a truly happy ending. At the end of their stories they are both left with a desire to grab a hold of their lives and go on and live them well, in a way that they perhaps haven't done, or been able to do, before. And surely in that, no one can deny there is ultimately a happy ending.

www.fayebirdauthor.com

Also by Faye Bird

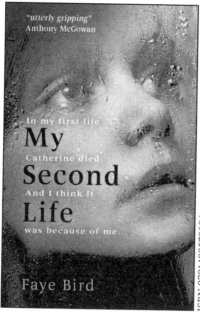

"utterly gripping"
Anthony McGowan

In my first life
My
Catherine died.
Second
And I think it
Life
was because of me...

Faye Bird

ISBN 9781409578604

The first time I was born, I was Emma. I was beautiful.
I had everything to live for. But I died.

Now I have been born a second time, and my previous
life haunts me. Because in it I think I did something very
wrong. I must find out what I did to Catherine. I must
uncover the truth about Emma...

Intriguing, compelling, *heartbreaking*!
What if your past life could shatter your future?

Praise for *My Second Life*

An astonishingly accomplished debut novel.
Highly recommended.
School Librarian

The plot is truly compelling, with the tension ratcheted
high. Faye Bird is very strong on characterization. Ana is
a great protagonist with very believable responses…
Highly recommended.
School Library Journal

A clever plot, defined characters, and fabulous writing.
There isn't much more you could ask for. *My Second Life*
is bound to be rushed off bookshop shelves very soon.
Reader review, The Guardian

I was completely gripped throughout the story.
Once Upon A Bookcase

This debut thriller gets off to a cracking start… Bird
looks like an enticing prospect if she can build on this.
The Daily Mail

An ingenious concept, an intriguing mystery and
a gripping story told with pace and passion…
An amazing and thrilling debut
Blackpool Gazette

My Second Life is heartbreaking, heartracing, has an
amazing lead character and the story is like nothing
I have read before. I can't recommend this book
highly enough.
Reading Away the Days

A rich, dense read which skilfully employs dramatic
tension to absorb the reader wholly into a constantly
shifting world of revelation.
Books for Keeps

YA
USBORNE
SHELFIES

And for more thought-provoking
Usborne YA reads, news and competitions,
head to usborneyashelfies.tumblr.com

@Usborne

@UsborneYA

www.usborne.com/youngadult